Ra

Outrageous hell-raisers let loose in Europe!

When London's most notorious rakes
embark on a Grand Tour,
they set female hearts aflutter all across Europe!

The exploits of these British rogues might be the
stuff of legend, but on this adventure of a lifetime
will they finally meet the women strong enough to
tame their wicked ways?

Read Haviland North's story in
Rake Most Likely to Rebel
Already available

Read Archer Crawford's story in
Rake Most Likely to Thrill
Available now

And watch out for

Rake Most Likely to Seduce

and

Rake Most Likely to Sin

Coming in 2016

Author Note

I hope you enjoy this second story in the Rakes on Tour miniseries. This is your chance to catch up with Archer Crawford in Siena as he embarks on his quest to ride in the famed Palio. I've tried to incorporate details about the race and to be as true to fact as possible. If you want to read more about the great race try *La Terra In Piazza*—the text I consulted.

What is true about the race the way it is depicted in Archer's tale:

1. The Pantera neighborhood *did* win the June Palio that year, with Jacopo's Morello.

2. The Torre neighborhood *did* turn around and win the August Palio that same year with the same horse. (It is fairly remarkable to have the same horse win both races in the same year.)

3. The neighborhoods (*contradas*) *did* have rivals. Torre was despised by Oca and Onda. Pantera was a neutral neighborhood with no set rivals. The neighborhood rivalry was strong and intense, and I've tried to be true to that intensity in the storyline.

What is *not* true (obviously) is that Torre's jockey is hurt before the race and Archer needs to ride in his place. You can look up lists of jockeys and see who really rode in the August race.

I hope you have a good time with Archer, and learning a little bit about a beautiful Tuscan city.

Join me online at bronwynswriting.blogspot.com or at bronwynnscott.com.

Bronwyn Scott

—

Rake Most Likely
to Thrill

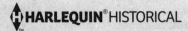

Recycling programs
for this product may
not exist in your area.

ISBN-13: 978-0-373-29845-7

Rake Most Likely to Thrill

Printed in U.S.A.

Bronwyn Scott is a communications instructor at Pierce College in the United States, and is the proud mother of three wonderful children (one boy and two girls). When she's not teaching or writing she enjoys playing the piano, traveling—especially to Florence, Italy—and studying history and foreign languages. Readers can stay in touch on Bronwyn's website, bronwynscott.com, or at her blog, bronwynswriting.blogspot.com. She loves to hear from readers.

Books by Bronwyn Scott

Harlequin Historical and Harlequin Historical *Undone!* ebooks

Rakes on Tour

Rake Most Likely to Rebel
Rake Most Likely to Thrill

Rakes of the Caribbean

Playing the Rake's Game
Breaking the Rake's Rules
Craving the Rake's Touch (Undone!)

Rakes Who Make Husbands Jealous

Secrets of a Gentleman Escort
London's Most Wanted Rake
An Officer But No Gentleman (Undone!)
A Most Indecent Gentleman (Undone!)

Ladies of Impropriety

A Lady Risks All
A Lady Dares
A Lady Seduces (Undone!)

Castonbury Park

Unbefitting a Lady

Visit the Author Profile page at Harlequin.com for more titles.

For Judi and Don and Nina and El Dorado Farms.
Thanks for helping Catie find Sharper Eagle.
There is no finer love than a girl and her horse.

Chapter One

The Antwerp Hotel, Dover—March 1835

There was going to be blood. It had become a foregone conclusion the moment the teamster brought the whip down across the hindquarters of the Cleveland Bay straining in the traces of the overloaded dray. How much blood, and whose, remained to be seen.

Archer Crawford had not stepped outside in the predawn darkness looking for trouble. Indeed, he'd been trying to avoid it. Inside, his travelling companion and long-time friend Nolan Gray's card game was starting to take a turn for the worse. But it seemed trouble had found him anyway. He could not stand idly by and watch any horse abused. From the looks of this horse's ragged coat, this wasn't the first time. But it might be the last if Archer didn't intervene. The teamster's whip fell again, the beefy driver determined the horse pull the load or die trying. The latter was highly likely and the horse knew it. The Cleveland Bay showed no fear. He merely stood with resignation. Waiting. Knowing. Deciding: death now, or death pulling a weight more appropriate for two.

The whip rose a third time, and Archer stepped out from the hotel's overhang. In a lightning move, Archer's gloved hand intercepted the thong of the whip and he wrapped it about his wrist, reeling in the teamster on his high seat like fish from the river. 'Perhaps you might try a sting or two of this lash yourself before delivering it to your animal.' Archer gave the whip a strong tug. Each pull threatened to unseat the teamster. The man leaned back in his seat, trying for leverage.

'Let go of the whip or come off the seat!' Archer commanded sternly, his eyes locking with the other man's as he gave another compelling tug.

'This is none of your business,' the teamster growled. 'That horse has to earn his keep and I do too.' But he released his end of the whip—forcefully, of course, probably with the hopes the force of his release would send Archer sprawling in the mud. But Archer was braced. The abrupt release did nothing more than seal his opinion of the man: bully, brute.

Archer wound the whip into a coil around his arm. 'Not with loads that are best drawn by a team of horses.' Archer jerked his head towards the horse. 'That horse won't finish the day, then where will you be?'

The man seemed to recognise the logic but his mouth pursed into a grim line. 'There's nothin' to be done about it, if you'll be givin' me my whip back, guv'nor, I'll be on my way.' The hint of a threat glimmered in the man's eye and he began to make his way down off the seat. That was the last thing Archer wanted.

He had a boat to catch within the hour. There was no time for fisticuffs. Archer was fast and light on his feet, thanks to hours of practice at Jackson's salon, but that didn't change the fact that the teamster outweighed him by two stone. Leaving on his Grand Tour sporting a split lip and black eye didn't exactly appeal.

The horse whinnied and stamped in the traces, his head rolling towards Archer as if in warning. The big man stopped a few feet from Archer and held out his hand. 'The whip.'

Archer grinned. 'I'll trade you for it. Give me the horse.'

The man spat on the ground. 'A whip for a horse?' His tone was derisive. 'That seems a bit unequal to me.'

'And for whatever is in my pocket.' Archer patted the pocket of his great coat.

'Maybe your pocket is empty.' The teamster's eyes narrowed. 'Show me.'

Archer nodded, careful to keep his body between the teamster and the horse. He could feel the horse's nose nudging his shoulder blade, perhaps in encouragement. Archer held up a gold money clip to the street lamp, letting it catch the light. He turned it, showing off the collection of pound notes folded together. 'It's fair. You can buy two horses for what's in this clip.' He was not going to doom another horse to the same fate simply by freeing this one.

Archer tried to assess the man's reaction. Money was usually the fastest way to settle a dispute, even if it wasn't the most moral. He waved the clip again in the beam of light. Behind him, he could hear the clatter of an oncoming coach, probably the one that was to take him and Nolan to the docks. He was running out of the time. 'The whip and the clip for the horse,' Archer pressed. What was there to think over? The man was letting pride get in his way.

'All right,' the man said gruffly, taking the money clip out of Archer's hand in a rough swipe. He jerked his head towards the horse. 'He's yours now, you unharness him.'

Archer had the horse free in short measure. There was triumph in knowing he'd rescued the animal from a certain fate, but what was he to do now? The coach he'd heard was indeed theirs and the driver was waiting. He had ten minutes to see the horse settled. He led the horse by a rope bridle towards the hotel's stable, sneaking a peek through the hotel's long street-front windows at Nolan. The situation inside didn't look good. Nolan and the other card players were standing. One of them was gesturing wildly at the cards and money on the table. Ten minutes might be a generous estimate.

Inside the stable, Archer roused the ostler, issuing rapid-fire instructions. 'This horse needs to be boarded.' He plunked down some coins on a small crude wood table. 'This will keep him until you can deliver him.' Money helped the ostler rub the sleep from his eyes. It was more than what was necessary. 'When the horse has been rested, have a boy deliver him to this address.' Archer pulled a card from a coat pocket. 'The man there will pay well. Here's additional money for the journey.' His nearest friend was a day's ride from Dover, but it was the best he could do under the hasty circumstances. Archer hoped the promise of more money would be enough to ensure the ostler didn't sell the horse instead of deliver it.

The sounds of commotion drifted in from the front of the hotel. That would be Nolan. Archer ran a friendly hand across the horse's ragged coat. The animal had been beautiful once, strong once; with luck he would be again. He dug in his pocket for more coin. Money was all he had to keep the horse safe. Archer pressed a third round of coins into the ostler's hand. 'This is for you, as my personal thanks for your efforts, one horseman to another.' Perhaps an appeal to the man's ethics would be enough. There was no time for more. The commotion was demanding his attention now. Archer gave the ostler a nod and strode into the courtyard, aware that the horse's eyes followed him out.

In the darkness, he almost collided with Nolan who was moving at a near run. 'Archer, old chap! Where did you get to? We've got to go!' Nolan seized his arm without stopping and dragged him towards the waiting coach, his words coming fast. 'Don't look now, but that angry man behind us thinks I cheated. He has a gun, *and* my good knife. It's in his shoulder, but I think he shoots with both—hands, that is. It wouldn't make sense the other way.' Nolan pulled open the coach door and they tumbled in, the coach lurching to a start before the door was even shut.

'Ah! A clean getaway.' Nolan sank back against the seat, a satisfied grin on his face.

'It doesn't always have to be a "getaway". Sometimes we *can* exit a building like normal people.'

Archer straightened the cuffs of his coat and gave Nolan a scolding look.

'It was fairly normal,' Nolan protested.

'You left a *knife* embedded in a man's shoulder, not exactly the most discreet of departures.' If Nolan had been discreet, he would have stopped playing two hours ago. The other players could have respectably quit the table, their pride and at least some money intact. But then he never would have had a chance to save that horse. 'You got away in the nick of time.'

Nolan merely grinned, unfazed by the scolding. 'Speaking of time, do you think Haviland is at the docks yet?' They were scheduled to meet two friends at the boat this morning to begin their Grand Tour. 'I'll wager you five pounds Haviland is there.'

Archer laughed. 'At this hour? He's not there. Everything was loaded last night. There's no reason for him to be early. Besides, he has to drag Brennan's sorry self out of bed. That will slow him down.' He and Haviland had known each other since Eton. Haviland was notoriously prompt, but he wouldn't be early and Brennan was always late.

'Easiest five pounds I'll ever make,' Nolan said something more, but Archer had leaned back and closed his eyes, blocking it out. He wanted a moment's peace. Between angry teamsters, rescued horses and irate gamblers, the late hour was starting to take its toll. Sometimes, Nolan wore a person out. Provoking a fight on the brink of departure wasn't exactly Archer's idea of *bon voyage*.

Still, whether he agreed with Nolan's choices or not, it was his job to have Nolan's back just as it was Haviland's job to have Brennan's. He and Haviland had divided up the duties of friendship years ago at school when it had become apparent Nolan and Brennan weren't entirely capable of exercising discretion on their own.

Back then, what couldn't be tamed had to be protected. These days, Nolan did a pretty fair job of protecting himself. He didn't need defending as much as he needed what one might call *support*. That was the gentlemanly way to put it. Needing a duelling second would be another.

It was times like this morning when Archer appreciated horses. He understood them, preferred them even. It was horses, in addition to his long-standing friendship with the others, that had provided the final, but not the only piece of motivation to leave Newmarket. Perhaps there were new breeds waiting for him in Europe, breeds he could send back to the family stud.

His father had charged him with purchasing any exciting prospects he could find and had given him *carte blanche* to do it. But Archer knew what that charge really was. It was his father's way of apologising. His father was very good at apologising with money. It was easy to do if one had a lot of it and his father, the Earl, had bags of it, rooms of it even. He'd never understood his family wanted more from him than his money or what it could buy. Not even at the last had he understood that and Archer had had enough of his father's aloof, uncaring reserve, enough of the coldness. He was off to seek warmer climates, warmer families: his mother's people in Siena.

Archer had never been so glad to be a second son.

His brother was the heir. He, as the eldest, was confined to the estates, whereas Archer had been given the stables, the racing string and that had been the avenue of a convenient escape when Haviland had delicately proposed the tour last autumn. He could be in Siena for the Palio, the town's grand tradition in the heat of August. He could be with his mother's family, horse breeders like himself. Perhaps that was what drew him most of all, these people he'd never met, only heard about in letters over his childhood; his uncle Giacomo, the breeder whose famed horses had won that race more than any other, a chance to be part of something great, a chance to keep the vow he had made to a dying mother. Her dreams and his promises were all he had left of her now.

There was the rustle of Nolan shifting, his body leaning forward to look out the window. 'I don't think he followed us, not with a knife in his shoulder,' Archer muttered, eyes closed. He heard Nolan's body relax once more against the squabs. Not quite relaxed, he amended. He could *feel* Nolan staring at him, those grey eyes boring into his head in a very one-sided staring contest. He would *not* open his eyes, he would not, would not, would not... Archer's eyes flew open. He couldn't stand it. 'What?'

Nolan crossed his arms over his chest, a wide smile taking his face. 'Archer, why is there a horse following us?'

'A horse?' It was Archer's turn to look out the window. He stared, he squinted, he looked at Nolan and then back out the window. It couldn't be. But it was. The Cleveland Bay he'd rescued was cantering down the road behind them. *Right* beside them, as if he knew Archer was inside the coach.

'I sort of rescued him this morning while you were playing cards,' Archer explained. What was he going to do with a horse at the docks? He couldn't take the beast to France with him. It would hardly be fair to make the poor horse endure a Channel crossing or to make him walk from Calais to Paris. He needed good food and rest. That didn't mean the horse's efforts hadn't tugged at his heartstrings. Nolan might laugh at the notion horses could and did communicate with their owners, but Archer had seen too many examples to the contrary. A horse's loyalty was not to be taken lightly. Horses would give their lives for the people they loved.

Their coach turned in to the docks, the horse slowing obediently to a trot to match the pace. Archer jumped down the moment the coach stopped. The horse still wore the rope bridle, but thankfully no lead line dangled dangerously at his hooves. Archer held out his hand and approached slowly. 'Easy, boy.' The horse blew out a loud snuffle, flecks of foam at his mouth. The running had started to wind him. A horse like him should be able to run for miles, but poor nutrition and hard labour had taken their toll on his natural endurance. They had not, however, taken their toll on the horse's sense of a good man. The horse stood patiently, letting Archer put a hand on his long nose and another on his neck.

Archer stroked the sweaty coat and spoke in soft, reassuring tones. 'I've got a good home for you. The ostler at the hotel is going to take you there after you have had a rest. There are green pastures. You can run all day and eat orchard grass.'

'He doesn't understand you, Arch.' Nolan chuckled, coming to stand on the horse's other side. 'He sure is a game fellow, though, to chase after you. Smart too. You've got to respect that.'

And wonder at it. Archer leaned his head against the horse's neck. People only left when there was no reason to stay. He knew that perhaps better than anyone. His mother had kept him bound to England when he would have left perhaps years ago. Now she was gone and so were his reasons. Were horses any different?

Archer walked the horse to the back of the hired coach and tied him on behind. He gave instructions to the driver and a few coins to deliver the animal back to the mews at the Antwerp Hotel. The ostler would be expecting him. He gave the horse a final pat. 'Trust me,' he whispered. 'Everything will be fine.'

'Except that you will be five pounds poorer.' Nolan gestured with a laugh towards a tall, dark figure standing alone on the pier. 'Haviland's already here. I told you he would be, and look, he's got his fencing cases with him. He couldn't be parted from them for even a night.'

Archer gave an exaggerated grimace and handed over the money, more concerned about the fact that Haviland was *alone*. 'Where's Brennan?' Nolan called out as they joined Haviland.

'Did you expect him to be here, scholar of human nature that you are?' Haviland teased and then his tone tensed. Archer could hear the worry. 'I had hoped he was with you.' Haviland motioned to the boat. 'We have to board. The captain is ready to leave. There's no more time. I was worried I'd be sailing alone.'

'Well,' Nolan said cheekily, 'we were rescuing horses.'

'And throwing knives at people's shoulders. Don't forget the knives part,' Archer added crossly. He was tired, concerned about the horse and Brennan. It seemed an ominous note to leave on. Perhaps it was an omen that he should stay behind? He could take a few days and deliver the horse himself to Jamie Burke over in Folkestone. He could find Brennan. They could catch a boat together. It was a sensible solution. He should offer...

No, he told himself firmly. He wasn't going to give in to the excuses no matter how practical they seemed. He'd put this off long enough, put others' needs ahead of his own long enough. He was getting on that boat. Perhaps he prevaricated out of cold feet at the last. If he took this step, there would be no turning back. His step would be larger than the others. He was going to find a new life, a new family.

The trio boarded the boat reluctantly and took up positions at the rail, their eyes glued to the wharf, each of them lost in their own worries about Brennan. The glances they exchanged with each other all communicated the same thought: What could have happened? Brennan had been with them last night at dinner. It wasn't, Archer knew, a matter of *where* Brennan was, but a matter of whether or not he was safe. Nolan tried to keep everyone's spirits up by wagering on Brennan's arrival, but to no avail. By the time the anchor's chains began to roll up, there was no sign of their fourth companion.

Archer bowed his head to the inevitable. Brennan wasn't coming. It wouldn't be the same the trip without him. It might be a whole lot safer, but it would lose something all the same. Wherever Brennan went, there was life and fire, he made everything exciting.

A blur of movement on the wharf caught his attention. Archer lifted his head. Beside him, Haviland saw it too. It was Bren! Haviland began shouting and waving madly. Brennan was running full tilt without his coats, white shirttails flapping like sails in the growing light. Haviland sprinted the length of the boat, yelling instructions: 'jump,' and 'don't jump here, it's too wide, jump at the back of the boat where it hasn't left the dock yet'. The back of the boat was flat for loading and there was a section that sported no railing. It would be Brennan's best chance.

That was when Archer realised Brennan wasn't alone. In his excitement, he hadn't noticed the two men racing behind, one of them armed. There was something more too. Behind the men was a horse, thundering past them, jumping knocked barrels, headed straight for Brennan and the drink. That wasn't just any horse. That was *his* horse. Archer exchanged a look with Nolan and they dashed off after Haviland.

The stern of the ship was chaos. Haviland was yelling, Brennan was running, the horse had pulled up alongside him, matching his pace to Brennan's, but the two men in pursuit were gaining. As long as they kept chasing him, they couldn't get a worthy shot off. It was when they stopped that worried Archer and that would be soon. There wasn't anywhere else to run. The ship had nudged away from the dock, leaving a gap of cold dark water between itself and the pier. Archer gauged the distance. Even with Brennan's speed, it would be close. Not close enough. Bren would need some help.

'Get on the horse, Bren!' Archer shouted into the wind, gesturing wildly towards the animal. It would be beyond dangerous. What if the horse refused to jump? What if they both missed the boat deck? Like him, Brennan had been born to the saddle. If anyone could do this, it would be Bren. There was no other choice unless Bren wanted to face pistols. Haviland and Nolan joined him in the wild charades. They held their breaths as Brennan Carr grabbed mane and swung himself up on the running steed. He put his feet to the horse's sides.

They leapt.

They landed.

Just barely.

Another foot and they would have missed. The shock of the landing and the uneven movement of the deck beneath him brought the horse to his knees. Archer and Haviland raced forward.

Brennan rolled out of the saddle. Haviland was there to catch him, but Brennan pushed him down with a rush of incoherent words. 'Stay down, Hav! Arch, the horse, keep him down!'

The first bullet whined overhead, missing Haviland by inches. Archer crouched beside the frightened horse, using his words and his hands to keep the big animal from becoming an accidental target.

Now that they were all safe, Archer wished the boat would move faster. There was suddenly not nearly enough space between them and the dock. It wouldn't surprise him to see Nolan's man from the hotel show up. Everyone else was here, even the horse. Thanks to Nolan and Brennan, the morning had got off to quite a start.

Assured they were out of range, the foursome picked themselves up cautiously, brushing off their clothes and exclaiming over Brennan. Archer exchanged knowing glances with Haviland. It was going to be quite a trip with those two along, but Haviland was smiling as England disappeared. Archer nodded to the reins in his hand. 'I'll go speak to the captain about where we can stable this boy.' As he moved off with the horse, Archer could hear Nolan drawl at the rail, 'The real question isn't where you've been, Bren, but was she worth it?'

Brennan's laugh drifted over the wind, as if the mad chase had been a simple lark, as if there hadn't been bullets fired. 'Always, Nol, always.' Sometimes, Archer envied Bren and Nolan their nonchalant ways, not seeming to care too much. They were proof that perhaps the unexamined life was underrated.

There was a makeshift stall above deck where the horse would be relatively safe. The Channel crossing was short. Just twenty-one miles of water separated England from France, but the water could be rough. Archer didn't want to risk the horse doing further injury to himself, so saw the horse installed and ran a hand down each of his legs to make sure there'd been no damage from his leap.

Satisfied the horse was no worse for his morning adventures, Archer placed a hand on the horse's neck. 'I guess you'll need a name if you're going to stay with me.' Archer thought for a moment. 'How about Amicus? It means *friend* in Latin, and you were that today. You stood Brennan in good stead when he needed you.'

'Especially since Cleveland Bays are carriage horses.' Haviland's voice was quiet behind him. Archer shrugged. He'd long since stopped caring if anyone heard him talking to the horses.

Archer smiled and stroked Amicus's long nose. 'Especially because of that.' He gave Amicus a considering look. 'I wonder if you might have been a hunter once, boy? It looked like you knew what you were doing when you made that leap.' Fearlessly, as if he'd taken hedges and logs, heights and wide spreads, before. Cleveland Bays were the preferred carriage horse of royalty, and Archer knew a few breeders who enjoyed riding to the hunt on them.

Haviland stepped up beside him and petted Amicus. 'Why do you suppose he did that? It was an extraordinary leap. I know horses that would have balked. He could have been killed.'

Archer gave Haviland a solemn look. 'He decided England could no longer hold him.'

'Like you, old friend?' Haviland ventured. 'Are you still determined to do this thing?' Nolan and Brennan might not know of his choice to stay in Italy, but he'd confided in Haviland.

Archer nodded. 'And you?' Haviland had done some confiding of his own. Archer wasn't the only one using this trip as an escape.

'Yes. I want to taste some freedom, I want to know

my own power, to see what might have been be-fore…' Haviland shrugged, his sentence dropping off. Haviland didn't have to say it. Archer knew how that sentence ended: before he had to go back and give himself in an arranged marriage to a woman who did not inspire his passions.

Archer silently thanked the heavens again that he wasn't firstborn. He at least had choices. He just had to make them. He and Amicus had something in common. He too had decided England could no longer hold him.

Chapter Two

The Pantera Contrada, Siena, Italy—early July, 1835

Tonight, nothing could hold her! Elisabeta threw her head back and laughed up to the starry sky. She let the wildness loose, humming through her blood in time to the musicians playing in the Piazza del Conte as she and her cousins drew near to the neighbourhood's centre. There was already a crowd gathered for the celebration and they were jostled on all sides by good-natured merrymakers filling the narrow streets. She didn't care. The press of people only added to her excitement. Tonight she was going to dance until her shoes were worn through and then she was going to dance barefoot. She'd dance until the sun came up!

It was her first real party since coming out of mourning and she was going to enjoy it, no matter what, which was no small thing in light of what had transpired this afternoon. Elisabeta grabbed her cousin Contessina's hands and swung the younger

girl around in a gay circle. 'I'm going to do something scandalous tonight,' Elisabeta declared, watching Contessina's pretty brown eyes widened in shock.

'Do you think that's wise? Papa just announced—'

'Especially because of that!' Elisabeta cut her
off. She wasn't going to think about *it*—the fact that
her uncle, Rafaele di Bruno, the *contrada*'s *capitano*, had bartered her off in a proposed marriage to
Ridolfo Ranieri, the relative of another neighbourhood's *priore* in order to secure an alliance for the
all-important Palio.

Like her first marriage, it was not a match of her
choosing and it wasn't fair. Five years ago at the age
of seventeen, she'd served her family and married
the very young Lorenzo di Nofri. It was meant to
be something of a dynastic connection for the family, and her feelings had not been considered. Then,
Lorenzo had died after three years of marriage and
she'd dutifully but begrudgingly done her year of
mourning for her adolescent husband.

Now, at the very first decent opportunity, she was
to be married off again. This time to a man in his
late forties, more than twice her age, heavy and gouty
from rich food and wine. Where would the chance for
a family of her own be in that? Elisabeta forcefully
shoved away images of what would be required of
her to produce a child in that alliance. There was no
place in this evening of celebration for dark thoughts.

She deserved better although her uncle disagreed.
He was quick to point out she was lucky to marry
again at all. She was no fresh virgin like Contessina, but a widow who'd been tried in marriage and
hadn't managed to prove her fecundity. Who would

want such a woman? She should be honoured by the Priore of Oca's attention and the chance to serve her family's greatness.

The Piazza del Conte came into view and Elisabeta pulled Contessina forward with her to take it all in: people, music, lanterns lighting the piazza like a magical fairyland. Celebrations like this were being held all over the town tonight, with every neighbourhood, or *contrada*, hosting its own party. It was Siena at its best and she'd missed it sorely in the years of her marriage spent in Florence. She'd missed her family, the festivals and, perhaps most of all, the horses.

It wasn't that Florence didn't have festivals or that Lorenzo's rich family didn't have horses, but they weren't hers and she was seldom allowed to work with them. Returning to Siena had been like coming alive again, which made the proposed marriage seem all the more cruel: to live again, only to face another sort of death.

Contessina tugged at her arm, slowing her down. 'What will you *do*?' she asked with a hint of worry.

'I don't know—*something*.' Elisabeta laughed. When the inspiration came she'd know it. Spontaneity was best left unplanned. 'Maybe I will dance with the next man I see!' Elisabeth announced, but that was hardly scandalous to her way of thinking. She'd have to do better than that to be truly scandalous. She'd made the remark mostly to shock Contessina, who loved her dearly, but didn't always know how to respond to her exuberance. Her uncle ran a strict household.

'You can't!' Contessina whispered a warning. Contessina's own dancing partners for the evening had already been arranged by her uncle and her brother, Giuliano. Even though it wasn't a formal ball, Contessina's partners were to be respectable young men from appropriate households in the *contrada*. 'What if the next person you saw was someone from Aquila?' Contessina dared to breathe the name of their rival *contrada*.

Elisabeta threw her a smug smile. 'I would even dance with an Aquilini.' She would too, but that was hardly likely. There would only be men of the Pantera *contrada*, her family's neighbourhood, here tonight. No one would dare venture away from their own neighbourhood celebrations. Still, stealing a dance was hardly the type of scandal she was thinking of, it was far too tame.

'What about your husband? What would he think?' Contessina was almost aghast at the thought of disobeying male authority. Her father had ordered her life to perfection. She had lived sheltered and protected to ensure she made a good marriage. Contessina had never thought to question the dictates of her parents. She was a good daughter and she would do what she was told.

Not so Elisabeta. She had played the good niece once. She was not ready to do it again, if ever, and certainly not to the fat cousin of the Priore of Oca, no matter how rich he was or what benefits it might serve the family when it came time for the Palio.

'He's *not* my husband yet. The engagement isn't even official,' Elisabeta said sharply, irritated with the conversation and what it signified. 'Perhaps I'll find a way out of it,' she teased, but she was only partially joking. If she could find a way out, she would.

Ridolfo terrified her with his beady, lecherous eyes. It was clear how he saw her: another thing to claim, to put in his treasury of earthly possessions. She did not relish the idea of being any man's slave, but especially not his.

'How would you do that?' Contessina, her brow knitting in contemplation, took her seriously. 'I can't see how it's possible unless you were to take a lover.' Contessina blushed as she said it. It was likely the most scandalous thing she could think of, an idea gleaned from conversations she wasn't supposed to overhear when her mother gathered with the other women of the *contrada* to exchange gossip.

Elisabeta gave her cousin a wicked smile. 'Exactly! What a perfect idea.' The thought held merit, just the sort of scandal she was looking for, but the list of candidates for such an affair was horribly short. She scanned the piazza, selecting and discarding the men of the *contrada*. 'Fabrizio is too old, I think I'd like someone younger, with more stamina. Alberto is young but he smells like garlic.' She wrinkled her nose.

'No!' Contessina was truly shocked now. 'I only meant to tease, to demonstrate how impossible it is.'

'How impossible what is?' Contessina's brother, Giuliano, sidled up to them, throwing an arm about his sister. He was handsome and wild, always in the throes of a grand affair, but life was different for a male. No one would condemn him for such promiscuity.

'Getting out of her engagement,' Contessina supplied.

Elisabeta moved to his other side and looped her

arm through his, feeling mischievous. 'Contessina suggested I take a lover.'

'I did not!' Contessina blushed furiously.

Giuliano's dark eyes sparked with mischief of their own. 'Ah, a last fling before settling down? A widow could do it, but not one who is affianced to another.' Giuliano thought for a moment. She could see her daredevil cousin puzzling it out. 'It could be pulled off, though, as long as you were discreet and the man you chose wasn't an enemy.' That meant not a man from Aquila or from Torre, the enemy of her would-be husband's neighbourhood.

Contessina looked frantically at them, waiting for them to give in and say they were only joking. 'Stop it!'

But Elisabeta didn't think she would stop. Why not take a lover? Perhaps just for the night? Perhaps it didn't have to be publicly scandalous, just a private interlude for herself. She deserved it and she'd been alone for so long. Even if her marriage had not been an intensely passionate one, she missed Lorenzo's presence. Was it so wrong to want one night in the arms of a strong, handsome man? To seek a little comfort, a little pleasure? No one had to know unless she wanted them to.

'Who would it be, Elisabeta?' Giuliano's playful pressing fuelled her madness. She would do it if the right man presented himself. Surely there must be one...

Elisabeta looked out over the piazza, towards the arch that marked the boundary of their *contrada*. Her breath hitched. It was as if the saints had conspired to present temptation and scandal personified. A man stepped through the arch. His height alone would make him stand out in any crowd—add to that those shoulders and it made for a remarkable sight. Good lord, they were broad, and that face! Even at a distance, the angles and planes were striking against the rich dark brown of his hair. It was longer than most of the men's present, skimming his shoulders and falling errantly over his right brow. She cocked her head and gave Giuliano a playful stare. This man wasn't a rival from an enemy *contrada*, he was something even more dangerous, a stranger, a man of unknown origins and family. That didn't make the man dangerous, it made him exciting, and it made him exactly the man she was looking for.

Did she risk it? It would be daring, even for her, but that was what tonight was for. The town's general spirits were high. The first Palio of the summer was behind them, her uncle victorious, his attentions already turned towards the Palio in August, and tonight people had gathered to celebrate the strawberry harvest: La Sagra del Fragole. Elisabeta doubted she'd be the only person present who allowed themselves to be swept away by the magic of a summer evening. Decision made, Elisabeta spoke her verdict.

'Him.' Her eyes studied the newcomer. 'I choose him.' Most definitely him. She wasn't the only one who'd noticed him, though. The attention of most of the feminine eyes in the crowd had gone his direction, she noted. He was *that* sort of man, the type who could command the female population of any gathering. The real issue was whether or not she could get there first. She would have to move fast. Signora Bernardi was closer and already edging near.

Elisabeta straightened her shoulders and tugged the square neckline of her gown lower, letting the tops of her breasts swell against the tightly laced bodice, to Contessina's dismay. She didn't have to reach him first, but she had to make her intentions known, had to convince him she was worth waiting for. She flashed Giuliano a competitor's smile and crossed the piazza, hips swaying, head held high.

Chapter Three

She was the kind of woman men crossed rooms for, or piazzas in this case, and she was headed directly for *him*. Archer couldn't say he didn't see her coming. How could he *not* see a woman like that; all those shiny black curls cascading down her back, the almond-shaped eyes that tilted ever so slightly at their corners as if they were always full of mischief and mystery, and the gown that set off the rest of her to perfection. The white of her shift peeked enticingly over the square bodice of a pale-green overdress laced over the full, rising curves of her breasts to a tight, slim waist before flaring out into provocatively swaying hips. The knowing smile on her lips suggested it was deliberate. She knew precisely what she was doing and what she wanted. At the moment, that was him.

The thrill of the hunt surged through him. Quicksilver eyes locked on his, and he held her sharp gaze, his own eyes communicating the unspoken message: *invitation accepted*. On his periphery, he was aware of women falling back, their interest averted by the advent of this woman's approach. She had staked her claim. If she meant to hunt him, she might be in for a surprise. Like any stallion worth his stud, Archer would be dominated by no woman.

She held out her hand, and he felt the full force of her attentions. 'Dance with me.' Not a question, then, she was too bold for that, but a summons, and he would honour it. Archer took her hand. That was where her supremacy ended. In his experience, a bold woman wanted a bold man and he could be that indeed, a commanding stallion to her flirty, teasing mare.

Eyes unwavering, he led her into the dance and fitted his hand to her back, swinging them into the polka without a word. Who needed words when they had eyes like hers? A body like hers, that communicated everything she thought and felt? She gave him a toss of her glorious dark head, tipping it up to meet his. Archer grinned, and she answered with a wide smile of her own, her eyes sparkling with the thrill of the dance.

Archer swung them into the turn and let the energy of the music claim them, his hand confident at her back as if it belonged there, as if they had done this before. He knew how to dance, how to navigate a crowded space, and she knew it too, recognised his skill and delighted in it, just as she was revelling in the sheer joy of the dance. The joy emanating from her was nearly intoxicating. She danced with her heart, her very soul, and it fired him, drove him to reckless abandon.

At the edge of the makeshift dance floor, he manoeuvred them sharply, bringing her up against him with the force of the turn, and did not relinquish her to the decency of distance. The pulse at her neck beat hard from the dancing and possibly from something more. She laughed up at him, confirming the latter. She felt it too, this surge of wildness, this connection between them although they'd not spoken a word— the dance was too fast, they were too breathless for conversation, too in love with the moment to contemplate the use of words.

What moments they were! Archer thought he would remember them for ever. It was an odd sensation given how many moments made up a lifetime, thousands upon thousands, most to be forgotten. Why these moments with a stranger who had lured him into a dance with only a smile and a touch? What made them different? What made them more valuable than all the other moments?

The music was ending. He took them through one last turn, his body memorising the soft curve of her hip where it met his, the straightness of her spine beneath his hand, his eyes discreetly taking in the rise and fall of her breasts beneath the tight-laced bodice just as he was aware of her gaze taking in him, studying his neck and throat where his shirt lay open. This was summer magic at its finest: a beautiful woman in his arms to enjoy the music and dancing with, a starry sky overhead, an arduous journey complete. He felt quite the king in these moments. Archer tilted his head to the sky and gave a howl of primal victory. And he knew.

He knew why he would remember these moments; because he was so alive in them, *she* was so alive in them. They were breathing hard and laughing, drinking in the simple pleasures of music and dance beneath a starry sky, the summer air warm around them. Did life get any better than this? His hand lingered at her waist in no hurry to set her apart from him and he thought that indeed it just might get better. His eyes drifted across her face, resting briefly on her lips. This woman was no stranger to pleasure, not with that body and those eyes, and the way she looked at him—with boldness and invitation. The rest of the piazza might as well have melted away for all that he noticed anything but her.

Archer's voice was low and private when he spoke, his gaze lingering meaningfully on the sensual curve of her lips. 'Who are you, *bella signora*?' They were the first words he'd spoken to her. She would know now that he wasn't Italian. She would hear it in his accent. Not just a stranger, then, from a neighbouring town, but a true outsider. Maybe it didn't matter where he was from for what they wanted of each other. 'My name is Archer.'

'Elisabeta.' She returned his signals, letting her own eyes wander over his mouth. Arousal stirred hard. She had understood the negotiation. She had consented. They were to be Elisabeta and Archer. No last names, no true way to trace the other once they parted. There would be no strings, no ties that would bind them beyond the immediacy of the affair.

'Well, *Archer*…' she smiled up at him '…you are just in time.'

Heat intensified in his groin. 'In time for what?'

She gave him a coy glance. 'For strawberries.' Elisabeta crooked her finger and beckoned with a 'come-hither' smile that left him aching. 'Did I mention there would also be cream?'

The innuendo was not lost on Archer. He was going to come all right. Between the dancing, the warm summer night, the elation of having arrived at his destination at last and the seductive beauty in his arms, his body was fully primed for more intimate thrills. He had every reason to celebrate. It had not been an easy journey from Paris on his own. He'd had to leave before Haviland's rather sudden wedding. He'd given up the summer in Switzerland with Nolan and Brennan. There'd been no choice. Time had been of the essence if he wanted to make Siena in advance of the August Palio. He'd known from the start he'd never make the first one in July.

Travel had been rough, the Italian inns rougher. But, oh, the journey had been worth it the moment he'd passed through the city gates, seen the town lit up and festivities under way, as if the party was just for him. He'd stabled Amicus, left his bag at the livery and headed for the central piazza, hoping to find someone to direct him to his uncle's. The piazza had been quiet, but he'd followed the music to this neighbourhood and found more than directions. He'd been in this piazza less than five minutes when this dark-haired beauty had pulled him into the dancing, all fire and beauty in his arms, her quicksilver gaze flashing with life and exuberance, her body moving into his as if they were made for one another. Dancing with her had been effortless, just as following her across the piazza was now. He had no doubts where this was heading: to the food tables and to a quiet space in the dark beyond the lights.

Archer's stomach growled, and he grinned. There was no choice to ignore it. Elisabeta smiled and passed him a plate. She gestured to each dish and offered an explanation, pleased when he nodded. While all of his friends had been studying French, he'd been studying Italian. His mother had seen to it that he had Italian tutors. It was paying off now, even if it was just to bring a smile to this woman's face.

'Risotto alle fragole, polenta con fragole, ravioli...' She rattled off the dishes, taking a serving for herself as they went. At the end of the table stood an enormous vat-like bowl of strawberries and tubs of cream alongside various tortes. *'La torta!'* Elisabeta beamed back at him over her shoulder, silver eyes gleaming in delight.

Archer took a healthy helping of everything. The smells alone would have been persuasion enough to try the new foods, but Elisabeta's smile stole any reservation he might have had. The way she looked at a man, the way her eyes lingered over him in appreciation, he would have eaten slugs for her. There was wine to pour from casks after that and slices of hearty dark country bread to add to his burgeoning plate.

She led him to a quiet spot off the piazza where the lantern lights didn't quite reach and the music didn't quite preclude conversation. There was privacy in the darkness. 'It's the strawberry festival, in case you haven't guessed,' she said between bites. 'We celebrate it every year. Most of the dishes of the evening are made with strawberries.'

'It's delicious.' Archer took another mouthful of the risotto. It truly was. The food was rich and warm. He'd never tasted anything as good as this, not even the fine food of Paris could compare. He took a swallow of wine, letting his tongue savour the full-bodied flavour, a perfect complement to the meal.

When his plate was nearly empty, she took it from him and set it aside. Her voice was a sultry whisper in the night. 'Now for *la dolce*.' She dipped a strawberry in the small pot of cream and held it to his lips. 'Lick,' she commanded as he took the berry between his teeth, laving the sweet cream with his tongue until her eyes locked with his and her lips formed the very erotic word: 'Bite.'

Two could play this game, as he knew she very well intended. Archer plucked up a berry and swirled it in the cream before he offered it to her, his own voice offering a seductive invitation of its own. 'Suck.'

She took the berry in her mouth, her tongue flicking across his fingers where he held the fruit, her eyes never leaving his, the message in them plain, *you're next*. Archer's throat went dry. He was going to love Siena, he just knew it.

Chapter Four

He would be an exquisite lover, and who would know what they had done? Who would care? He would just be passing through. He could give her something of pleasure to carry into her marriage. Elisabeta leaned towards him on their narrow bench, her eyes caressing his mouth with their gaze, offering him a moment's preparation before her lips slid over his. She tasted him, tempted him—or was she tempting herself?

His mouth answered hers, hungry for more, his body straining in acknowledgement that they were not private enough for 'more'. Elisabeta drew back. It would be up to her to initiate, this was her territory. 'Perhaps a walk? There's a lovely fountain not far.' It was a ruse, an excuse to seek that privacy, to be alone, and her heart thundered in knowledge of it. There would be more to come with this man.

'Which direction? I'll go first.' His concern for preserving at least a facade of decency spoke to her. Here was a man of experience.

'To the right.' She motioned to the street veering

off from the piazza. 'It's not far.' She watched him slip into the night and counted the minutes in her head before following.

He'd gone deeper into the curving street than she'd anticipated. There was a moment when she thought she might have misread him, where she thought he had taken the opportunity to disappear. Then the whisper came in the darkness. 'Elisabeta!' An arm reached out to seize her about the waist, dragging her into a curve of a little alcove. She gave a startled yelp as he spun her about and drew her against him, his mouth stealing a laughing kiss. He felt as a man should, all heat and hardness where their bodies melted together.

'What took you so long?' He was grinning in the darkness. She could hear that grin in his words as his hands rested at her waist, so comfortably, so naturally as if they were long-time lovers well used to one another's bodies.

'I didn't expect you to go so far.' Elisabeta twined her arms around his neck, her hands fingering the ends of his hair where it brushed below his collar.

'I was looking for the perfect spot.' His mouth was at her neck and his words came between kisses along the column of her throat, his mouth latching over the pulse beat at its base, sending a trill of excitement down her spine.

'For what?' She managed to breathe, although she could guess, and the guessing made her giddy with excitement. She was thankful to note there was a wall at her back should she need it. At this rate, her legs wouldn't hold her much longer. This man was a consummate artist in the craft of *amore* with his subtle touches, the lingering of his gaze, the temptation woven in his kisses.

'For this.' His mouth returned to hers, his body pressing hers to the rough brick of the wall. She was fully protected here by the breadth of his shoulders and the height of his body. They blocked her from view should anyone stagger down the street or come looking for privacy of their own.

She should have *known* such a master of the art would not resort to a base, rushed, dark-alley coupling, or be carried away by the heat of the moment and his own need. She should have been *ready*. The kisses to her neck, to her throat, should have primed her, warned her that here in the privacy of the dark and the quiet of the night, the music and noise of the festivities far behind them, these moments would be different than the frenzied excitement in the piazza. But still, the kiss took her unawares.

This kiss was a long, languorous exploration of her, his tongue probing and tasting, his mouth opening to encourage her to do the same, and she did. She tasted the remnants of rich wine on his tongue, smelled the last vestiges of his morning *toilette* beneath the sweat of the day, the scents of a man. Wherever he'd come from, he'd come on horseback. The smells of leather and horse were evident too, on his skin, and most pleasantly so. She preferred a man smell like a man than a flower garden. A man's scent should above all be an honest representation of him.

As should his body. There was honesty aplenty in that dark alcove. His want was in evidence, his erection hard at her stomach where their bodies met. He was not alone in that evidence, only more obvious. There was wetness at her core, an ache that rose in her, demanding to be assuaged. He nipped at her lip, tugging at it gently, and she moaned, her body pressing into his, her hips grinding in suggestion against his.

Archer groaned his response into her mouth, his kiss becoming possessive, the slow tempo between them quickening, turning primal. His hands bunched the folds of her skirts, pushing them up. 'Let me lift you.' The command was hoarse with need.

His hands slid under her, cupping her buttocks and hefting her to him, her legs wrapping around his waist as he balanced her between himself and the wall. Her skirts fell back, her private flesh bare against him. She felt the hardness of him through the barrier of his trousers, the contact erotic, and she moved on him in instinctive response.

She was rewarded with a fierce nip at her ear and the feel of the strong muscles that held her, trembling. 'You will have me spilling like a green boy.' The rasped warning was both caution and accolade and it spurred her on. The heat and frenzy was returning, stoked to life once more. Her hips sought him again, but he had other ideas, better ideas.

He shifted his weight, his hand finding the core of her, his palm pressing against her mons until she cried out in pleasurable frustration. She was far beyond it being enough. But he knew. 'I can make it better,' he promised against her throat, his fingers parting her folds. His breath hitched as he felt her wetness, found the tiny bean of her pleasure and began to stroke. Her pleasure was exciting for him, she realised. The knowledge that her delight roused him was intoxicating, heady, and she gave herself over to it, fuelling them both, driving them both towards the cliff of madness. She reached for him, her hand taking him through his trousers as he stroked her. *Dio caro!* The man was big, and long and, oh, so deliciously hard.

Elisabeta worked the fall of his trousers open. The best way to tell him what she wanted was to show him. Her hand found the naked length of him, and he gave a low, guttural groan. 'You will kill me yet, Elisabeta.' Her name was a groan on his lips, his body straining.

'Take me,' she whispered fiercely at his ear. She too had become primal in these moments. She had never been so lost in the madness of lovemaking before, had never been this far and yet something more loomed on the horizon of this pleasure. All reserve, all rational thought had been stripped away by his hands, his mouth.

'Yes,' Archer rasped and the response was immediate; the slide of his body into hers. She was tight but ready, the slickness of her tunnel easing his way until he was fully within her. There was the glorious sensation of stretching, accommodating. Then he began to move, and she with him, her hips matching the thrusting rhythm of his body, slowly at first, the pace growing with their intensity.

Moans and gasps became the sum of her vocabulary, his body the sum of her world. She muffled those gasps against the fabric of his shirt and still he brought them closer and closer to the undefinable something that lay just over the edge of madness. All she had to do was…

'Let go, Elisabeta,' came the hoarse command. 'Let yourself go, we are nearly there.' The words came in pants and broken fragments, but that he had any power of speech at all was miraculous to her—she had none. He gave a final thrust, and she let the madness take her entirely. She was over the cliff, claiming pleasure in its fullness, her heart pounding, her pulse racing, and Archer was there too, his own heart pounding hard against hers, proof of his efforts spilling against her thighs, a hot reminder of glorious life.

She rested her head against the brick of the wall, Archer's head on her shoulder, his own shoulders heaving from his exertions. Her hands were in his hair, absently stroking, soothing. Her mind was still in an incoherent fog where thought came in incomplete scraps. What did she know of such things? She'd known nothing of this pleasure before tonight, only that it hypothetically existed. How was she to have known it would be so bone-shattering? Her experience was limited to the adolescent skills of a fumbling but well-intentioned virgin. Later, her marriage bed had known the comfort that comes with familiarity, but never this overwhelming pleasure that left her drugged; sapped and satisfied all at once.

Curiosity began to ignite as reality slowly settled on her. It made one wonder. If this man's lovemaking could be incredible up against a wall in a dark alcove of a city street, what would it be like in a feather bed? What would it be like with a woman he *knew* or perhaps even truly loved?

No, she couldn't let her mind travel that direction, not even under the excuse of this pleasurable fog. To know the answer to such a fantasy meant knowing him, learning his last name, his history, his people. She was not looking for that. She could not have that, it was far too much temptation. Her uncle had promised her to another. What a cruel temptation it would be to know he was out there in the world somewhere and to have the tools to find him, while being married to the *priore*'s gouty relative. There was only hurt down that path, and shame.

The thought of shame sparked too the reality of what she'd done. For all of the nuances he'd provided with his laughter, his touch, his sexy knowing mouth, his intimate possession of her body, for all that he'd never made her feel that this was a cheap encounter or she was nothing more than a *troia*, there was no disguising what this was: sex in an alley with a stranger. *Extraordinarily* good sex, apparently, and with a *very* handsome stranger, but adjectives didn't change the blunt truth. She'd set out to act scandalously and she had.

Archer's head moved against her shoulder and he set her down slowly, as if warning her legs they would need to stand on their own. He moved away from her long enough to restore his trousers. In the dimness, he was even more attractive after sex than he was before, if that was possible. His hair fell rakishly in his face as he concentrated on his clothes, his hands sure and competent in their tasks. She'd never found a man's hands sexy before, but even in the dark, his hands carried a certain quality to them, she'd thought as much when they'd danced and eaten. Those moments in the piazza seemed a lifetime ago.

'Elisabeta.' His voice was soft in the darkness,

his face close to hers, his eyes half-shut. One arm bracketed her as he leaned against the wall. His lips touched hers in a light brushing, not a full kiss. He was formulating ideas, deciding what happened next. She couldn't allow that. She gathered her reserves.

'Archer,' she answered in equally soft tones, her hand gently cupping the firm line of his jaw. She wanted to touch him until the last, to give her body every chance to remember him. 'I have to go.' With that, she ducked under his arm and ran into the night.

Just like bloody Cinderella in the children's tale. Archer took a few steps forward into the street after her, but he stopped himself. Women who fled without provocation didn't want to be followed. He would not make a fool of himself by running after her. Or worse, put her in danger of discovery. Elisabeta, if that was even her name, was gone with not even a glass slipper to trace her. If Nolan was here, he'd tell him he'd got a fair bit luckier than the prince. That poor fellow had only got a dance after flirting with her all night. To which, Archer would acerbically remind him it *was* a children's tale after all. As such, it was also a tale of true love.

Sex in an alley wasn't true love, not even close. It wasn't meant to be. Yet nothing in the encounter had been casual. Archer leaned against the wall, his active mind imagining the brick still warm from her body. He'd had casual sex before. It was physical and fast, a game for the moment, a way to pass the time at a ball or masquerade. The arousing quality of those liaisons usually came from the heightened risk of discovery. Certainly, those qualities had been somewhat in evidence tonight. A street was public no matter how dark. But there had been more. Even now, arousal gave an insistent stir at the memory of her head thrown back at the last as she claimed her pleasure, her hair spilling, her breasts thrust forward against her bodice, her cries of release, the squeeze of her legs, holding him. Never had he seen an abandon so complete, so beautiful in its naturalness.

She had been stunned, surprised when it had come. He'd had the sense in those moments that while she was no virgin, this was new to her. New seemed an apt but inadequate description of what he'd seen in her face, felt in her body. His ego preened at the thought. He'd given her that exquisite release for the first time. It was silly, he hardly knew her, but he prided himself on putting a woman's needs at the centre of his lovemaking. It was what had made him one of London's rather more successful lovers.

And yet, his body hadn't been without its own pleasures there against the wall. His body hummed for more of the same even now with having achieved repletion. Once was apparently not enough. Then again, perhaps it was understandable. He'd been on the road and alone for quite a while.

He was going to be alone quite a while longer too if he didn't put this fanciful nonsense out of his head and find his uncle's house. He'd left Amicus at the livery near the *campo*, the town centre, with plans to return for him once he'd located his uncle's home. He'd had no desire to tramp through narrow cobblestone streets with a horse in tow, in the dark, looking for a home he wasn't familiar with. His best bet would be to return to the party and ask for directions to Giacomo Ricci's home in the Torre neighbourhood.

Archer shoved off the wall and began walking back to the festivities. His other best bet would be to put his Cinderella out of his mind. He wasn't here to fall in love; he was here to make a new start, to help his uncle with horses for the Palio and to fulfil a promise to his mother. Taken together that seemed quite enough to keep a man busy without a woman to complicate things. The mysterious Elisabeta would have to remain just that—a mystery and a memory.

Chapter Five

'*La famiglia è la patria del cuore*! Family is the country of your heart. Of course you've come.' Giacomo Ricci rose from his chair and came to embrace Archer, kissing him on both cheeks the moment Archer entered the *loggia* where a late breakfast was being served the next morning.

'*Buongiorno, Zio.*' Archer bore the effusive greeting as graciously as he had last night after finding his uncle's *contrada*, Torre. It hadn't been far from the town centre, just to the west of where he'd come from. Everyone had known his uncle and it had been easy to find Giacomo among the throng of revellers. Apparently each neighbourhood had been hosting its own celebration.

His uncle had kissed him publicly and spirited him away to his home where a new party commenced as he was introduced in whirlwind fashion to cousins, spouses of cousins and their offspring. There had been neighbours and friends after that, all eager to greet him and kiss him. He'd never been kissed by so many men in his entire life. Archer couldn't recall the last time his father had kissed him. Had his father *ever* kissed him?

Archer filled a plate with bread, cheese and fresh strawberries and took a seat at the table where he could look through the arches of the *loggia* into the street. The *loggia* was open by design, so that people passing by could wave to his uncle or stop to conduct brief business or even partake of some food. He knew enough from what his mother had told him about her home that the arrangement spoke to the power and position of her family in the *contrada*. To be seen with Giacomo Ricci was important. It was the sort of news people would share over dinner later in the day.

For now, though, Archer was thankful the *loggia* was empty and the streets quiet after a boisterous night of festivities. He was still reeling from last evening. His uncle retook his seat. 'Did you sleep well? I want to take you around the neighbourhood and show you everything, have you meet some people.' His uncle's eyes shone with warm pride as he paused, gripping Archer's hand firmly. 'I cannot believe you are here at last, my sister's son, here in my own home.'

Archer felt his throat tighten unexpectedly at the warmth and sincerity of his words. 'I cannot believe it either. I wish it had been sooner. I promised her I would come.' These were promises only his brother, Dare, knew about, promises he'd made that last day in his mother's final hour and not spoken of to anyone, not even Haviland. He and Dare had been with her, all three of them simply waiting, knowing the end was so very close, that all the sunshine, all the open windows letting in the crisp autumn afternoon, couldn't hold back the inevitable. She was going on without them. They were grown men. They should have been able to handle the reality. But Archer's own throat had been tight with emotion as it was now.

'What did you promise her?' his uncle prompted gently. Archer struggled to find words to tell this man he knew and yet didn't know. 'She said, "Promise me you will go to Giacomo, Archer. Go to my home. I think you will find what you're looking for."' He was looking for so much. A father figure who could replace the one his father had become, a place of his own where he could be his own man as opposed to the second son, where he could live his own dreams among the horses.

'This is a pilgrimage for you?' Giacomo asked quietly.

'In part,' Archer confessed. 'I come here to honour her, to remember her, to know who she was before she was my mother. But I have also come here for the future, for *my* future, to see what I can be.' His mother had not told him explicitly to stay in Siena, but the idea suited him, this concept of striking out on his own and under his own power.

His uncle smiled, his grip on Archer's hand tightening. 'The past and future are often intertwined in this way. She was right to send you to us. You are a good son to honour her and you shall be like a son to me.' Even if the past ten hours weren't enough to confirm it, Archer knew from years of letters how his uncle and his wife had despaired of any children of their own.

Archer could see now, surrounded by the big brick home of the Riccis, how disappointing it must be for his uncle not to have the home filled with children.

His uncle was a well-built man, tall in the tradition of the Riccis, but his temples were greying and his years for child rearing had passed. He was a local statesman now, his days consumed with running the family cloth business and training horses. Archer understood now with vivid clarity how his mother's last wish had been a gift for him and for her brother. Even facing death, she'd thought about what would be best for the family, for others. He would not fail her.

Giacomo was smiling now, already planning. 'There are people I want you to meet, places I want you to see. I'd like to show you around the *contrada* today if you're up for it.'

'I would like that, if it's not too much trouble. I can show myself around,' Archer offered. Perhaps there was a chance of running into Elisabeta. But he would like it in other ways too. It would give him time to spend getting to know this uncle of his. The warmth of his uncle's welcome was overwhelming, the sincerity and emotion of it touched him. It reminded him of his mother, of the warmth she extended to everyone she met. She had been a generous woman in the way that his uncle was a generous man.

His uncle waved an adamant hand in the air. 'No, no, it's not any trouble. You are one of us. Everyone must understand that.' Archer nodded graciously. His mother had warned him, had she not? In an Italian family, one was never alone, never 'forced' to make one's way on one's own. His uncle was not done with his plans. 'Perhaps tomorrow, we can ride out to the country and see the horses. It is why you've come, isn't it? Your mother mentioned you loved the animals in all of her letters.'

Archer smiled. Ah, this would be easier than he could have hoped. His uncle understood. 'It is. I am interested in the Palio. I want to be part of it.'

Giacomo beamed and laughed out loud. 'And so you will! I am the *capitano* this year,' he said proudly. Archer felt the man study him for moment, dark eyes assessing. 'Maybe I could appoint you as one of my *mangini*.' He nodded as if the decision was made. 'Yes, you would do nicely and it would give you a chance to learn about the race.'

The *mangini* were supporters of the *capitano*, his lieutenants in seeing his commands carried out. Archer knew it was a position of honour, but it was not what he'd hoped for himself. Archer leaned forward, holding his uncle's eyes, amber-brown like his own, in all seriousness. 'The honour would be mine. I will serve the *contrada* however I may, but I had hoped to offer myself to you as a rider.' Surely his mother had mentioned his skills in that regard if she'd mentioned him in the letters that had been exchanged over the years.

'A *fantino*?' his uncle asked before shaking his head. 'It is not possible. The riders are not from the *contradas*, or even from Siena.' He gave another wave of his hand. 'It makes it too difficult to arrange the *partiti*. It simply isn't how it is done.' Perhaps he saw Archer's disappointment. He gave a gentle smile. 'Everyone in the *contrada* is part of the Palio and you will be too, you will see. I will need you as a *mangini*, someone to help me with the Palio arrangements.' He nodded, affirming his satisfaction over the arrangement.

It was not what Archer had wanted. He'd come all this way to ride in the Palio. He'd given up Haviland's wedding to make the journey on time. But his uncle was done with the subject for the moment. He sat back in his seat. 'You have your mother's eyes, the Ricci eyes, and her chin.' His tone softened and lowered. 'My sister, your mother, was a beautiful woman. She stole hearts wherever she went, your father's included, and his was not an easy one to steal. But he saw her and it was all over for him. I remember that summer as if it were yesterday; the grand English earl had come to Siena for the races to see the Italian champions, and he went home with a wife, the most beautiful woman in Tuscany.'

He gave a nostalgic sigh. 'It was a heady summer, watching Vittoria in the throes of her courtship. It was a time full of victories and romance, and now the earl's son has returned.' He smiled benevolently at Archer. 'Perhaps we will find you a wife too? Someone worthy of a Ricci, no?'

Archer tried to refuse politely. 'My path is unclear to me. I don't know that I'd be much of a catch at the moment.' He didn't need his aunt and the troops of his newly introduced female cousins matchmaking for him. Marriage was the last thing he wanted. He'd just gained his freedom, he didn't need a wife. And yet his reckless conduct in the alley last night suggested he needed something. Had last night been about sowing wild oats, or had it been about a desire to make a connection?

His uncle drummed his fingers on the table, a

knowing gleam in his eye. 'Young men all think they know what they need. I know, I was a young man once too. That's why young men have female relatives. Women can see what a man needs better than he can himself.' His eyes moved to Archer's empty plate. 'If you're finished eating, let us be off.

'Have I completely overwhelmed you?' Giacomo asked as they stepped out into the street and the sun.

Archer laughed, shading his eyes and appreciating the easy camaraderie that flowed between him and his uncle. He'd missed his friends during this last leg of the journey, even Nolan's goading and endless wagers. It was good to be back among people he could trust. 'You mean despite the fact that you've tried to get me married off in less than a day? And you've appointed me to be a *mangini*? Overwhelmed hardly begins to describe it. I am overcome with your generosity.'

'That doesn't please you?' Giacomo asked as they turned towards the *contrada*'s central piazza.

'It does please me, it's just that I had hoped to ride,' Archer confessed. He would be honest with his uncle. The sooner his uncle learned he was determined and wouldn't accept no for an answer, the better. 'Although I understand to be a *mangini* is a great honour,' he added, not wanting to appear insulting.

'Ah, I know the feeling. I would have loved to have ridden but it isn't how it's done for the Palio,' his uncle commiserated. 'The *fantini* don't come from the *contradas* themselves. It's no matter.' Giacomo shrugged. 'If Torre wins, you will still be a hero.' He gave a mischievous wink. 'The women will go crazy for you since you were part of the negotiation team that helped us win.'

They came out of the street into the piazza with its fountain. It was busier here, people starting to go about their daily errands. Although, Giacomo informed him, that wouldn't last too long once the afternoon heat peaked. Everyone would retreat behind shuttered windows into cool stucco rooms for siestas. 'My favourite part of the day with your *zia*.' He gave Archer a knowing look. 'In the evening everyone will come out again for strolling, *la passegiatta*, do you know it?'

He didn't wait for an answer. 'Everyone strolls within their neighbourhood or in their allied neighbourhood.' He pointed to a banner hanging on the wall of one of the tall buildings surrounding the piazza. It depicted an elephant in the foreground, a tall tower in the back, done in crimson. 'That's our symbol. We are Torre, the Tower.'

'Does neighbourhood matter so much?' Archer asked, thinking of Elisabeta and the neighbourhood he'd wandered into last night before finding his uncle.

Giacomo threw back his head and laughed. 'The *contrada* is *everything* if you are Sienese. You are *born* into the neighbourhood. If you ask anyone who they are, they'll tell you their neighbourhood first, city second. If you know someone's neighbourhood, you know everything about them; who their allies are, what they do; most of us in Torre are in the wool trade. You know where they live, you know who their enemies are.'

'Enemies? Really?'

'Oh, yes.' Giacomo was in earnest. They strolled

the perimeter of the fountain, stopping occasionally to greet people and exchange a little news. 'Valdimonte's enemy is the Nicchio Contrada, Aquila's enemy is Pantera and so on. Our enemy is Oca, which is rumoured to be striking an alliance with Pantera. Pantera won the July Palio.'

Archer did his best to follow Giacomo's conversation. It was a lot to take in, especially in a second language. English families and English neighbourhoods were far simpler entities by contrast. He wondered which neighbourhood he'd stumbled into last night? Would that make Elisabeta an ally or an enemy? 'Do *contradas* ever intermarry?'

Giacomo gave him a keen look. 'Of course, but during the Palio, husbands and wives often separate and go home to their own neighbourhoods.' He grinned and wagged a finger at Archer. 'You will learn. It's the *contrada* above all else. My Bettina, though, your *zia*, was the old *priore*'s daughter so we are never separated.' There was no mistaking the pride in Giacomo's voice in having married a Torre woman. This was a new world indeed, his mother's world, Archer reminded himself. She'd grown up in the *contrada*.

Giacomo clapped him on the back. 'Do you have your eye on a pretty *signorina* already? Perhaps you refused my help because you have spied a pretty girl for yourself?'

Archer was tempted to tell him about Elisabeta, but thought better of it. If she had been from an enemy *contrada* it would only make trouble if he pursued her. Anyway, he wasn't looking for a permanent relationship. But that didn't stop him from

thinking about her as they stepped into a few shops
to meet some of the family's especial friends. Was
Elisabeta out in her neighbourhood doing errands?
Talking with shopkeepers? Was she with friends?
Another man?

Had he merely been an escape for her? Maybe
he'd merely been part of a fantasy or the madness of
the summer night? She'd not wanted to be followed.
There were only so many reasons for that; none of
them suggested she was unattached and free to make
her own decisions. He *should* let it be and accept it
for what it was: a few glorious moments. Yet, the
thoughts persisted. Where was she? What was *she*
doing? Archer chuckled to himself. He knew already
he couldn't just let it go. Against his better judgement, he was going to find her.

She was picking petals off a rose like a silly school
girl. 'He loves me, he loves me not.' The foolishness
made her laugh. Elisabeta snipped the roses and put
them in her basket. To be honest, love had nothing to
do with it. All right, then, she amended: he lusts me,
he lusts me not. Even here in her uncle's garden in
the full light of day, thoughts of last night managed
to bring a blush to her cheeks and a heat to her body
that had nothing to do with the sun. Those thoughts
made her want.

More.

Of him.

Pleasure once tasted was proving to be a potent
elixir with a power, she suspected, to addict. Once
was not enough. What a lovely addiction that would
be. What an unexpected one. When she'd sought out

her stranger, she'd not expected this wanting as a consequence. He was to remain a stranger, a man to whom she had no ties. But she'd come away with a name and a longing to have him again. Already, she was wondering if that name would be enough to find him. Over breakfast she'd reasoned an English name couldn't be terribly hard to find among all of these Italian names. Nor was Siena so big that she wouldn't be apt to run into him if she went to the city centre often enough. Surely, those odds would be in her favour if she chose to exercise them.

By the time she'd wandered out to the garden to pick flowers, the issue was no longer a question of finding him, but a question of did she truly want to? Her curiosity said yes. It was her curiosity that had driven her to distraction this morning with its questions filling her mind: Where was he now? What was he doing? Had he woken to thoughts of her? Had he dreamt of her? Did he too regret their veiled identities?

Then again, perhaps it was better to wonder than to know. The pleasure he'd offered might only have been the luck of the night, the work of the stars and summer magic. Surely such pleasure was not commonplace? It most certainly didn't happen all the time. She'd lived her entire marriage without it and she would likely live through another without it, proof enough that Archer's pleasures could not be conjured on a whim nor by just any man or woman. It would be a shame to have him again only to be disappointed by the ordinary nature of their lovemaking. Better to let him become memory.

'Cousin! There you are. I've been calling for you.'

Giuliano came striding down the path, playful mischief sparking in his dark eyes. 'Have we been daydreaming over our handsome stranger?' he teased. 'You were quick to disappear last night.'

She gave Giuliano a saucy grin in return, her good spirits making her reckless. 'I told you I'd have him.'

Giuliano leaned in close, a grin on his face. 'And did you? Have him?'

Elisabeta gave him a light punch on the arm. 'You're wicked. Besides, a lady never tells.' She paused and gave him a considering look. 'What of the lovely Widow Rossi? Did you have her?'

Giuliano groaned and had the good grace to look down at the ground. 'Point taken.' But a moment later any penitence he felt over probing into her personal affairs had vanished. 'Will you see him again?'

Elisabeta shrugged and moved on to a new collection of flowers, trying to keep her actions nonchalant. She did not want to give too much away to Giuliano. He was reckless and there was no telling what he might do. 'Of course not. We didn't exchange enough information for that.'

Giuliano followed her, far too astute in the games of *amore* to take her response as a direct or even accurate answer. His voice was low now, his tone compelling. 'But would you? If you could?'

Elisabeta fixed her cousin with a cool stare, trying to keep her pulse from racing. 'What do you know?'

'There's an Englishman in town. There was word of it when I ran my errands this morning. He's the nephew of Giacomo Ricci, the horse trainer who lives in Torre.'

The information was better than a name and it was

worse. She could find him, she knew who his people were and where. But it didn't help her cause. Her eyes held Giuliano's and a silent message passed between them. Both of them were serious now. Love stopped being a game once the *contradas* were involved.

She could go to Archer. But did she dare? Beside her, Giuliano gave a short nod. 'It's probably best your answer is no.' The Oca *contrada*'s sworn enemy was Torre and while that might not matter to her uncle, it would matter to her future husband's *contrada*.

'Then why did you tell me? I do not think of you as generally unkind,' Elisabeta scolded quietly. Perhaps it was far crueller to know she could not have him. It was not like Giuliano to tease meanly.

He ducked his head. 'Forgive me. Last night you said you were desirous of avoiding your engagement. I thought only to give you a choice, Cousin.'

'Your father would never forgive me.' Elisabeta played idly with the stems of the flowers in her basket.

'My father need not know,' Giuliano countered. 'You have done your duty for the family in marrying Lorenzo. You may even do it again in another marriage very soon, but in the interim, perhaps you owe yourself some pleasure?' The argument was so very compelling, maybe because it was the same argument she'd made with herself. To hear it validated by another made it all the more persuasive.

'No one can know,' Elisabeta said out loud, more to herself than to Giuliano, but it was Giuliano who replied.

'He is English. He is not one of us. He will leave.

He will be a thousand miles away. While you think it over, say you'll come with me to see the horses for the August Palio. Father wants me to go out to the farm tomorrow.'

Elisabeta barely heard the invitation. She was too focused on the unspoken rationale. *No one will ever know.* Suddenly the risk seemed minimal against all that stood to be gained. Only two questions remained: Did she dare? What would she risk to see Archer again? And perhaps more importantly, what did it mean to her and why? What had started out as a spontaneous dare had taken on something much deeper and more significant if she cared to explore it.

Chapter Six

Archer didn't dare press his uncle's decision immediately. No man liked to be countermanded outright. Challenging his uncle would hardly be the way to ingratiate himself to his new family. But he could make an effort to change his uncle's mind about the Palio. Archer kicked Amicus into a trot to pull up alongside Giacomo, determined to start on that good impression today at the horse farm.

If his uncle could see him handle the horses or see him ride, his uncle would change his mind. Seeing was believing after all. His uncle had nothing to go on in reference to him except his mother's letters and mothers were inherently biased. Based on that, Archer understood his uncle's reticence to make him a rider.

'Tell me about this beast of yours, *mio nipote*,' his uncle said as Archer pulled even with him. The traffic had lessened on the country road. They were able now to ride side by side and enjoy some conversation. 'He's a fine-looking animal, strong through the chest.'

'He looks much better these days,' Archer agreed. Even considering the rough travel from France, Amicus had blossomed from good care and affection. He told his uncle the story of Amicus's rescue and his heroic jump on to the boat, keeping his attentions covertly alert to his uncle's reaction.

'No!' Giacomo cried in happy disbelief. 'That's incredible.'

Archer patted Amicus's neck. 'It is incredible. But he's an incredible horse. He had two months to rest in Paris and I worked him with a fine group of riders while I was there. Paris has a surprisingly strong group of enthusiastic riders. I had not expected it. They were a pleasure to train with and I was able to give Amicus some more refined skills. He'll make a good hunter.' Although he intended to stay in Italy, Archer still wanted to make the trip north to the Spanish riding school in Vienna. It would be a treat to see Amicus join their training regimen and it would be a good opportunity to look for new horses. He shared as much with his uncle. 'Perhaps next year's Palio horse will be among them.' He winked.

'Could be. We haven't had a horse from that far away for quite a while, but it wouldn't be unheard of.' Giacomo nodded, the idea becoming more interesting as he thought about it. That had to be a good sign, a sign that he could trust his nephew as an assessor of horses. One step closer. Archer had no intentions of taking no for an answer on the Palio. Just because his uncle thought he wasn't going to ride in the race didn't mean he was going to accept that decision any more than he was going to accept the mysterious Elisabeta simply disappearing into the night, lost to him.

He'd come too far to let these challenges get in his way. He was going to ride in the race. He was going to find Elisabeta because he wanted to, and Archer Crawford was a man used to getting what he wanted.

'We're nearly there. The farm is just over the hill.' His uncle gestured ahead of them. 'Let's be clear on what we're looking for today. This man is a horse breeder. He's bred more winners of the Palio than anyone else currently living. I train them, of course, but they spend their early years with him. I've had two horses in his care since they were yearlings. They are four years old now. I want to see if they're ready to be recommended for the race, but I also want to see which other horses might be brought in either by Torre or by the other *contradas*. We are not the only ones who use him.' This was to be a test, then, of his skill, Archer thought. His uncle would listen to his opinions and decide if he knew his business. But the visit was more than a test for him. It was also a subterfuge.

Checking on the two horses was merely the surface of his uncle's agenda. Archer saw that immediately. This was a reconnaissance mission. They were here to ascertain the level of competition. 'I understand,' Archer nodded. He was enjoying this easy camaraderie with his uncle, finding it a novel contrast to the terse, succinct conversations he had with his father. His father rarely asked for opinions. The man just gave them. But his uncle seemed to genuinely care what his opinion might be. 'This is not all that different than wandering through the Newmarket stables during race week to see the other horses.'

Giacomo gave a friendly laugh. 'That's where you're wrong, *mio nipote*. At Newmarket, it is straightforward; a man races his own horse with his own rider. Anyone who wants to enter a horse can as long as they can pay the entry fee. Not so, here. We have to make it more dramatic. We can recommend horses for the Palio, but we do not control which horse we get. We do not enter a horse for Torre, our horse is drawn for us, assigned to us, out of the final pool of horses. All we can do is recommend the best horses possible for that pool.'

That was news to Archer. He was starting to see that his mother's stories of the great race had left out certain details. It was easy enough to do. When one lived in a particular milieu, there were nuances that one took for granted and assumed everyone else did too. 'I think I understand, but give me an example.'

Giacomo grinned and warmed to the subject. 'Consider the horse that won the July Palio, Morello de Jacopi. He is owned by Lorenzo Jacopi, but the Pantera Contrada drew him for the race. It doesn't matter what *contrada* Jacopi is aligned with, if any. For the race, the horse is Pantera's. If the horse is selected again for the August Palio, another *contrada* might draw him.

'Hopefully us.' Giacomo leaned in although there was no one on the road to hear. 'He's the best-looking horse this year and I think we could put a better *fantino* on him than any of the other *contradas*.'

The remark wounded Archer although he knew

it wasn't his uncle's intention. He could be that rider if his uncle would give him a chance. 'If the horse has proven himself by winning, surely he's an immediate choice for the August race,' Archer put in.

'You Englishmen are always so direct.' Giacomo laughed. 'You're thinking just like your father, that speed matters. It does to some extent. But now, you must think like an Italian, like a Sienese. If we all know who the fastest horse is, the race is less exciting. Why race if the outcome is certain?' He gave Archer a sharp look, daring him to debate the proposition.

For all that his mother had taught him about her city and her language, she'd not taught him that. Archer had no answer. 'First you tell me a *contrada* doesn't enter its own horse and now you tell me the race isn't about speed? I'm afraid it all seems a bit counter-intuitive.'

'It's like this,' his uncle explained, clearly revelling in the chance to delve into the intricacies of the great race. *This* Archer was prepared for. His mother had told him that for many in Siena, the mental exercise of the Palio was raced all year. 'Every *contrada* should have an equal chance to win the Palio. To that end, the horses are selected to give everyone the best chance for an equal race. Obviously, horses who are hurt or not in good physical condition are not considered. They would obviously put the *contrada* who raced them at a disadvantage. But also, a horse who is too good might give a *contrada* who drew it an unfair advantage. When the *capitani* vote for the horses that should be in the drawing, we vote for the horses that will create the most equal race.

The horses that are chosen for the honour are neither too fast or too slow, but just right. They fit well with each other.'

The fastest horse didn't race? That sounded crazy to Archer but he did not dare to say it out loud. It would be imprudent to question a centuries-old tradition. Who was he to say it was wrong? It was merely different, *vastly* different than the straightforward tradition of speed he'd been raised to.

'Of course, a good *fantino* isn't going to let a horse go all out in the trials if he's too fast,' Giacomo put in cryptically. 'There are ways to ensure your horse fits in.' Good lord, Archer thought. This wasn't a horse race, it was a chess game. Based on the statistics, Torre played the game well. His uncle's *contrada* had won the Palio eleven per cent of the time over the past three hundred or so years. Many of the successes of the past twenty years had been his uncle's doing as the *contrada*'s *capitano*.

The farm came into view, a lovely spread of flat green pasture fanning out before them with a brown-brick farmhouse rising in Tuscan style in the background. The age-old desire of man to claim land and to make it his own surged within Archer, so compelling was the scene spread before him. *This* was what he wanted—a home of his own where he was master, not of the land necessarily, that was rather egotistical, but master of himself and his destiny, where his children ran alongside the horses in the grass, where his sons and daughters would ride bareback through the fields, where he worked hard each day and retired each evening to a table full of fresh country food and a wife to warm his bed and his heart.

It was an entirely fanciful notion. He had some of that in Newmarket but there, he was always the earl's second son and the stables had been part of the family long before he'd taken over. There was also the issue of wealth and social standing. There were appearances to keep up at Newmarket. He could not muck out the stalls or work too closely with the stable hands. He could hand out orders, design breeding programs and instruct the riders who exercised the Crawford string. But that was all. Heaven forbid his father heard his son had been out riding like a common jockey or cleaning stalls. And his father always heard. How many times had he been told by the earl that gentlemen *rode* to the hunt? That they *bet* on the races?

They swung off their horses as the man they'd come to meet strode out to greet them. Michele di Stefano was a man of middling stature and easy confidence, dressed in farm clothes. There was handshaking and cheek-kissing, something Archer didn't think he'd ever get used to. He couldn't imagine Haviland ever kissing his cheek, although he could very well imagine Nolan doing it just to goad him. Nolan would like Tuscany with all its touchy rituals. Nolan was a great believer in the idea that people were more inclined to trust you if you touched them.

They tromped out to the stables and the paddocks where his uncle's two horses—both high-spirited chestnut beauties—were running the length of the fence. Giacomo and the man talked briefly before the man excused himself to see to other guests. For the first time, Archer noted how busy the stables were. They were not the only guests who'd come to see the horses. 'I see you're not the only one who thought to come out and view the horses,' Archer said slyly.

Giacomo elbowed him teasingly. 'Everyone is interested in making the race equal. There are three weeks until the horses are chosen. The *capitani* from the different *contradas* will spend the time travelling to the different stables looking for horses and *fantini*. Naturally, the *capitani* have been looking all year, but now that we've got one race behind us, we know what must be done for the next. We're looking to fill in gaps.' Giacomo lowered his voice. 'What that really means is that we're all looking for a horse to beat Jacopi's Morello.' This last was said with more seriousness than it had been on the road, a clear indicator that they were in earnest on this mission.

'Tell me, *mio nipote*, what do you think of the horses?' Here came the first test. Archer was ready.

'I think they run quite nicely, but at a distance that is all I can tell. Let's go in. I want to look at their legs.' Archer was already heading into the paddock, slices of apple retrieved from a pocket and at the ready in his outstretched hand, his voice low and sure. It was an irresistible invitation. Both horses wasted no time making his acquaintance.

Archer stroked their manes and played a bit with them before beginning his examination. He checked teeth and ran his hands down their legs, finding the bones strong and the muscles cool. 'They are in good shape. Now, how they'll do with a rider remains to be seen.' He brushed his hands on his riding breeches and stepped back.

'We should take them to my farm, then, to join the

others?' his uncle asked. 'I have riders there who will work with the horses we want to nominate.'

'Yes, definitely take them,' Archer said confidently, his blood starting to hum at the mention of a horse farm. He'd not realised his uncle had a place outside the one in town. 'Perhaps I could deliver them for you if you're busy?' He was suddenly anxious to see this place.

His uncle smiled and Archer grinned, laughing at himself. He had taken his uncle's bait quite easily. 'You're just like your father when it comes to horses, eager as a school boy.' His uncle clapped him on the shoulder. 'You may pick them up tomorrow and deliver them to our villa.' There was something else in his uncle's eyes too, something that said he had passed the first test.

'Just like my father?' Archer queried, not sure if he liked the sound of that. He'd spent most of his life trying to avoid such a comparison.

His uncle studied his face for a moment, his happy eyes sobering a little. 'Like he used to be the summer I knew him. I don't know the sort of man he became, but I know what he was like at your age.'

'And what was that?' Archer ventured, finding it odd and novel to think of his uncle knowing his father, knowing a man different than the one Archer knew.

A small smile returned to his uncle's face. 'A man who wasn't afraid to live, to embrace life. A man like you, who wasn't afraid to get his hands or boots dirty when it came to horses.' Really? Archer didn't know that man.

There was movement across the field, and Archer

followed his uncle's gaze as it flicked across the paddock to another holding pen farther out. 'Pantera's here. The *capitano* has sent his son and that niece of his to survey the competition. Rafaele di Bruno must be feeling the pressure now to win two. Wouldn't that be a feather in Pantera's cap to win both Palios in a single year? Of course, it won't happen.'

Giacomo uttered something about the statistical possibility of that being unlikely, but Archer didn't hear it. He was too focused on the woman across the field. He'd been ready to ride the breadth of Tuscany to find her and here she was. She could not have been delivered to him any more neatly.

'His niece is a beauty,' Giacomo put in idly. But Archer wasn't fooled. He'd better tread carefully. His uncle's next words confirmed it. 'Perhaps you might spend some time with her this afternoon if you're interested.'

Archer was interested, all right. She was perhaps even lovelier by daylight. Any worries he might have entertained that his perception of her beauty had been influenced by the night and the lighting were immediately banished. Her black hair was neatly coiffed beneath a straw hat that showed her profile to advantage; the curve of her jaw, the firm jut of her chin. She wore an exquisitely tailored riding habit done in blue. The white of her lacy jabot stood in striking contrast from the dark fabric, but even from here Archer could see that the jabot was loose, the neck of her blouse undone against the warmth of the day. She walked arm in arm with her cousin, stopping now and then to watch the horses and comment to their host. Archer imagined he could catch hints of her laughter. But thoughts of Elisabeta had to be set aside until later. There was work to do now. *Pranza*, or lunch, was to be served only after everyone had viewed the horses. There would be time to meet her then. He could possibly manoeuvre a place beside her at the table, perhaps a walk after the meal while his uncle conducted the rest of his business.

Archer's blood began to hum with the knowledge of her presence and with plans. He let a smile of satisfaction spread across his face. Today was shaping up quite nicely in terms of his goals. His uncle had been impressed with his story about Amicus and Elisabeta was here, standing a hundred yards away.

Chapter Seven

He was here! Elisabeta felt his eyes on her before she dared look for him. She didn't want to be disappointed. She didn't want to look up and see that she was mistaken, that her fanciful imagination had simply made up a girlish whimsy. You couldn't really feel someone looking at you and if you did it was unlikely to be the man of your dreams—for her literally the man of her dreams the last two nights. It was unlikely the man she'd been thinking of nonstop had suddenly materialised at a Tuscan horse farm. Her life didn't work that way. She wasn't that lucky. And yet, the illusion she was indeed that lucky was a pleasant one. She could maintain it if she didn't look up. She shouldn't look, she wouldn't look. Looking would shatter it. She would not commit the Orphean crime of looking.

She looked.

He was watching her.

She blinked in the sun and then feared the image would disappear. Perhaps she'd only seen him because she'd wanted to see him standing there. No, that was him. It was definitely him. She'd recognise that nut-brown hair skimming his collar, the set of his jaw and that kissable mouth anywhere, even at a distance.

Their host had left them to see to other guests and she was aware of Giuliano watching her too. Elisabeta averted her gaze, careful to school her features. A suspicion took root. 'Did you know he would be here?' She thought of Giuliano's request that she join him on this visit.

'It was guesswork only,' was all Giuliano would admit. 'We should go in for *pranza*.' He grinned and took her arm. 'I'm hungry, how about you?'

She was undeniably hungry. She only hoped forbidden fruit was on the menu. If it was, would she eat of it? All her hypotheses were about to be tested. She had a chance to see him again. Would she pursue it? Why did it seem to matter so much?

The meal was laid out at a long table beneath the trees for shade. Michele di Stefano's wife had outdone herself. There was a white cloth on the table, and an abundance of food; bowls of fresh pasta, trays of round mounds of mozzarella and sliced tomatoes, bowls of olives and loaves of bread to dip in the dishes of olive oil. And of course there was wine, the rich local red wine of the region.

Perhaps it was all in an effort to impress Pantera, Elisabeta thought. Pantera had won the Palio. It would be good to be in their favour. Or perhaps it was to impress the influential *capitano* of Torre and his nephew.

Elisabeta allowed her eyes to land on Archer as they took their seats. He had not been able to finagle the seat beside her. Giuliano had seen to it that it wasn't possible. 'It is better for your reputation,' he murmured, but she could hear the laughter beneath his words. He understood the irony of having arranged this opportunity only to keep her from Archer at the meal. 'Make him watch you, build his anticipation and wait for your moment,' Giuliano coached quietly.

'I can't decide if I love you or hate you,' Elisabeta said quietly, sliding into her seat at the benches lining the long the table.

Giuliano winked. 'You love me, Cousin.'

Elisabeta lowered her voice. 'I'll let you know after lunch.' She eyed Archer surreptitiously over the rim of her wine glass. Lunch was going to be… interesting.

'Would you like to go for a ride?' The question caught Elisabeta off guard, just when she'd thought she had successfully navigated lunch. She coughed and the wine she'd swallowed nearly made a reappearance in a most unladylike fashion.

'On a horse?' Her reply came out with a slight rasp as she dabbed at her mouth with a napkin. What was Archer thinking to make such a bold reference? Perhaps the real question was what was she thinking to infer the nuance was there to begin with? Lunch had been a polite, careful affair with conversation drifting between talk of horses and of goings-on in town. Both parties were careful not to give away too much while still appearing to be friendly.

Archer's dark eyes twinkled just for her. 'You do ride, do you not?'

'Yes, I do.' Elisabeta took a swallow of wine in the hopes of conveying a sense of normalcy. 'Is the bay in the courtyard yours?' She'd noticed the animal on the way to lunch. He was a magnificent creature.

'Yes.' Archer reached for another slice of bread. Elisabeta took consolation in having limited his speech to monosyllabic responses. If he was going to make references to riding or 'riding' as the case might be, she had to have some recourse.

Archer's uncle jumped into the awkward breach. 'It's quite a story how he came by that horse.'

'Do tell.' Elisabeta smiled at Archer, returning the mischief in his eyes with her own. 'I love a good horse story.'

It was a good story too, and a dangerous one. By the end of it, Archer was no longer a stranger, but a man she was beginning to know and respect, a man who shared her interest in horses. Such knowledge was the very last thing she wanted. It meant an end to 'no ties', but perhaps that concept had ended the moment she'd spied him across the paddocks. Maybe it had even ended sooner than that, or perhaps it had never truly existed at all. It might have just been a convenient rule to justify what she'd wanted to do.

Now she knew him. Here was a man who loved animals, who cared about their well-being as she did. It would have been easier to resist him if he'd merely tolerated horses or seen them as merely a means to an end.

Archer finished his story and rose from the table. He held out a hand for her. 'Shall we take that ride while the others finish their business?'

For protocol's sake, she waited for a consenting

nod from Giuliano, who was acting in the role of chaperon, something she only nominally needed. She was a widow after all, but his presence communicated to others that the family valued her, although her uncle would be appalled at the nature of Giuliano's chaperonage. In that regard, he was a miserable failure. They would laugh about it on the way home.

She took Archer's hand and let him lead her away from the table. His move had been nicely played. His offer appeared generous. The other men at the table would appreciate her absence so they could 'talk' without a female present, never mind that she knew more about horses than most, and Archer, as the outsider, was expendable to their conversation. It was only logical that he be the one to temporarily take over as her escort.

They took their own horses, of course. It would somehow be unfair if they rode any of the horses who might be eligible for the Palio in August. His bay was indeed magnificent and her mare whickered in appreciation.

'What sort of horse is she?' Archer asked as they turned on to the bridle path leading away from the paddocks.

'She's a Calabrese. They originated south of here, in Calabria as the name implies.'

Archer studied the horse as they rode. 'Probably cross-bred with an Arab? Her head is distinct. Perhaps another breed has been used too? There aren't any other strong Arab features. Arabs are smaller in build with a tighter body construction. The mare has a larger quality to her.'

He was musing out loud. She recognised the trait.

She often thought out loud when she looked at horses too, wondering what their antecedents were. 'Likely there's an Andalusian in her family tree somewhere.' Elisabeta patted her mare's shoulder. 'She's twelve, I've had her since I was seventeen.'

The mare had been a wedding present from her uncle for doing her duty by the family. The mare had gone with her to Florence and back again. The two of them had weathered the past five years of life together. She pushed the reminders aside. Talking of horses was better than calling up sad memories of the past. They would only lead to thoughts of a future she wasn't ready to contemplate, not with this handsome man beside her. But apparently the subject was depleted. Silence fell between them. They could not speak of horses for ever.

'I did not think to see you again.' Archer braved the topic, showing none of her awkwardness with the silence. Then again, he was not an awkward man.

'Did you want to see me again?' She wasn't sure how to interpret the remark. Was this afternoon a good surprise or a bad one?

'What a leading question,' Archer teased, fixing her with a merry stare, the amber lights of his eyes dancing. '*I'm* not sure how to answer for fear I might appear too desperate. Let's just say I'm not in the habit of women running off on me.'

He was far too handsome for his own good. Women probably threw themselves at him. 'Well, there's a first time for everything and all that,' Elisabeta responded with a laugh. Flirting with him, exchanging this teasing banter, was easier than pursuing the conversation in a more serious vein, but the question remained: What next? Was there anything between them worth pursuing? And the ever-returning question: Would she dare?

Her mare turned her neck towards the bay and nipped at him. The bay nipped back, causing each of the horses to sidestep. 'She's in season,' Archer commented, reining his horse to one side of the path until the big bay settled down.

'Most likely.' Elisabeta turned the mare in circles. *She's not the only one*, Elisabeta thought. She'd been hot since she sat down for lunch. Archer had the most seductive eyes, the most kissable mouth, she'd ever seen on a man. Every word he spoke seemed to conjure up hot images in her mind, reminders of their bodies entwined in the alley, and the possibility for more.

'Is there a place where we can run?' Spoken like a true horseman who thought of the safety of his mount first.

Elisabeta nodded. 'There's a meadow just ahead. We can gallop there.' She kicked the mare into a fast trot and moved ahead of Archer on the path. A run was exactly what she and the mare both needed.

At the edge of the meadow, Elisabeta let the mare go, let the wind take the hat from her head, her hair from its pins, the very thoughts from her mind until there was nothing but sky above her, horse beneath her. This was as close to flying, as close to freedom as she was ever likely to get. In these exhilarating moments it was close enough.

The thunder of hooves alerted her to Archer's approach, his bay coming alongside, his body stretched out in the gallop as they pulled slightly ahead, just enough for her to appreciate Archer's form low over the horse's neck, his body out of the saddle, his heels down in the stirrups, presenting a magnificent pose of man and beast in synchronicity together.

Her mare would have nothing to do with it. No stallion was going to outrace her. They pulled even and Archer flashed her a grin of sheer delight, content to let the horses sort it out between them. Or the meadow. The far edge of the meadow settled the race for them, declaring it a tie. The horses could not race safely any farther and both of them pulled up, breathing hard. Archer swung down from the bay and came to her side. 'Let's walk them.' He reached up, his hands at her waist to help her down, and she let the thrill of his touch run through her body.

The horses were more obedient after their run and walked patiently behind them along the shaded path. 'Speaking of first times, was it your first time in an alley?' Archer boldly picked up the threads of their conversation before their mad gallop. She'd hoped he'd forgotten.

'Now who's asking the leading questions?' she replied, but the bantering fun of earlier had disappeared between them. It was time to be serious. What did they know of each other? What did they *want* to know? 'Just as you are not in the habit of having women running from you, I am not in the habit of, um…' She cast about for a delicate word, not wanting to be crass.

'Alleyways?' Archer supplied. 'Then why? Why that night? Why me?' His voice was quiet in the still of the afternoon.

She could say she didn't know, but that would be

a lie and she suspected he would know it. He'd been different, safe, a convenient outlet for her anger over the betrothal and for her discreet rebellion. But he'd not been different enough, not safe enough and not nearly convenient enough. He was associated with an enemy *contrada* and the beloved nephew of its *capitano*. He was not going to go away as she'd first thought. She opted for a simple answer. 'I wanted you.'

'*Me?* Or what I could give you? A dance, company, *pleasure*?' He held her gaze, and she didn't look away. She let him see the honesty. Her eyes could confess for her what she dare not put into words.

His own eyes darkened in response. 'And now, Elisabeta di Nofri?' He'd added her last name to make a point; now that they knew more about one another; now that they were no longer strangers; now when she would have to think about why she wanted this. Once, it could be about rebellion and recklessness, but twice was something else.

She dared further boldness. She would think about those reasons later. 'Now, *Archer Crawford*, I want you still.'

But…

She didn't need to speak the 'but' for Archer to hear it. That one small word screamed in the silence of the trees around them. From here on out it would be different. The anonymity of the alley no longer protected them. The magic of the night, of two strangers coming together, could no longer prevail without also giving credence to other considerations. An affair was not impossible, but it came with consequences. She had family. He'd sat across the table from it at lunch, understanding full well what Giuliano di Bruno represented—a protective male presence who would not tolerate anyone dealing unfairly with a female associated with the family.

'You've only answered half the question,' Archer prompted. He took her reins and led the horses to a grassy patch and picketed them, hoping the action of doing something, of moving away from her, would encourage her to say more and encourage his body less. His mind understood the need for renegotiation, but his mind was holding on to that by the slimmest of threads while his body thundered with want and clamoured for satisfaction.

Whether she meant to or not, she'd been teasing him since lunch with those eyes covertly watching him over the rim of her wine glass, her mouth forming around a rich red berry not unlike it had the night they'd fed one another berries in the piazza. And now she'd confessed she wanted him still, wanted him again.

He could have her, his own rules would allow it. She was a widow and this was no romance. He'd not lied to Giacomo when he'd said he wasn't looking for a wife. He hadn't the time right now for romantic entanglements and all the effort a proper courtship required. His priorities lay with the Palio and starting his new life. A wife would come eventually, but not now. The lovely Elisabeta di Nofri wasn't looking for romance either, only company and pleasure. He could do that.

'You still haven't told me why that night.' He strode back to where she leaned against the trunk of a tree. Her hair had come down, a result of the ride, and her cheeks were flushed. The collar of her blouse was open, her jacket unbuttoned to her waist. Taken together, it created an enticing picture. Hell, yes, enticing. He'd just lost the battle and gone from 'possibly aroused' to 'definitely aroused'.

'I've answered the most important part of the question: Why you? Surely the rest doesn't matter.' She gave him a coy smile that took his arousal the rest of the way.

Archer braced an arm against the tree trunk, letting his eyes drift over her mouth. 'Maybe I disagree. Maybe I think the most important part of the question is "Why that night?" I do wonder why a beautiful woman would suddenly pick that night of all nights to wander off with a stranger for the *first* time.' That particular thought had kept him awake for two nights in a row. If it was not a habit, then why that night? What had happened to compel her to take what could only be viewed as a *rash* action? 'What you did was reckless. There has to be a reason.'

She gave a throaty laugh. 'Recklessness has a reason? Are they not the antithesis of each other?'

'I think one spurs the other on.' He was pressing her for an answer. She looked away, uncomfortable with the conversation, but he needed that answer before he could let things progress, before he could claim the kiss that lay inches away on those lips.

She had no such compunction. Elisabeta moved into him, sliding her mouth over his, a hand slipping under his shirt. He felt her touch against his skin, felt his body give in to the temptation. His hand closed around her wrist, his mouth broke from hers with a firm, 'No. Not until I have my answer.'

Her grey eyes hardened to flints. Ah, he *had* read her aright. The kiss had been a distraction, an attempt to make him set aside his questions. She was not pleased in having been thwarted. Her tone was sharp. She was not afraid to stand her ground. 'I doubt my answer will change your mind if you're determined to play the noble hero.'

Archer knew then it was going to be complicated. She'd been using anonymity as a means of protecting him. He could not be blamed for what he did not know. Neither could he be blamed for what he didn't understand. Perhaps she'd been using his status as a stranger for protection too. But Archer was not accustomed to hiding behind anyone's stratagems, female or not. He tightened his grip on her wrist so she would not be tempted to flee. 'I will not be used to cuckold another.'

'Nothing is officially decided.' She did not like his choice of words. Her chin went up defiantly. 'I've betrayed no one. Your honour is intact. I have not compromised you.'

Not yet, Archer thought. He wasn't compromised *yet*. Even though she'd spoken the words in defence, there was an admission in them too. His intuition had been right. There was someone. This was followed by the other realisation he'd shied away from since she'd run into the night. She'd used him, damn it, as an escape. Elisabeta di Nofri was a *femme fatale* of the first water. She might not make a habit of alleys, but Archer doubted he was the first man who'd been lured by her. 'Tell me, who is he?'

The only thing that kept his temper in check was the shadow that crossed Elisabeta's face as she uttered the words. 'There is a man my uncle wants me to marry for the sake of the *contrada*.'

'You are opposed to the match?' Archer asked, not willing to assume her brief facial expression told the entire story. Duels were often created that way.

'I wasn't asked.' Elisabeta's tone was fierce, her grey eyes flashing her indignation. She yanked her wrist from his grip, and Archer let it go. Her own temper had the better of her now and he let her stride about the clearing, venting her wrath.

'I am to be bartered again in service of the family, this time to an old gouty man, without even my permission given. My uncle is the head of the house and the *contrada capitano*. It is his right to do so.' Her eyes had gone from flashes of indignation to full fires of righteous anger. Archer could feel their heat from where he stood, his body firing along with them.

Elisabeta was not done. She marched towards him with forceful steps until they stood toe to toe like two boxers at the line. 'I am supposed to be honoured by the opportunity to grace his bed and let his fat, hairy body rut over me for *his* pleasure.'

Archer was not unmoved by the vivid crassness her words conjured. She would be wasted on such a man. She would never throw back her head and embrace her passion as she had done in the alley with him.

Her eyes narrowed in challenge. 'I've had a young boy barely able to do his duty and now I'm to have an old man. So if you want to stand there and condemn me for seeking a little pleasure, so be it.' Her voice broke at the end. 'All I wanted out of life was one good man.'

'And you shall have one.' Archer's response was swift, his voice hoarse as he seized her about the waist and drew her to him, his mouth claiming hers in a rough vow of its own, tasting her anger, her desperation and, somewhere beneath it, her hope and that was the fire he stoked and fed. She would have a good man for the moment at least. He would see to it. He could not give her for ever, but he could give her pleasure for the now.

Chapter Eight

Pleasure for now. Elisabeta gave herself over to the kiss in all its rough, hungry glory. At the eye of her angry tirade was desperation and she gave herself over to it, let it drive her recklessness. She was desperate for so much; desperate to forget, desperate to see if the magic between she and Archer was still there.

Heaven help her, it was and it transported her out of desperation into seeking. In Archer's arms she was no longer reacting, but actively seeking…something, the elusive, explosive end of pleasure, and so was he. She gave a soft moan and pressed against him, revelling in the feel of his erection and that he made no gentlemanly attempt to hide his arousal from her. She was not alone in this; she was not the only one affected so thoroughly by the fire he conjured between them. It was heady knowledge to know she had a partner, that it wasn't all just for her. She didn't want pity of any sort, certainly not the sexual pity of a handsome man.

She ran her hands up under his shirt, drawing her

thumbs across the flats of his nipples, feeling them pucker at her touch, and then down again over the rippled ridges of his abdomen, wishing she could see what her hands felt. He must be exquisite naked, this well-made man of hers.

Yes, *hers* for the moment. That was the promise communicated in the meeting of their mouths, the caress of their hands. Her hands reached the waistband of his trousers. They belonged together for the moment. She reached for him through the fabric of his clothing, running her open palm along the hard ridge of his stalk. He gave a deep groan, his mouth pressing against the column of her throat as he shuddered his appreciation.

His response drove her on. She wanted to give him pleasure, to take his delight further. She caught his eyes, a dark, deep amber that reflected the depth of his arousal. Her hand stalled on his phallus as she whispered, 'Let me give you pleasure.'

She flicked open the flap of his trousers, her hand closing around the hot, hard flesh of a man. Oh, this was heady indeed, the feel of this virile man in his prime and knowing he desired her. Elisabeta stroked down from the tender tip of him and up, and then again, and again until she had a rhythm that had his tip wet and his breath coming in ragged pants. She felt his body clench, heard him give a long groan as his body gathered itself for its release and then it took him, sweeping through him in a shudder as he spent, her hand still clutched around him.

Their eyes held as his body finished and a thrill passed through her at what she saw there: awe. The experience had shaken him as much as it had shaken

her. Perhaps *shaken* wasn't the right word. Δ, perhaps, was a better word. This was a shockingly bold
and new intimacy for her and apparently for him too.
It wasn't always like this. She knew it wasn't. And
yet it had been like this twice with him now, this man
she hardly knew.

He hardly knew himself. Archer handed her his
handkerchief and took an unsteady step backwards,
trying to regain his mental equilibrium. In the distance, he was aware of the soft nicker of the horses, a
reminder that they'd been gone a while. People were
waiting for them. 'I'll get the horses,' he offered to
give her privacy in these moments of post-intimacy,
and perhaps to buy himself time too, time to think
through what had transpired.

These reckless encounters were not his usual style.
Not only that, he hardly knew *her*. Perhaps that was
the most reckless and surprising aspect. He'd been
reckless before in the way young bucks about London are, but always with women he knew. There was
a certain safety in that. He would not be ambushed
for his recklessness by angry brothers or other males.
He did not have that security here. Yet he'd found
an overwhelming pleasure with her twice that was
nearly beyond words, so different was it from his
other experiences.

To feel her hand intimately on him had been exquisitely primal and private, something that would
bind them together. In truth, being the sole recipient of pleasure in an encounter was new territory for
him. In all his encounters, he was the one in charge
of delivering pleasure for them both. There was a

reason the London ladies who sought his bed had dubbed him the Rake Most Likely to Thrill, and he did, time and again. But today, Elisabeta had brought him pleasure that was for him alone without asking for pleasure for herself. Her pleasure had been giving him his.

That didn't change the fact he didn't know her beyond the pieces he'd gleaned from their conversations and, maybe most telling, from her rant in the clearing. Nor did it change the fact that while he'd known nothing of her, he'd been willing to offer her pleasure, to offer himself in the hopes of fulfilling her wish—*all I want is one good man.* That remark alone birthed more questions; clearly she was referencing her marriages both past and pending.

Archer took the horses by the reins and led them back to where Elisabeta waited, cheeks flushed, but her gaze none the shyer for what had passed between them. What he did know of her was that she was a bold woman with honest passions. He liked that. Honest passion often spoke of honesty in other dealings as well. A woman lived her truth in the expression of her feelings and that boded well for Elisabeta.

He cupped his hand and tossed her up on to her mare, neither of them in a hurry to race back to the farm, both of them content to leave the other alone with their thoughts. But Archer was unwilling to waste the entire ride in silence. How was he to learn of her if he kept the questions in his head?

Archer held a branch back for her so that she could pass along the trail. She smiled her thanks, and he took the opening in quiet tones that rivalled the stillness of the summer afternoon and the lingering intimacy between them. 'Was it bad? Your first marriage?' It was a bold question, but the two of them had done bold things together. She would tell him if he presumed too much.

Elisabeta gave a small smile and a shake of her head. 'No, we were just poorly suited for one another. We didn't know each other. We met for the first time at the wedding. Even the engagement was conducted by proxy. He was young, just fifteen. Neither of us was interested in being married, but we were interested in being dutiful, so we tried to make something of it. Perhaps we were even successful to a degree. After all, I missed him when he died. It might not have been a grand passion or a perfect marriage but we became friends, unified by the understanding that we were in this together. Perhaps in time, that friendship might have borne a grand love.' She gave a shrug that spoke eloquently of genuine regret.

Archer nodded solemnly, grasping implications of that regret, of all that she'd lost, of all she'd never had the chance to explore. 'I am sorry, but I'm glad it was not an entirely miserable arrangement for you.'

'No, not entirely miserable. Lorenzo tried his best to make me happy, but I missed home. I belong here with the horses. It wasn't so hard being married to Lorenzo as it was being in Florence. My darkest days were after Lorenzo died. Without him, I had no reason to stay. All I wanted to do was come back. It seemed for ever until his family agreed to let me return.' She paused and Archer sensed he'd reached the borders of what she would share. Then she added rather suddenly, holding his eyes in a brief, meaningful exchange. 'His family had hopes, you see.

They would not let me go until those hopes were fully quashed.'

Archer could imagine what those hopes were: that their beloved son had left behind an heir in his wife's womb. He could imagine too the pressure she might have been under to make those hopes come to life for them and even the cruelty she might have endured afterwards when those hopes were quashed. She was granted her freedom, but at what price to herself? The grieving family would not understand that in their disappointment.

'I am sorry,' he said again. She'd been so very young to bear those burdens. She was young still, too young to be bartered off in a second marriage, too young to be a widow. 'How did it happen?'

'A summer fever,' she said simply. 'All of us had gone to the family villa in the hills of Fiesole above the city, but Lorenzo had stayed in town to look after some business. He was always trying to prove himself.' She knitted her brow as if she were debating whether or not to tell him something. 'You have to understand Lorenzo had never been in good health. I think his family was eager for him to marry so soon in life because of that.'

Archer felt his heart go out to the young man he'd never know, a young man never destined to make old bones, as the expression went. A stronger man would not have been as susceptible to such a fever.

'It's hardly a subject for today.' Elisabeta gave a little laugh. Her cheeks flushed and she pressed a hand to them. 'I don't usually talk about Lorenzo to anyone. I must apologise for burdening you. You don't want to hear about all of that.'

'But I do, and I asked,' Archer protested. 'I have a lot of questions about you.' He said it lightly, not wanting to scare her away. She'd run from him once. Of course, she couldn't literally run this time. He knew where to find her. He had a name and an address. But there were other ways to run.

The fences of the outlying paddocks came into view. His time was running short. He was a man who believed in asking for what he wanted and he'd best get on with it. Archer drew Amicus close to Elisabeta's mare, his voice low. 'I have one more question. What next, Elisabeta? Will I see you again or is this the end?'

She lowered her gaze, her attentions focused overmuch on the reins at her horse's neck. 'I am promised to another.'

'That's not an answer,' Archer pressed. Perhaps he should feel guilty for being so bold, but she had confessed to being against the match, had confessed to wanting pleasure if only for the short term. If she wanted it, he would give her no quarter in neglecting to go after it. Perhaps, too, this was why London considered him a rake. He understood there were people who would not see the honour in his actions.

A true gentleman would give way in face of an impending agreement, but Archer would not give such an agreement, one made without the woman's consent, any sway. If she chose to honour the agreement, he would not gainsay her, but if that was not her choice, he would not be a party to forcing it upon her.

They were near enough now to make out the figures of his uncle and her cousin leaning against the fences. 'Elisabeta, when shall I see you again?' Archer asked once more, his tone urgent.

She kept her eyes forward, fixed on Giuliano, and raised her hand to wave, signalling their arrival. When she spoke, her voice was so low, Archer nearly missed it. 'There is a party at my uncle's home to celebrate the Palio victory. It will be a large party, a summer masquerade, with a lot of people in attendance.' She put her heels to the mare and spurred her horse on ahead.

They left soon after that, eager to be on the road now that the afternoon heat had started to cool and travel would be more pleasant. His uncle rode beside him, telling him about the afternoon discussions. Plenty of wine had been passed during those discussions. Archer half-expected to have to take the reins.

'Now, it's your turn, *mio nipote*.' Giacomo clapped him on the back, the suddenness of the gesture causing Amicus to jig. 'What did you learn this afternoon? Was Signora di Nofri full of information? Did you *pump* her for it?'

Archer tried to ignore the innuendo and the fact that he might have been set up. His wily uncle had wanted him to pursue her for information. 'I hardly know her. I doubt she has anything of worth to impart.' There was no lie in that. He did hardly know her. It wasn't as if he was denying having met her prior to lunch. Thankfully his uncle hadn't asked that.

'That's all to the good,' his uncle said. 'A woman should be loyal to her *contrada*. Signora di Nofri honours her uncle with her circumspection. If she was gossiping about his strategies and his Palio dealings with everyone, she would be a discredit to him and to the family.'

Uncle Giacomo leaned towards Archer in his saddle. 'However, while she is not sharing secrets willy-nilly, she might be inclined to share a little something if she knew you better. Pantera and Torre are not sworn enemies. Perhaps there is something we might cultivate there? It would be helpful to know what Pantera's plans are for August. Will you see her again?'

Archer thought of Elisabeta's rage over being married for a Palio alliance. No, he would not share that. It wasn't official. But there was something he could share, something he would need their help with if he was to see her again. Archer grinned at his uncle. 'It seems I've been invited to a party.'

His uncle raised an eyebrow. 'Torre hasn't been invited,' he said slowly, sharply, for a man who'd spent the afternoon drinking wine, his mind making lightning connections.

Giacomo's laughing eyes narrowed in contemplation. 'It would be good to know who was invited. Perhaps Oca? We could not possibly attend if Oca was invited,' he explained to Archer. 'Torre and Oca are bitter rivals. Pantera would not invite us both, but neither would they seek out Oca on purpose. Oca is not their natural ally and they had no dealings with Oca for the last Palio.' His uncle was thinking out loud, his ideas mixing with his explanation. 'Palio winners will invite those who helped them win to their parties; other *contradas* with whom they had *partiti*, or secret negotiations, will be rewarded with invitations.'

Archer laughed. 'I thought *partiti* were illegal? It's in the rules.'

Giacomo laughed along with him. 'My dear *nipote*, that's why they're *secret*.' Giacomo returned to his thoughts. 'Perhaps Pantera seeks a secret alliance with Oca?' He eyed Archer. 'You must go to this party, but be very careful. One Torre smuggled in with a mask will not be noticed, but more would stand out.

'Yes...' Giacomo chuckled '...you will crash the party, it will be your first official duty as a Torre *mangini*.'

These were exactly the machinations his mother had told him about. There was a certain adventurous thrill about crashing a party, something Nolan and Brennan would have thrived on. He was missing his friends right about now. He would have welcomed them with him. There was Elisabeta to consider too. He didn't want her compromised should the two of them be caught. At least this way, he wouldn't betray Elisabeta's secret. If Giacomo learned of the arrangement with Oca on his own, it wouldn't be Archer's fault. Besides, if it was official soon, everyone in the town would know of it.

Giacomo waggled his dark brows. 'You'll be able to spirit your pretty widow away to a dark corner without anyone being the wiser. Just think of all the trouble you can get up to with a mask on?'

That, thought Archer, was precisely the problem. There could be trouble aplenty.

Chapter Nine

So far so good, but there was still plenty of opportunity for something to go wrong. Archer adjusted his mask and surveyed the brightly lit courtyard of the di Bruno home. Like most well-to-do Italian homes, the di Brunos' featured a large, square, internal courtyard in the centre of the home that served as an al fresco drawing room surrounded by arched colonnades leading to the private internal rooms of the occupants. Tonight, that courtyard was full of masked guests dancing while others strolled the colonnades on the perimeter.

His job was easy. He just had to blend in. The sheer number of people present made it likely no one would even know he was here. It made him wonder how many other 'uninvited' guests were here too. He'd wager he wasn't the only one. But it also pointed out the flaw in his plan. If no one noticed him, perhaps Elisabeta wouldn't notice him either. How was she to spot him among so many? How was he to spot her?

What had started out as simply slipping into the

party had turned into a major reconnaissance mission. His uncle was using him to spy on the Pantera *capitano*. In hindsight, Archer saw now why his uncle had encouraged him to take Elisabeta out for a ride after lunch: it had been good for *contrada* business, just as accepting her covert invitation to the party was good for business.

Still, he was here and he had his own agenda for the evening aside from his uncle's: find Elisabeta. How would he do that among all these people and all these masks? He only had until midnight when the masks come off. Then he had to be gone. Archer scanned the room, considering what sort of mask Elisabeta would wear. There were glittery suns, and silvery moons, jet-beaded cat masks, a few long-beaked birds, half-masks and full masks of all varieties. He had wanted to send her a note confirming the masks they would be wearing, but Giacomo had been rankly against it, saying, 'If it's a trap, they will know who you are immediately.'

Archer wasn't used to such machinations. London ballrooms seemed rather straightforward by comparison. Then he saw her, a woman in a deep-red gown, wearing a red-and-blue mask in the form of a panther's head. It began to make sense; red and blue were the colours of the Pantera *contrada* and the panther their animal. The event was to celebrate the *contrada*'s victory, so it followed that the *capitano* as host would pay tribute to the *contrada* with this sort of symbolism. Probably the whole family wore panther masks and sported some combination of the *contrada* colours. Archer chuckled to himself. He was starting to think like Uncle Giacomo.

Archer approached. If he was wrong, the worst it cost him was a dance with a stranger. But he wasn't wrong. He would know her anywhere from the way she moved; all graceful confidence communicating in every step that she was a woman who knew what she wanted. Archer stepped into her path and bowed over her hand. *'Buona sera, signora.'*

Would she know it was him? They had not had time to arrange a signal greeting. No secret code word, no pre-identification of masks—he was doing this socially blind. It was not the way he handled his usual assignations. Brennan, of course, would thrive on the unknown, but Archer preferred preparation and plans. Fewer things went wrong that way. Fewer feelings were hurt. It seemed imperative that she know him, that she be able to pick him out of a crowd, as if that spoke to the quality of their relationship in some way.

Clear grey eyes met his through the holes of her half-mask, a smile taking her face in a recognition that had him stirring. If he hadn't known her before, he knew her now by that sensual mouth, that confident smile. *'Buona sera, signor.'*

Archer closed his hand about hers and led her to the dance floor. 'We should have planned this better.' He grinned, his spirits lifting now that he'd found her.

'What's the fun in that? You found me, didn't you?' She tossed him a saucy look as they joined a set for a lively country dance. Archer threw back his head and laughed. That confirmed it. She definitely wasn't safe and for the moment he didn't have to do anything about it except enjoy her.

Masks had their benefits, or maybe the benefit was

just simply being in Italy where the rules were different. No one seemed to care how often he danced with Elisabeta. Perhaps it was simply too hard to keep track of everyone in masks let alone who they partnered with. By the third dance, Archer didn't care what the reason was. He was intoxicated with her; with her laugh, her knowing looks, her sensual smile, the feel of her body moving in rhythm with his to the music, providing a powerful reminiscence of how their bodies moved together in other intimate rhythms.

Would they seek those intimate rhythms tonight? Was that all she wanted from him? These were the questions populating Archer's thoughts as they stepped from the dance floor, breathless from their efforts, and found their way into the darker realms beyond the colonnades. Others strolled here, oblivious to those around them. It would be easy to disappear from the throng, to slip into the shadows.

Elisabeta tugged him farther from the dancing, into a darkened foyer. There was no one about now and opportunity aplenty. Was that what she wanted? For him to take her against the wall? A hunger rose in him to have her in a bed, to have a night to linger with her, to see her naked beneath him and to savour it, no more rushed encounters pushing them at record speed towards pleasure.

Archer pulled her to a stop. 'Elisabeta, wait. Where are we going? What are we doing?' Two questions he was sure Brennan never asked a woman, but Archer had to know. The alley he could justify as a one-time occurrence, the heat of the moment. Her hand on him during their afternoon ride was harder to justify except for the fact that it didn't involve penetration. That was just indecent fun, with no consequences. There would be no justifying a third time. A third time was outside the scope of what constituted a random encounter. A third time constituted a relationship.

Elisabeta looped her arms about his neck, her body pressed against his, her voice sultry. 'We can go wherever you want, do whatever you want.'

A woman wanted him for sex and he was about to say no. Had the world turned upside down? Nolan and Bren would be laughing their asses off. The Rake Most Likely to Thrill was about to turn down a thrill of his own. 'Perhaps we should talk first. We can't keep doing this. Once, maybe, twice, but…' He didn't get to finish.

She put a finger to his lips. 'You cannot deny we have a talent for pleasure between us.'

He tried to speak around the press of her finger, to form the argument that having a talent for it didn't make it right. But she would have none of his protest.

'Shh, Archer,' she whispered right before she stopped his words with a kiss, a far more effective measure than a mere finger since the kiss stopped his words *and* his mind. It was impossible to think logically with her in his arms, firing his blood, firing his body, obliterating his thoughts. It mattered very little in the moment that she did not fit into his plans, his dreams, that he wasn't in the market for a permanent woman in his life. But he had his standards and the desire to bed her appropriately ran hot and fierce in his veins.

She reached for him through his trousers, but he

stayed her hands, his voice a raspy imitation of itself. 'I would have you in a proper bed, Elisabeta, if we are to be proper lovers. I would at least honour you in that way.' And then, because his body was driving this interaction and not his mind, 'Let me come to you tonight, after the revels.'

She relented, her forehead bent to his, her eyes downcast, her body pliant where it had been strung tight. 'I'll leave a candle in the window.'

'Come back to the party and dance with me until then,' Archer said softly. He took her hand, and they made their way back to the lights and the music in companionable silence. Much had been settled between them. They were to be lovers. The knowing of that took away the stress of ambiguity, of wondering if they would see one another again.

If he had not been so content, perhaps he would have noticed the man in the mask charging towards him. As it was, he saw the danger too late. The man yanked at Archer's mask, tossing his own aside as Archer's identity was revealed, a curse erupting from his lips. 'What the hell are you doing here? What are you doing with her?' He was older and heavy. Archer did not recognise him, but he could guess. This was Elisabeta's intended.

'Ridolfo, leave him be.' Elisabeta had removed her mask.

The man's gaze swung to Elisabeta. 'What are you doing with him?' he accused, lunging forward to drag her away. But Archer was faster, stepping in front of her, instinctively acting as a shield.

'Leave her alone,' Archer warned. 'I am here on my own accord.' It was true. She might have proffered an invitation but no one had compelled his attendance.

Ridolfo spat on the ground. 'Torre scum!'

'Stop this!' Elisabeta protested from behind him. She was trying to get around him to stand between him and her unofficial bull of a fiancé, but Archer kept her effectively blocked. He didn't trust Ridolfo, who seemed equally mad at both of them and he was not one to let any woman play his protector.

'What are you thinking to entertain this man under my nose? Do you think to play the whore in front of me? Oca will not tolerate such a blatant disregard for virtue,' Ridolfo snarled, a dagger flashing in his hand.

Archer reached for his in response. He'd thought his uncle too wary to suggest he bring one. Now he was glad for it. 'Watch your mouth when you speak of her.' If Ridolfo wanted a fight, he'd give it to him. They were drawing a crowd, the guests sensing a fight was inevitable.

Even Archer, new as he was to the machinations of the *contradas*, recognised the danger in this. A fight there might be, but not a fair one. Torre was on enemy ground here. He was outnumbered. Around him the guests started to shape a circle, forming into allies and enemies. If only he knew who the Torre allies were. This was going to be bad. There was going to be a brawl and he was going to be at the centre of it.

Over a woman.

There was a first time for everything. 'Elisabeta, go,' Archer warned, wanting her to find safety. Then he swung his fist straight for Ridolfo's jaw. It was the catalyst for all-out chaos. Fists flew along with a few chairs and quite a few goblets as the *contradas* engaged one another. Insults were hurled with punches all around Archer, but here at the centre of the fight, there was just he and Ridolfo. And their daggers. Ridolfo had no compunction about using his. His first swipe made it clear he was out for blood and a lot of it. The rules of first blood would hold no sway here. Ridolfo would stop only if he was knocked out cold and unable to fight. Archer set aside any hopes of fighting defensively. He had no desire to feel the cut of a blade. He danced backwards out of the way as Ridolfo made a mad slash with his dagger. The older man was slower on his feet. Before Ridolfo could recover, Archer swung at his chin with an upper cut. The big man went down. It was time to go.

And Archer went. Not because he was a coward or because he wasn't capable of more fighting, but because it made sense. With him gone, the fighting might stop. He took a step backwards towards the darkness of the colonnades and sprinted for the door.

He'd almost made it when the cry went up. 'There he goes!' The core of the fighting turned from the centre of the room to the door and as one, the mêlée surged towards him. Archer ran into the night, scaling walls and vaulting fences as the mob chased him. His dancing shoes skidded on the slippery cobblestones, he put down a hand for balance, readjusted and kept running. He was breathing hard now but he gave himself no quarter. He didn't want to find out what the mob would do if they caught him. He sped across the *campo* in the centre of town and hazarded a glance behind at the mob. They were closing in on him, but he was nearly there. The safety of Via Salicotto loomed in front of him, the boundary into the Torre *contrada*. The mob wouldn't dare take their chase into foreign ground. It was one thing to chase an intruder through the streets of Pantera, but quite another to invade a *contrada*.

He sped across the boundary and down a twisting alley, losing himself in the darkness. He heard a collection of disappointed yells go up behind him and knew the mob had given up the chase. But that didn't mean Pantera wouldn't seek vengeance. It would just take another form.

Archer bent over, catching his breath. This was the height of foolishness, being chased through the streets by a mob. It was something that would happen to Brennan. And yet, beneath the foolishness, Archer felt alive. The thrills of the kisses, the fight, the escape, were heady ones. There was some excitement lurking in the unpredictability of it all. It was unlike him. He was a planner. Elisabeta's laughing words came back to him: *Where would the fun be in that?* He hoped she would be all right, that Ridolfo wouldn't turn his frustrations on her.

There was no question of going back to Pantera tonight. The streets would be full of thwarted revellers looking for a fight and Pantera would be on guard. Did he even dare go to his uncle's? Would his uncle be angry? He'd started a fight and ruined a prestigious party. His own father would be appalled. It was one thing for his son to be famed for his bedroom exploits as a lover, but it was another for his son to be embroiled in vulgar scandals. Would his uncle feel the same way? Would his uncle ask him to leave? The full implication of what he'd done tonight, of what he'd caused, was starting to settle on him. He might have ruined his chances. Well, he was no coward. Archer turned his feet towards home. He might as well face his uncle and get it over with. Waiting never solved anything—it usually only served to make things worse.

Chapter Ten

'Well?' His uncle's face was stern as Archer entered the *loggia* and Archer feared the worst. The news had arrived just ahead of him, the bearer not having to dodge a mob in the streets. Archer could only imagine the report Giacomo had been given: how he'd thrown the first punch, how he'd drawn his dagger in defence of a Pantera widow, how he'd not been the least penitent when Ridolfo Ranieri had called his presence into question.

It was hard not to wince at the thought of it. But his uncle's next words surprised him entirely. 'Was she worth it?' Then his uncle's face split into a wide grin and his loud laugh filled the quiet *loggia* and spilled into the silent streets of Torre. 'Good God, *mio nipote*, you've the makings of a fine Ricci yet! Come have some wine and tell me all about it.' His uncle's eyes twinkled. 'I have heard part of it, but I want to hear your version.'

Three glasses of wine later, Archer was more confused than ever. What had struck him as singularly scandalous behaviour on his part had his uncle slapping his knee and eyes brimming with tears of mirth as if it was the best of larks. His uncle raised his glass. 'We'll make a Torraioli of you yet.'

Then his uncle sobered. 'But there is still the issue of the Widow di Nofri. You fancy her and they mean to marry her to our enemy. *This* is serious.' As if drawing daggers at a party and being chased into the night wasn't. He looked sternly at Archer. 'The *signora* is lovely. I understand the attraction. But she is not for you. She *cannot* be for you. Pantera will be our friend no longer. They have chosen to align themselves with our enemy.

'This will go down in our records as a conflict of equal fame with Pantera's interference with Aquila in the 1752 Palio. The friend of our enemy is also our enemy.' Giacomo tapped the side of his temple with his finger. 'The Torre memory is a long one. We will not forget.' He fixed his dark eyes on Archer. '*Mio nipote*, you have had your fun and there is no shame in it. Romance is part of life, is it not? But it ends tonight. For the sake of the *contrada* and peace in the streets, you must not see her again.'

The next moment he was jovial once more. 'Besides, I have good news. The horses Torre wants to volunteer for the Palio need you. I need you. I want you to start working them. There is less than two weeks before the drawing of horses for the race.'

He was to ride! The import of the news was not lost on Archer. If his uncle could see him ride in exercise, he might change his mind about allowing him to ride for Torre in the Palio. He was one more step closer to his dream. It seemed the fight tonight had done for him what his ability to ride had not been able to achieve: convincing his uncle to give him a chance with the horses. But he was too astute to not recognise there were other agendas here as well. This was also being dangled in front of him as a carrot. Should he not abide by his uncle's edict to leave Elisabeta alone, the honour of riding would be removed. There was the practical consideration too. If he was working the horses in the country, he would be effectively removed from the city. Those conditions would not be spoken directly, of course, and his uncle would deny those strings to his face, but Archer would know they were there.

His uncle walked with him to his room on the second floor. To make sure he actually went to bed instead of going back to Pantera? Or just because it was the fatherly thing to do? Archer was learning quickly that the family might love you, but they seldom did anything without multiple reasons.

'It was a good night.' Giacomo clapped him on the back. 'You did well. It is too bad about the widow, but we'll find you another woman if you want.'

'Of course,' Archer said because it was all he could think of to say as he bid his uncle goodnight. He shut the door behind him and leaned against it with a sigh. This was shaping up to be something out of *Romeo and Juliet*. Too bad he'd only paid attention to the Shakespeare plays that had horses in them. If Romeo had had a horse, he might have been better prepared for this turn of events; Ridolfo's attack this evening, his own crashing of a party, and now the potential of street warfare between the neighbourhoods, all over a forbidden woman.

Archer began to strip out of his clothes for bed. Why should he care if he saw Elisabeta again? He'd known her for a week and very little of her at that. His uncle wasn't asking him to end a dear friendship or to throw away the love of his life. Why did he feel as if he were? The evening was warm and he lay on top of his covers, naked and hard and wondering if a candle still burned in a certain window in Pantera?

There would be no candle tonight. Elisabeta stood before her uncle and Ridolfo without flinching. A fiercer tribunal she could not imagine. She'd been on her feet, answering questions for half an hour. Had she known who was behind the mask? How had someone from Torre got into the party? Her uncle had been ready to accept her vague explanations, it was a masked ball after all. Who was to prevent unwanted guests? But Ridolfo was not as easily pacified. He kept watching her with beady eyes, waiting to catch her in a lie. Ridolfo was sporting a large bruise on his face where Archer's fist had left its mark. It might be petty, but she took some satisfaction in that.

'Tell me again, had you met him before?' Ridolfo questioned for the third time.

Giuliano intervened from his position against the wall. He came forward. 'She's already told you. How many times do you have to ask? How was Elisabeta to know she was dancing with a Torraioli? She was merely doing her duty as a good hostess. If the Torraioli seemed taken with Elisabeta, who could blame him? It was hardly her fault. You seem taken enough with her, surely you can understand the attraction she might hold for another man,' Giuliano managed to sneer. 'Have you thought that perhaps you should blame Torre for this and not Elisabeta? You seem quick to condemn her, but not the man who gave you that bruise.'

Ridolfo snarled and turned to her uncle. 'Your niece is a harlot, no matter what she says,' Ridolfo accused from his chair at the table. She watched her uncle flinch. 'Do not sit there and tell me she is a dutiful niece because she would not have done this if she was. She does you no credit.'

'I am sorry, *signor*,' her uncle began, and she felt guilty for making him have to say those words. She didn't want him to beg a man like Ridolfo Ranieri. Her uncle was a proud man. He might not be as wealthy as Ridolfo, but he had standing in his own right. She had endangered that tonight with her daring invitation. She'd not thought...

Ridolfo brushed away the words as if they meant nothing. 'It is not your fault. She needs a man to take her in hand. Clearly, her first husband was too lenient with her.' His eyes flicked her direction, narrow and assessing as they looked her up and down, his fat sausage fists flexing and releasing. She willed herself not to look away, not to show him her loathing, her fear. He would punish the loathing and he would use the fear.

'I am her fiancé now, I should have the handling of her since I am soon to be her husband and her behaviour reflects on me,' he said, and her stomach went cold. She shot a glance at Giuliano who stood alert, his gaze encouraging her to stay calm.

'I shall see to her punishment. She will know who

her master is.' His eyes never left hers and her skin crawled with the knowledge of it.

Giuliano spoke up. He could risk being less diplomatic than his father. 'I do not think it is your decision. You are not her husband yet. The engagement has not even been formalised.' Giuliano's challenge drew his eyes from her, and she allowed herself to feel a little relief, but it was short-lived.

'If this is how she will behave in the interim, I want the engagement announced immediately and I want the wedding to take place two weeks after the Palio at the end of August,' Ridolfo announced, throwing down his terms like a gauntlet.

'It is too soon,' her uncle prevaricated. 'We need time to plan. We are so busy now with the Palio.'

Ridolfo fixed her uncle with a stare. 'Shall I tell my cousin the *priore* that Pantera does not mean to keep its word?'

Those were fighting words. Her uncle could not let them pass. He rose from his chair. 'We will keep our word.'

Ridolfo rose as well, sensing the interview was over. 'I will expect an announcement shortly.' He gave her an insincere bow. 'I will also expect planning your wedding, Signora di Nofri, will keep you too busy for further scandal.'

When he had gone, Elisabeta waited only a moment to launch her protests. 'Uncle, you cannot allow this. You see what kind of man he is.'

But her uncle held up a hand to stop her words and raised tired eyes to her face. 'No more, Elisabeta. Go to bed. You've done enough for one night. Giuliano will see you up.'

Giuliano took her arm and she allowed it until they were out of sight. 'Take your hand off me!' Elisabeta hissed, at the top of the stairs. 'I will not be escorted to my room like some sort of prisoner.' She was taking her temper out on him and it was unfair. Somewhat.

She fairly *burned* with angry indignation. If anyone shared responsibility for the debacle of the party, it was Giuliano. He'd encouraged this affair. He had arranged for them to meet again at the horse farm.

Giuliano opened the door to her bedchamber and stepped inside with her, his own anger simmering. 'Stop with this posturing, as if you're the wronged victim here.' His body vibrated with tension. 'I protected you down there. I gave nothing away, although Lord knows you deserve it for taking such a risk.'

She did have to give him that. He had stood up for her during Ridolfo's repetitive inquisition. Her uncle had sighed and accepted the story as truth because Giuliano spoke it. It wasn't implausible that events had happened as Giuliano stated. It wouldn't be the first time a *contrada* had stolen into another's party.

'I do thank you for that,' Elisabeta offered politely. 'You did protect me.' She astutely kept the thought to herself that in protecting her, Giuliano was also protecting himself. Uncle Rafaele would not like to hear of Giuliano's part in encouraging her association with the handsome Torre *mangini*.

Giuliano leaned against the door. He had protected her and in doing so had admitted privately, between the two of them, his own culpability in the fiasco. But she could see in the set of his body he wasn't ready to accept all of the blame. 'What were you thinking to invite him *here*…?' Giuliano began, his anger not yet spent.

'It was a masked ball. I didn't think he'd be discovered. He would have been well away by midnight. It was just supposed to be a few dances,' Elisabeta defended her decision with crossed arms. She might confess, but she wouldn't be penitent over it. She was not sorry she'd done it.

'Your future husband was in attendance. Surely, you had to know he would notice if you danced so often with the same partner, masked or not. If not that, he'd notice if you were absent for an extended time,' Giuliano pointed out.

'We weren't gone that long. Nothing happened.'

'You sound disappointed by that.' Giuliano pushed off the door and began to pace the room. He pushed a hand through his hair, and Elisabeta winced. That meant he was thinking, perhaps too hard and too much. She liked her cousin when he was more spontaneous. When he thought he became too responsible and that was dangerous, especially to her freedom. 'Is the Englishman worth so much you would risk dishonouring our family?'

'I do not want the marriage your father has arranged.' It was an indirect answer and it was complicated. Of course she didn't want to dishonour her family, but neither did she want to dishonour her freedom. 'When I am with him, I am alive. I am not a pawn, not someone else's currency to spend.' Could Giuliano, a young man raised with freedom and privilege, understand that?

Apparently not. 'The *priore*'s cousin is wealthy. You will have a nice home in town and a villa in the country. There will be fine horses. He is besotted with you. He will give you anything you ask for,' Giuliano reiterated the benefits. She'd heard them all before when the match had been first put to her. They were even less appealing now that she had Ridolfo's measure.

'Your answer disappoints me. I had hoped for better from you,' Elisabeta shot back fiercely. 'I get all that in exchange for what, do you suppose? Not for "free". It is not just about horses and the Palio, Giuliano. It's about me being with him for ever. His wealth does not make the prospect more palatable.'

'But the prospect of pleasure with the Englishman is more than palatable.' Giuliano countered. 'This is why I suggested him. Now, you have had your pleasure where it belongs, in the countryside, in an alley. But that's where it ends. Your *discreet* foray into pleasure does *not* take place in this house in front of the man you would marry or under my father's nose. *Those* are flagrant insults and not to be tolerated.'

Elisabeta swallowed. What she had done had been dangerous. She'd been lucky. Giuliano had been able to deflect the issue away from her downstairs tonight. She would not be punished. Giuliano had persuaded her uncle and fiancé any punishment that was meted out be directed at Torre and the Englishman. They were the ones responsible for what had happened, Elisabeta was merely a casualty. Yet, her mistakes did not validate being sold into marriage against her will.

'Perhaps Ridolfo will cast me off now,' Elisabeta said hopefully. Casualty or not, tonight had drawn attention her way and that was hardly a commodity valued in a politely bred Sienese woman of virtue.

It would be one good thing to come of the evening's travesty.

Giuliano shook his head. 'That's doubtful. If anything, tonight verifies for Ridolfo and the Oca *priore* that you are a beautiful, sought-after woman, a credit to their house. They are fortunate to have won such a lovely bride. Men want what other men covet. You heard Ridolfo—he is more eager than ever to move the marriage up.'

There was a scratch at the door followed by a whisper. 'It's me, Contessina, let me in.' Elisabeta sighed. Her room had become as busy as a posting inn. All she wanted was to go to bed and wallow in her misery and her memories. Giuliano opened the door, and Contessina slipped in.

'Are you all right? I came as quickly as I could,' Contessina said, slightly breathless as if she'd run up the stairs. Elisabeta smiled in spite of herself. The very proper Contessina had been eavesdropping. 'You are to be married early. I heard the news.'

Elisabeta felt panic start to rise. She'd done a fairly good job of convincing herself she'd have more time, until tonight and Ridolfo's announcement. Hearing Contessina say it made the reality far too real, far too close.

Elisabeta shot a desperate glance at Giuliano. 'Can't you do something? Can't you talk your father out of it? There is no shame to back out of the agreement, nothing has been announced. No face will be lost if it's not public. Ridolfo and Oca need not be embarrassed yet. We only dislike Torre on behalf of Oca. Torre is not our enemy,' she argued.

Giuliano shook his head slowly. 'You know I cannot. My father has made up his mind. Perhaps it will not be so bad, Elisabeta? Ridolfo is rich.'

'Yes, I know,' she all but shouted. 'He will deny me nothing as long as I reciprocate in kind.' She was tired of being told to endure, that the money was worth it, the prestige was worth it. Did no one see that this arrangement was nothing more than church-sanctioned prostitution—a woman taking a man in exchange for money? No matter what vows were traded, that fact could not be erased.

'Perhaps you should stay with her tonight, Sister,' Giuliano suggested quietly as he slipped from the room before she could strangle him. He thought she would run.

'I will. I will stay with you, tonight, Cousin,' Contessina offered sweetly. 'Let me brush out your hair. You will feel better.'

It was hard to be mad at Contessina. Elisabeta sat and let her take out the hairpins. There *was* comfort in the ritual and in Contessina's presence. The girl meant well. They all meant well. Her uncle, Giuliano. Her uncle had arranged one wealthy marriage for her and when that had failed, he'd brought her home and arranged another. Her uncle was fulfilling his promises to her father to see her taken care of for life.

She should not ask for more. She felt badly that she could not reconcile herself to this marriage, that she selfishly wanted something different. Sometimes she wished she could be more like Contessina who accepted; who did what she was told.

Contessina helped her into a nightgown and they settled into her big bed. She didn't want to desire the Englishman, but she did. To pursue him was to pursue folly and yet her gaze went to the dark window. Was he out there, looking up from the ground even now, waiting for a sign? Was her Englishman that foolish? To brave the streets tonight would be far too perilous. He would risk more than his safety if he tried to make his way back to her uncle's home.

Elisabeta tucked the pillow more firmly beneath her head and rolled on to her side. He was not down there. Coming back risked not only his safety, but her reputation. Archer had understood that tonight. His first inclination had been to protect her with his words and his actions. He'd drawn a dagger on *her* behalf and he'd been quick to take the blame upon himself, quick to divert any of that blame from her. Archer's own words had given Giuliano the grounds for his arguments later that night. A gallant lover was her Englishman and she could not have him not even once more.

Her uncle and even Giuliano, her champion, had made that request explicit. To see Archer again would undermine Giuliano's arguments regarding her innocence. It would make them both appear as liars to her uncle. More than that, to see him again would lead to blood. She knew how these family feuds went and a duel was where it was headed. The upcoming Palio had diverted that course of action for now. Plotting against Torre in the race would serve in the stead of duelling. But a duel would not be escaped if she were caught with Archer again.

She sighed, and Contessina rubbed her back consolingly. 'It will all look better in the morning,' Contessina comforted. What did Contessina know? Nothing went wrong in her world.

Elisabeta doubted it. Nothing would ever be better again. Seeing Archer again definitely involved no small amount of risk. But not seeing him again carried its own risk too. She had found a very private, personal sort of pleasure with Archer. She wanted to explore how deeply that pleasure ran, how long it could last.

Her cousin's hand stilled for a moment. 'Elisabeta,' she began tentatively, 'why does the Englishman matter so much? You hardly know him.'

Ah, but she did! She'd ridden with him, watched him with animals, danced in his arms, seen him vulnerable to pleasure as she held him intimately in her hand. How did she express that to Contessina? Elisabeta turned to face her cousin, taking the girl's hands in hers. 'When I am with him, I'm not alone. There's a connection.' The words seemed apt, if not inadequate. In truth, being with Archer was unlike anything she'd ever known.

Contessina's pretty face turned sad. 'You have us. You don't need to be alone.'

Elisabeta shook her head. 'It's not the same.' It would be so much easier if it was. Tonight, she was just beginning to realise that what had started out as a single venture into discreet sexual experimentation had moved far beyond that. Her curiosity had been satisfied. Pleasure had been achieved. Those had been her goals—to experience that which had eluded her in her marriage. Now that she had, the adventure should be over. But Archer had become more than a sexual partner.

Contessina was looking at her patiently, waiting for her to say more, to explain. Elisabeta tried the idea forming in her mind, the words coming slowly, her brain peripherally aware that her grip on Contessina's hands tightened with the intensity of her thoughts. 'What makes him important is that he makes me feel alive. He is *my* choice.'

He represented something she'd never had before—the liberty and the luxury to choose. The most significant events in her life were not things she'd chosen to happen to her. She'd not chosen to have her parents killed in a coaching accident. She'd not chosen to marry Lorenzo. She would not have chosen to marry Ridolfo on her own. She'd not chosen either of the men who had been or would be given sanctioned intimate access to her body. But she'd chosen Archer. He was the physical embodiment of her freedom. He was *hers* entirely.

'What are you going to do?' Contessina asked softly, perhaps divining the dilemma such an acknowledgement created—the personal good pitted against the greater good.

Elisabeta shook her head and gave her cousin a small smile. She had no answers and she'd kept the girl up too late tonight as it was. 'I don't know. But *you* should definitely go to sleep.'

Elisabeta blew out the light next to their bed and settled down to her pillows. It was a futile exercise. Her mind was too alive to find sleep immediately. Which risk did she take; the risk that exposed her family to Ridolfo's revenge and scandal or the risk that asked her to give up a chance at claiming her freedom? More than that, it asked her to give up the right to a choice. It would make her a pawn once more.

Chapter Eleven

Archer was a man who liked having choices. He'd grown up learning that while one must always consider others in one's decisions, ultimately a man's choices were his own. Not so in Siena. The individual respected the wishes of the family in theory *and* in practice. It was the one rule Archer could not entirely bring himself to live by. He would go to his uncle's villa and train the horses, but on his own time. He had something to do first. He would see Elisabeta regardless of his uncle's edict to the contrary. He was a grown man of twenty-nine, not a boy in leading strings who could be told what to do.

His conscience demanded no less. He could not leave the city without knowing Elisabeta was safe. If it had only been his own safety he risked, he would have gone back to Pantera last night. But he'd been astute enough to realise he jeopardised her as well. He would take his chances this morning in the hopes that his note had reached her. The route it had travelled was rather circuitous and relied on her cousin, Giuliano, giving it to her.

Archer paced the small upper room he'd rented on a street not far from the busy *campo*, checking his watch yet again. There'd been no question of trying to approach her publicly, not with the rumours of last night on everyone's tongue, nor without his uncle knowing. He doubted too that she would appreciate the attention either. But the confines of the room were chafing on him and waiting made him feel impotent.

He'd been here an hour already. It was market day and the streets were bustling with customers and vendors. Surely, if the note had reached her, Elisabeta would be able to slip away in the crowd. If she wanted to come at all. There was always the possibility that she'd decided he was too dangerous, or that she couldn't come. Archer wasn't sure which option concerned him most—wouldn't come or couldn't come. If Ridolfo, or anyone, had hurt her, vengeance would follow no matter what his uncle thought.

There was a quiet knock at the door, a whispered question of a name through the door. 'Archer?' He snapped his watch shut with a smile, his anxiety fleeing. She had come.

Elisabeta stepped into the room, flushed and breathless. Relief swamped him at the sight of her so vibrantly alive and unharmed. He'd been ready to feel such relief, but he'd not been prepared for the intensity. He had not realised just how worried he'd been. 'You're all right?' Archer crossed the small room and took her hands, searching her face, her eyes, to assure himself she was unhurt. 'I feared last night that Ridolfo might turn his anger on you after I left. I hadn't wanted to leave.'

She stepped into him then, her arms wrapping around his neck, her body pressed against his, wanting more from him than the touch of his hands on hers. 'You would have been hurt or worse if they'd caught you.' She kissed him, her mouth lingering on his. 'You should see Ridolfo's jaw. He has the most magnificent bruise,' she murmured.

'He'll get a lot more than a bruised jaw from me if he ever seeks to do you injury,' Archer growled fiercely. He bent to kiss her, but the tentative quality in her eyes stopped him. 'What is it? What has happened?' Had she been hurt after all?

She stepped away from him. 'You won't always be able to protect me.'

'Let me decide that.' Archer's answer was terse. He reached for her hands. 'I'm one of the best boxers in our London club. I've left more than a few opponents on the ground when the need arose.'

Elisabeta shook her head. He saw sadness in her eyes, which had been alive a short time ago. 'You can't fight a husband over his wife.' She paused. 'I am to marry him at the end of August, after the Palio. It was decided last night.' By others, not by her, that much was clear, but that didn't stop a cold pit of dread from spreading in his stomach.

He could feel her hands start to shake in his before he saw the fear take root in her eyes. She was starting to break, this beautiful, strong, woman who loved with abandon. 'I don't know what I'm afraid of most, being married to Ridolfo or of not having a choice in the matter. Perhaps it doesn't matter which I fear most. I am trapped either way. There is no place to run.'

'You can run to me,' Archer said in deadly, measured tones. He'd seen Ridolfo last night, a hulking, stinking ogre of a man whose only recommendation was his wealth and social connections. It wasn't that Ridolfo was a fat man that made him repellent. It was his lack of manners, his lack of regard for Elisabeta and likely for any woman that made him distasteful. Archer had been more than glad to take a fist to his face.

'I don't want your pity,' Elisabeta said solemnly. 'You hardly know me. You are not required to do anything, to feel anything…' Her words dropped off, her thought incomplete.

Archer felt his temper start to rise. 'Pity? Is that what you think exists between us? That night in the alley was pity? The horse ride was pity? Drawing a dagger for you in the middle of my enemies was done out of pity? It was done out of choice. I am not required to do any of those things. I chose to do them, *for you.*' He would do more for her too if she would allow it.

The rashness of that realisation struck him hard. How much more? Today, with her trembling before him, he was willing to do it all, to give her the protection of his name, of his body. That was the power of his anger at her for not understanding what had passed between them, of his anger towards Ridolfo who saw her as nothing but a possession, anger at her family too for not seeing what she needed or what they doomed her to with their plans. He turned from her and strode to the window, trying to wrestle his emotions into compliance. He had not counted on a reaction like this. Then again, he hadn't counted on a woman like this.

'I'm not a horse to rescue like your Amicus.'

'Of course you're not,' Archer answered sharply.

'But the premise is the same, isn't it? This is what you do. You rescue animals and people,' Elisabeta challenged. She was getting angry too and that fuelled his own temper. How dared she be angry when he'd made her such a generous offer of protection? She was the one throwing it back in his face, rejecting him outright. He was going to lose her before he'd really found her.

Archer turned from the window and let her see his anger. 'What did you come here for if you won't let me help you? Did you simply come to say goodbye?' He wanted to hear her say it and yet a part of him held out hope that she wouldn't. Coming had required a certain risk. Why would she take that risk if only to leave him again? It hardly seemed worth it.

'I came because you asked me to. I came because I wanted to. I didn't come to quarrel.'

'What did you come to do?' Archer asked, his words quietly cutting. Coming wasn't enough. 'Did you think to have one last romp in the sheets?' He gestured to the iron bed in the corner with its quilt. He tugged at his shirt, pulling it out of his waistband as he began to undress.

'Archer, stop!' Elisabeta cried as he tossed his shirt on the bed, standing before her half-naked.

'Oh, so you're *not* using me for sex? My mistake. I thought you were.'

'That's not fair!' Elisabeta's eyes blazed. She strode to the bed and balled up his shirt. She threw it at him. Good, she was willing to fight. He was getting to her now, getting her to move past the paralysis of her fear. It was what he wanted. She was no coward, but currently she felt cornered. She didn't know what to do, or what she was capable of doing, and she wouldn't know until she tried. He knew all too well from dealing with his father how it felt to be cornered, to feel there were no options. He hadn't known his power until the day he'd chosen to step out of the corner. But that had come with consequences too. What was she willing to risk?

'What is not fair is what you're letting them do to you,' Archer replied. 'It's simple really. Either you marry Ridolfo and accept it or you don't.'

'You forgot the part about what happens if I don't.' Elisabeta's eyes narrowed. 'You forgot how scandalised my family will be, or that I'll become a social outcast, or that my uncle might be forced to send me away. I would be exiled from everything I know. I've already done that once. You can't possibly know how it feels to be so entirely alone in a new world.'

Archer raised an eyebrow, challenging her assumption. 'Don't I? And yet here I am with a family I have never met, in a country that doesn't speak English, a thousand miles from home.' He softened his tone. They hadn't much time left. She would be missed soon and he needed resolution. 'You wouldn't be alone, Elisabeta. I would be there for you.'

Archer or Ridolfo. When the argument was boiled down to that common denominator, the choice was easy. The thought that she could have him made her knees weak. This bold, handsome, kind man was offering himself to her. Not as a husband, she wasn't that naive. There'd been no talk of marriage between them. They would be lovers—she would be his mistress. He stood there before the window, a veritable Adonis without his shirt, the sun behind him, representing everything she craved: pleasure, freedom, respect, choice. But to get it, she'd have to give up all she'd ever known.

Elisabeta moved towards him, daring to touch him since their quarrel began. She placed a flat palm against his chest, feeling his heart beat strong and healthy beneath her fingers. 'You do understand, Archer, that you represent everything I want as well as everything I fear.'

His hand covered hers, his eyes holding hers with their amber lights. 'Not everything you fear.' He smiled. 'I wanted to tell you that I am going to my uncle's villa in the country for a couple of weeks to work with the horses before the Palio selection. The villa is near San Gimignano, not far, I hear, from the di Bruno villa.'

Her pulse quickened, with hope, with the prospect of pleasure. She heard the implied invitation. In San Gimignano they would be anonymous. In the Chianti countryside they would be free to pursue the possibility of what they could be. They could buy themselves some time. *She* could buy herself time to consider what she would risk, what her freedom was worth to her. In those moments as they said farewell, Elisabeta could barely speak, so great was her gratitude. Archer had given back the one thing that mattered most right now—her choice. It gave her strength, strength she needed far sooner than she would have anticipated.

* * *

Ridolfo was waiting for her when she and her cousins returned from the market. He'd arranged it very neatly, intercepting them on the street before they gained the house. He fell into step beside her, forcing Giuliano to move ahead with Contessina on the crowded street. He had her by the arm, steering her away from Giuliano.

'They can manage without you,' he replied when she protested. 'You and I have unfinished business to settle from last night.'

'Where are we going?' She was instantly wary. He was leading her back down the street away from Pantera, away from the people she knew.

He smiled, showing all of his yellowing teeth. 'We're going to Oca, to my home. It occurred to me that you will be mistress of all of it and you've seen none of it. It's a big house. It will, however, require a woman's touch. You will want to make changes.'

'Shouldn't my aunt be with us? I am sure her advice would be useful,' Elisabeta suggested, not wanting to show any of the trepidation that surged through her. No one knew where she was at. She would run if she had a chance, no matter how childish that would look—a grown woman running in the streets. She couldn't imagine how she would explain such an action to her uncle but that was the least of her concerns at the moment. She counselled herself to stay calm. Ridolfo had done nothing now or ever to directly harm her even though he'd implied it last night with his talk of punishment, something she thought he'd enjoy meting out. Still, she had no proof he intended anything other than what he said. Perhaps he meant only to win her over with a display of his wealth. His was the nicest home in Siena after all.

Still, all the tapestries and fine furniture couldn't erase the heavy clamp of his hand at her back as he ushered her through the home, couldn't make up for the sour smell of his breath at her ear as he told her about each piece of art and how he acquired it. She was acutely aware of his closeness, of his touch, of her body's judgement on that: he was repulsive. Her body couldn't relax, she was on edge.

He saved the bedroom for last. It was a large, opulent room done in thick, heavy wood pieces that had been passed down for generations of Ranieri. 'It's done in the Turkish style,' Ridolfo boasted, waving a hand in the air. 'Everything here is from Constantinople.' His voice dropped. 'Even the bed linens are from a pasha's harem.'

His hand ran down her spine, and her skin crawled. 'I think you will come to enjoy this bed, if your behaviour with the Englishman is any indicator of your passion. I saw last night how I had misjudged you. I was waiting around, trying to be the delicate gentleman when, in reality, you were ready for a man. You have passion that needs to be spent.'

Elisabeta said nothing. He must have taken the silence as acquiescence. 'I assure you, there are ways we can help your enjoyment,' he drawled. He was playing with her now, she realised with a sick drop of her stomach. He went to a drawer next to the bed and opened it. He held up silken cords. 'Some tricks from the harem. You may prefer to be tied down, blindfolded, as you learn to take your pleasure in my bed. Being deprived of the senses can heighten that.' He drew out a jar. 'There are lotions too that I can spread on you before I enter that eases your passage. You cannot say I won't be a considerate lover. I have a physician on staff to see to your every need as well. You'll meet with him once our engagement is announced and he can ascertain your special needs.'

He gave the drawer a firm shove and approached her, forcing her to back up to the wall. She would not flinch. He would like that too much. He would have his victory. He'd brought her here to warn her, to punish her with words, with visions of her life to come in his house. His fat fingers gripped her chin roughly. 'You will never shame me like you did last night with the Englishman. I am to be the only recipient of your attentions. Once you are mine, I can do with you as I please. Whips, ropes, potions. Do you know how many nights I've lain in this bed imagining you in it? You naked before me, tied and helpless, rousing to me, begging me to give you release? And it will happen.'

Elisabeta spat in his face. 'I will never rouse to you.'

'You naive bitch!' He wiped at the spittle. 'You have no idea what I can make you do.' He gave her an evil look that nearly took the last of her resolve. 'The next time you think about your Englishman, think about this. The potions work, the drugs work. I can make you rouse to me whether you like it or not.'

He stepped too close, and Elisabeta saw her chance. She brought her knee up, hard and fast, thrusting it into his groin. Ridolfo went down, hands clasped over his privates and screaming expletives.

She didn't stop to listen. She ran through the streets, dodging vendors and passers-by. Her side ached as she tore through alleys and shortcuts to Pantera, not caring who cursed her as she bumped into them, or who called after her. She would not be safe until she reached her room. Upstairs, she bolted the door. Even then, with the heavy door and the bolt to keep out unwanted intruders, she wondered if she'd ever be safe again.

Ridolfo would get up eventually and he would come for her. He might not be able to tell her uncle what had transpired without implicating himself—after all, women don't knee men in the crotch without a reason—but he would come for her, he wouldn't let this pass without retribution. The longer his temper cooled the less severe that retribution might be. She needed to leave, needed to get out of the city. She needed time to think, to discover her options. She needed a friend.

You can run to me. The words came to her as she leaned her head against the strong oak of her door, her breath coming in gasps and sobs. Archer would keep her safe. He had given her all the power to decide her fate. Perhaps he might also have some ideas about what to do with that fate, or better yet, how to avoid it. A girl could always hope.

Chapter Twelve

If there was one thing Archer knew, it was horses. He could feel the heat in their legs if they were lame and which ones had 'kissing spine' when the girths were fastened. He could treat them too, and he did, spending hours massaging liniment into the muscled shoulders and strong backs of the horses at his uncle's villa in the Chianti countryside. The horses became his full-time occupation, along with waiting for Elisabeta.

Letting the horses absorb him was the easy part. Waiting for Elisabeta was not. Archer lay back in the grass and looked up at the sky, watching the first evening stars come out. This had become his nighttime ritual—lying on the grass in front of the villa. It had only been three days since he'd seen her. Logically, he knew he couldn't expect her to appear so soon. She had arrangements to make, assuming she could get away. Would she choose to come? Even if she wanted to come, would she be able to? It was the thoughts of what might keep her in town against her will that bothered him most. Those ranged from the benign—being unable to arrange transportation, being unable to get out of whatever previously arranged social commitments she had—to the more harmful: being locked in her room, being forbidden to leave the house, being forced to endure the odious company of Ridolfo to please her family.

Restless, the early stars unable to hold his attention tonight, Archer sat up and reached for his whittling knife, another nightly habit. Sometimes, like tonight, he did some carving from the scraps of wood lying about the stable. He hadn't had much time to indulge his little hobby since leaving Dover. Now, he had time to spare. Keeping his hands busy also kept his mind busy, kept it off Elisabeta.

Archer laughed to himself. He should be careful what he wished for. There'd been times in the past four months he'd wished for aloneness. Now that he had it, he missed the companionship that had surrounded him since his trip had begun. In Paris, he had shared lodgings with the others. In Siena, he'd been surrounded by his uncle's family, cousins upon cousins, that had filled in the absence of his friends. He had not been alone for quite some time.

Now, he was alone and his thoughts had him all to themselves, a privilege they were exercising ruthlessly at the moment. Archer shaved off an edge of the wood with extra fierceness. Every thought went back to one central theme: what to do about Elisabeta? He'd meant it when he'd told her she could run to him. But what did that mean? In the heat of the moment he'd not thought about what he was willing to offer her, only that he would protect her. Certainly, she could claim the protection of his body.

But that was easy. It required the skill of his fists. It didn't require matrimony. The protection of his name, however, did.

Archer held the little carving up to the lantern light, the form of a horse starting to take shape. This was familiar territory. He'd been carving horses since he was a boy. A stable hand in his father's barn had shown him how, much to his father's displeasure. Whittling was not a gentleman's pastime. It had become a boy's quiet rebellion against his father, against rules that made no sense except to separate people from one another.

Even here in Italy, his father haunted him, intruding into his thoughts about Elisabeta. If he married her to protect her, it would mean going home, the one thing he did not want to do. Going home meant going to his father; it would mean making amends and facing the past. Not just facing it, but accepting it. Elisabeta had talked of the price of pursuing him, the price to her of leaving Ridolfo. Archer understood the price of her choice was considerable. But she was not the only one to pay. He would pay, too, for his offer. He would not be able to keep her and stay in Italy. Probably, he wouldn't have to marry her to be banned from Siena. Any association would be damning since both his uncle and hers, and her fiancé, had forbidden contact. Was the protection of a woman worth his dream?

That dream had become real to him in the days since his arrival in the Chianti countryside. He'd seen first-hand the possibility of his uncle's horses and the villa. This was the life he wanted. He loved the routine of his days here and already he was earning the respect of his uncle's grooms. He rose early before the heat of the day, oversaw the morning feeding and walked the stalls, checking on each horse. Over a group breakfast, he assigned each groom a set of horses to work out. He spent the morning watching those workouts and even riding himself. The hot afternoons were spent in the cool of the indoors at a desk, writing down his observations in a log that recorded each of the horses' progress. The evenings were his own spent under the Tuscan sky.

Archer looked up into the sky. It was fuller now, the stars having emerged in force. He could pick out the Plough and the Pleiades. In his mind, he could envision evenings like this with a child or two, or three, or even a horde of them beside him picking out constellations too, their mother holding the newest addition in her arms. He'd always a wanted a family, but it had been a goal for later. Since arriving in Siena, in spite of his plans to the contrary, it seemed 'later' was intent on being 'now'.

Maybe it was Italy that prompted such thoughts. His mother had warned him often enough with a laugh that in Italy family was the most important thing and it was infectious. One could not be in Italy and not feel that yearning. He'd not truly believed her. Or maybe it was Elisabeta that prompted such yearnings. He was missing Haviland. Haviland would know how to talk through this with him. For now there wasn't any more he could do. He'd made his move. Now he had to wait for Elisabeta to make hers. He hoped he wouldn't have to wait much longer. Perhaps in the morning there would be word…

* * *

She was not good at waiting. Elisabeta's pulse raced. Her horse pranced beneath her, picking up on her nervousness. She scanned the wide open space of the countryside, looking for Archer. He would have got her note this morning with his breakfast. If he was there. He could be out. There could be any number of reasons he was late or wouldn't show up. Had he felt this way waiting for her that day in Siena?

Perhaps he'd changed his mind? Perhaps he realised how foolish his offer had been up in that little room? Or perhaps she had truly convinced him she wasn't worth it, this woman whom he hardly knew when it came right down to it. Had he gone home and weighed the cost of his offer? Had he truly thought about what it would mean if she took it and concluded he would not pay that price?

A horse and rider appeared on the horizon and she knew a special relief. It was him! She knew by the way he sat a horse, by the way the horse moved beneath him, at one with his rider. She knew him too from something that had nothing to do with physical recognition. Safety, protection, was riding towards her. Her belly was warm with it. Here was a man she could trust, who was fine and strong and good, with the ability to make his promises a reality.

Her conscience whispered one last reminder before she let herself be swept away. *You've come to discuss your options, nothing more. Already, you know that one of those options is unacceptable even if he offers it. You cannot run away with him. Remember what he will cost you. It cannot be for ever. It can only be for now.*

But still, he might know a way out that didn't involve dishonouring her family.

Archer's eyes were merry as he pulled close alongside her mare. 'I thought you would never get here.' He leaned from the saddle, angling for a kiss.

'Me?' She laughed, the tension that had plagued her these past few days starting to lift. '*I've* been waiting on *you*.'

'But I'm the one who has been here three days already,' Archer argued pleasantly. She liked the way his eyes settled on her face, the smile on his lips. He cocked his head and studied her, seeing too much, she feared. His smile disappeared. 'What is it? What's wrong?'

'When you offered me protection, what did you mean?' She watched him carefully, knowing those words changed everything. They'd gone from being a casual *affaire* to expectations. He would know now that among her reasons for coming was her desire to claim his promise, one he might not want to have made.

But there was no hesitation from Archer. He was off his horse and at her side, swinging her down. The reins of both horses were in his free hand as he said, 'Let us walk and you will tell me everything. Hold nothing back, Elisabeta, it will do no one any favours.'

She told him all of it; the bedroom full of a harem's furniture, its restraints and potions, its drugs, all of it designed to strip away a participant's choice, none of it meant for mutual pleasure, but instead the pleasure of one man whose satisfaction came from the submission of another. 'He wanted to punish me for the fight at the ball.' She worried her lip as she made her admission. 'I hate that he succeeded. I haven't been able to forget about that room, about the images of what he intended.' They'd haunted her sleep. He'd had his revenge.

'The bastard should be castrated,' Archer ground out when she finished. 'I'm glad you came to me.' He was looking at her with his gaze intense, his mind whirring behind those dark eyes.

'I have to find a way out. I need you to help me think of options,' Elisabeta explained.

Archer gave her a rueful smile. 'Ah, then it's more of a case of running *from* Ridolfo than running *to* me. It's rather a blow to my ego.'

'No, not entirely,' she said quickly, realising her mistake.

Archer stopped walking, the horses halting behind them. 'I would help you regardless. Don't think for a moment my assistance is predicated on having you in my bed. I'm not that sort of a man.' Not a man like Ridolfo who thrived on submission. 'We will think of something. Perhaps there is information that can be leveraged against him, information that he would rather protect in exchange for giving up this marriage. If that fails, I can challenge him to a duel, and should *that* fail, I can always spirit you away.'

He would too, Elisabeta had no doubt. That was something she had to prevent. 'I don't want you ruined in the process, Archer.' She had to draw the line somewhere. This was her mess, not his. 'It is too much to ask of someone who hardly knows me.'

Archer grinned for the first time since she'd begun talking. 'We know each other better than you think.

Still, there is more to learn and we have a week.' He squeezed her hand in reassurance. 'Don't think about him and his lurid promises any more. How much time do we have?'

For ever. No, she couldn't think like that. Her hands played with the reins. 'Just the week. I need to be back in town before the *tratta*. My uncle has business and he expects Giuliano to watch the early horse trials. Giuliano will want my opinion, privately, of course.'

'Of course.' Archer grinned. 'Don't worry, Giuliano's secret is safe with me. How did you manage to get away?'

'I told my uncle I needed to come to terms with the changes in my life. I thought the quiet of the country would do me good, help me clear my mind.'

'And when our week is up? Do you mean to consent even after all Ridolfo has revealed?'

She lowered her eyes. 'I suppose that depends on the options we come up with. Don't ask me for any answers. I came, didn't I? All I know is that I can give you this week.' This week to explore one another along with the options.

'Elisabeta—' he began, but she cut him off, raising her eyes to his once more. Her voice was strict but soft. She wanted no more talk of running away. It was the one option she couldn't allow herself to think of.

'Archer, don't. Don't rail at me for answers I won't or can't give. You know any decision we make will cost dearly. We have a week. That is all that is certain.' Who knew, maybe in a week the bubble would be off their wine. Maybe she'd realise he was only a man with a man's faults, no better than any other. But there was also the risk that after a week, she'd realise something else altogether—that he was *the* one, the *only* one.

Archer smiled, his posture easing. He understood the dilemma even if he didn't want to accept it. 'If it's only a week, let's make it count.'

They did make it count, every hour, every day until the week became a blur of memories: luncheon picnics on hillsides surrounded by olive groves, dinner picnics amid vineyards popping with this season's grapes. Evenings spent in his arms, staring up at the stars. The carriage ride back to her uncle's villa. For all the days she had with him, there were no nights. If there was one blight on the week, that was it.

The servants at the villa expected her to be out visiting or walking to the village, or riding. It was nothing unusual for her to be gone during the day. With no one else to care for at the villa, it was a relief to them to have her taking dinner with one of their neighbours or enjoying a quiet evening entertainment. But it would be irregular indeed if a woman pledged to another did not come home at night. So each night, she left Archer with the promise to see him in the morning.

That didn't mean the days were bereft of passion. There was plenty of opportunity to make love in the outdoors, on picnic blankets during the lazy heat of the afternoon, or in the evenings with early stars overhead. Perhaps more than the picnics and the lovemaking, there was the talk. The week was a chance to learn about Archer and for him to learn about her.

She treasured each trinket of information; he had an older brother, Dare, who would be an earl some day. He had had a mother he'd loved. He talked of his Newmarket horses and of his home in England. He was like her in that regard. She loved her home in Siena, her life in her uncle's home with Giuliano and Contessina. She had missed it thoroughly when she'd married Lorenzo.

'How can you stand to leave it all?' she murmured one night as they lay together under the stars, their bodies relaxed after wine and love on a blanket, the warm summer breeze passing gently over them, their clothes open and rumpled. She traced a circle around the aureole of his breast with a fingernail. 'It sounds lovely. Don't you miss your family? Surely your father needs you.'

She felt him tense and wished she could take back the words. She'd inadvertently hit on a sore spot and yet some perverse sense of peeling away his layers urged her to go on.

'My father needs no one.' His tone was gruff. 'That's why I left. I'd had enough of jumping into the breach for him time and again, making excuses for him when he was absent. I couldn't live with someone who treated people so callously as if they had no particular worth.'

She knew he meant for her to hear resentment, but Elisabeta heard something else beneath the gruffness. 'You can't stop loving him anyway?' she ventured. She had a little experience with that. Her uncle wasn't perfect, but she knew in her bones that he was the best he could be for her and she loved him anyway.

'Maybe. I don't know if I'd call it love exactly.' Archer paused, his eyes riveted on the stars. 'The thing is, I feel guilty about caring for him. I should feel nothing for him after the last time. What he did was unforgivable.'

She was close to something now, something that defined him at his core. If she could just know it, she would know him. Elisabeta raised up on an arm, lifting her head from his chest. Her voice a mere whisper. 'Tell me, Archer, what did he do that was so bad?'

Archer's eyes glittered in the dark, full of raw emotion. 'He left my mother to die without him.'

The words tumbled out before Archer could stop them, eight words he'd never spoken out loud to another, not even Haviland. These eight words embodied the belief that had driven him from England. He could not stay where his hatred was rooted, could not stay with a man who had so callously disregarded his wife in her last hours, a woman who had given him her life, her love, for thirty years without question even though it had meant leaving her own family behind.

To her credit, Elisabeta said nothing. Another might have tried to soften the thought with useless phrases: you don't mean that, or, surely you're mistaken. But he did mean it, he believed it. He was there. He knew. Elisabeta only nodded her head solemnly and in expectation. There was no going back once the words were out. One could not utter such a sentence and declare the conversation over. The horrible statement deserved explication.

He turned on his side to face Elisabeta, copying her pose. She waited patiently for him to begin, her neutral silence giving him strength. If he could just hold her gaze, focus on her eyes, on the beautiful soul he could see in them, maybe he could get through the telling.

'My mother had consumption.' He began with the facts. Facts hurt less. 'The end was bad, it always is with consumption, and it lingers far past the patient's strength.' It was the first time he had talked of those days. Not even Haviland knew how beautiful, how terrible, those last days were. They were private and painful.

'I sat with her for hours, helpless to do anything more than that. I held her when she coughed and the pain racked her thin body. She had lost so much weight. I gave her water, and later laudanum when the pain was too bad for consciousness. I told her stories, telling back to her all the stories she'd told me in my childhood, taking her back to the home of her youth and the family she hadn't seen in thirty years. When I ran out of stories, I read all of Uncle Giacomo's letters. It was what she'd wanted that last day.' He had to stop and collect himself. Elisabeta reached for his hand and held tight. 'My brother, Dare, sat with us,' he said, able to go on. 'The two of us took turns reading to her.'

'And your father? Where was he?' Elisabeta encouraged softly.

'In Newmarket. His prize mare was in foal.' The bitterness in his tone was unmistakable. Even after all these months, it still rankled that he could have walked out on her for a horse. 'The mare gave birth to a fine filly. He named her Vittoria in my mother's honour.

'It was the last straw for me. All my life, he'd been absent when we, or others who claimed friendship with him, had needed him. Dare tried to stop me, but I wouldn't listen. When my father arrived home that night, I took a swing at him. I knocked him to the ground.' They had fought until Dare and some footmen had been able to separate them. He had some regrets over that choice—a son does not hit his father easily—but those regrets were not enough to stay. 'My father knew when he made his decision that morning that she would not be there when he returned,' Archer bit out. 'He said it was too hard to watch her die, so he left—' he scoffed here '—as if it was any easier for the rest of us to watch it, to participate in it.' He held Elisabeta's gaze.

'She was the beauty in our lives, the light. She kept the three of us united. Unity is not an easy thing to come by in a household of stubborn males who only got more stubborn as they got older. What we wouldn't do for each other, we'd do for her. *Capisce?*' Archer said softly. 'My uncle says she was always like that. She could get a man to do just about anything.'

'She sounds like a wonderful woman,' Elisabeta said softly, her tone urging him to go on, and he did. He couldn't seem to stop talking.

'Oh, she was. It's been almost a year since she passed. Part of me hopes missing her will get better. But part of me hopes it doesn't. If I am missing her, I am also remembering her.' Archer paused and gave her a considering look, his mind working behind his dark eyes. His voice was quiet, almost reverent when he spoke. 'Sometimes I feel that if I stop missing her,

I'll stop remembering how much she meant to me, how much she did for me and for my brother, how much she must have given up.' He shook his head. 'I had no true idea how much she must have sacrificed to come to England until I came here. She had a family, a good one, and she never saw them again.'

'She had a new family in you and your brother and your father. Perhaps that was enough, or perhaps it was all she wanted,' Elisabeta said. 'I often think if I had a family like that of my own, it would be enough.' It was her turn to hesitate. Archer watched her worry her lip, choosing her words carefully as if voicing them for the first time. 'You might find me selfish, but I think it would be wonderful to have a small family, just a husband and children, all to myself, to never have to worry about cousins and aunts and uncles and how everything I did affected every one of them. There would only be my nose in my own business.' She shuddered. 'It sounds so ungrateful when I say it out loud, forgive me.'

Elisabeta sat up and reached for the forgotten bottle of wine and their empty glasses. She sloshed the bottle. There was a little left. She split it between the glasses and handed him one, a smile on her face. 'Drink a toast with me, to her memory, and to her sons.'

They drank before Elisabeta set aside her glass and moved over him, straddling his thighs, her hand cupping him. He could feel himself rouse to the squeeze and caress of her fingers, of her nails, running along the inside of his thigh.

'What did I do to deserve this treat?' Archer put

his hands at her waist, his thumbs pressed low on her hips.

She bent over him, her hair brushing his nipples as she took his mouth in a generous kiss. 'You told me. Thank you.' She stroked him hard then, his arousal flaring to full life. She rose above him and came down on his cock, confident and sure of its entry. She moved on him, and Archer groaned. Had anything felt this good? Felt this full of life? Of hope? When she rode him, when they were together, anything was possible. He let his climax come hard and swift, his body bucking against hers, his head arched to the sky, the stars witnessing his pleasure even as they witnessed the silent realisation of his mind. He had only one night left and he had yet to convince her she had options.

Chapter Thirteen

It was to be their last night. Elisabeta's hands trembled as she fastened a necklace, a simple gold chain with a gold heart-shaped locket, about her neck. The week had flown. In the beginning it had seemed like an abundance of time, but now the hourglass that held the sands of her freedom was rapidly emptying. They'd not spoken again of her choices, opting instead to speak of themselves and getting to know one another in a fuller sense. She knew what it meant: there were no options that allowed her to deny Ridolfo without shaming her family.

She pushed the thought away and stepped back from the mirror, running her hands over the folds of her skirt. She would not sully the evening with thoughts of the future. Tonight, she couldn't think of what came tomorrow, only what came now. She'd dressed carefully with that in mind. Archer had said only that he had something planned, something special. Although that was true of everything they'd done this week. Every picnic, every walk had been special. Every day had been special, but this evening the night would have its moment. The arrangements had demanded a little subterfuge. She'd told the staff at the villa she was spending the night with friends. The entire week, she and Archer had been careful to plan their days away from the villas where no one would see them, where no one was likely to recognise them and pass that sighting on to family members.

Elisabeta stepped back from the mirror. She'd brought the dress on a whim, a bold red silk cut tight through the bodice and full through the skirts. It wasn't exactly the kind of dress one took to the country. It was better suited to a grand ball, or a seduction. Elisabeta smiled. That made it perfect for tonight. It was time to go.

Archer seemed to be of the same mind. When she arrived, he came out to meet her dressed in dark evening clothes, immaculately groomed. 'My lady.' He helped her down from the carriage. 'You have rendered me speechless with your beauty.'

'As you have rendered me with yours,' she replied, liking the way his gaze lingered on her in appreciation. That alone made hauling the dress out to the country worthwhile. She let her own gaze linger too. She had seen him in formal attire before. The night of the Pantera party he'd come dressed up, but there'd not been time to drink in the sight of him. She was not in the habit of thinking of him as the son of an English lord. It was easy to forget all that when she saw him working with the horses or tramping through the countryside in dusty boots and a loose shirt. On those occasions, he was only Archer Crawford, and this week she'd only thought of him as hers. Not as a lord's son, not as a member of a rival *contrada*, just hers. It was a dangerous way to think of him.

'I have set up our meal al fresco. Shall we?' He tucked her hand through his arm and led her to the olive grove where candles were lit on a white-clothed table. Wine stood uncorked, waiting to be poured, and covered dishes couldn't quite hide their delicious smells.

'Oh.' A little gasp of delight escaped her. 'Archer, it's wonderful.' She couldn't imagine a lovelier setting, the stars coming out overhead, the candles flickering in their protective glass.

He held out her chair and poured the wine, serving her before he raised his goblet in a toast. 'To one more night with the most beautiful woman in the world.'

She blushed. He had a way of making her believe it was true, of making the words sound like more than empty flattery. Perhaps that was part of his charm, part of the reason she'd found him irresistible from the start. He gave a woman his attention, and in doing so, he gave her his sincerity. The woman he loved would never feel like a possession. She would feel cherished.

Archer lifted the cover off a gorgeous green salad of arugula and pear sprinkled with slivers of pecorino.

'We are entirely alone. I've sent everyone home, so you'll have to suffer my poor attempts to serve.'

He gave her a wink and took her plate, filling it with the summer greens. They ate in the slow Italian style of courses, moving languorously through the dishes, savouring the tastes and the conversation. *Insalata* gave way to pasta with bits of mushroom and pancetta mixed with it, and more pasta, this one with a meat sauce. The loaf of bread disappeared slice by slice, one bottle of wine gave way to two. The candles burned down, the stars twinkled, the night deepened.

She could not recall a time when she'd laughed so much. He told her stories of his childhood, the things he'd done that he probably shouldn't have, such as the time he'd skipped out on lessons with his tutor to go swimming. 'I got out of the river to find my clothes missing.' Archer chuckled. 'My tutor was standing there, though, looking none too pleased. When I asked where my clothes were he said, "You took away my time, so I have taken away your clothes." He gave me a choice. I could either walk home naked or I could give him double time the next day on my Latin.' Archer made a face. 'I gave him double time on my Latin, of course, but it was the last time I skipped lessons. Four hours of Latin is a horrible punishment to inflict on a boy.'

Elisabeta smiled, imagining the boy in the man seated at the table. 'Were you always so rebellious?'

'Only when there's something I want badly enough. Rebellion is most useful when used sparingly, otherwise it loses its point.' Archer's hand closed over hers, his eyes holding hers, his meaning clear. He wanted her, was willing to fight for her if she would let him.

He let her hand go and reached for a small box tied with a ribbon. 'I have something for you, I almost forgot.'

A present. For her. She felt the sudden sting of

tears over the little wood box. It was silly and yet when had someone given her a gift for no particular reason? She couldn't remember. Elisabeta untied the ribbon, almost reluctant to ruin the idea of a present by opening it. Inside was a small, carved wooden horse, polished with a chestnut stain. She smiled, recognising it immediately. 'It's my mare.'

Elisabeta ran her hand over the smooth lines of the carving, a suspicion taking root. 'Did you make this? It's beautiful.' She could see that he had. The praise made him uncomfortable. The ever-confident Archer squirmed slightly in his seat.

'It's just a little thing, it's not fancy.'

'It's a *treasure*,' she corrected. Because it was from him. Because it might be the only thing she ever had of him after tonight. 'Every time I look at it, I'll remember our afternoon ride, and I'll remember this evening when you gave it to me.' She was nearly beside herself with the pleasures of the evening. Never had she been romanced so thoroughly, or so well: the food, the wine, the stories, the laughter, the gift. But it was his next words that had her melting.

Archer rose from the table and held out his hand to her, his eyes an amber smoulder. 'Elisabeta, come to bed with me.'

She met his gaze evenly and slid her hand into his with a single whisper of the word 'yes'. She knew even as she said it, as they climbed the stairs, tonight was a watershed. Tonight's intimacy would be different than any of the intimacy they had previously shared. Tonight would push them closer to resolution one way or another.

Everything that had transpired between them had

led to this. To this room lit by candles, and scented with sage and thyme, to this bed with its quilt drawn back revealing clean, simple white sheets. To this moment, with this man. Elisabeta swallowed. Tonight they would be naked together in a bed. This would be unlike anything they'd done so far. The thought came to her suddenly. It would be like a wedding night, a real wedding night, with a man who knew what he was about and who cared for her. It made her nervous and excited all at once. But Archer was all confidence, guiding her to a chair near the bed, stepping away from her to remove his coat and his shoes.

His hand worked his cravat free, drawing it from around his neck before his fingers deftly worked the cufflinks at his wrists, making his intentions plain. He meant to disrobe for her, meant for her to watch him. 'Look at me, Elisabeta.' His voice gave the low command. 'Tonight, I would come to you as Adam came to Eve.'

Her throat went dry, expectation replacing her nerves. He made an offering of himself then, stripping off his waistcoat and shirt to reveal the muscled planes of his torso, the broad shoulders, the tapered waist where his hands rested in provocative suggestion, his thumbs hooked at the waistband of his trousers, his hands spanning his hips, fingertips pointing towards that most manly part of him. She could not ignore it, nor did she want to. She was eager for it, to see with her eyes the unadulterated sight of the phallus that roused to her touch. She had felt it, massaged it, seen it in part, but always his clothes obscured it in some way. Tonight, it was to be completely on display for her, every glorious inch.

Archer pushed his trousers past lean hips, his eyes watching her watching him, his movements confident, but she caught a flash of caution in his eyes. He wanted to please her, wanted her *to be* pleased by the sight of him, she realised. It was rather novel to think of the competent, self-assured Archer as having doubts of his appeal. But he need not have worried. He did not disappoint. She inhaled sharply, a reverently breathed 'oh' escaping when she exhaled. 'Oh, Archer. *Che bello, molto bello*.' The words were entirely inadequate. This was no sickly adolescent boy who stood before her. Fully naked, he was Adam and Adonis, Prometheus and Apollo all in one, his phallus a gorgeous jutting obelisk, a pillar of masculine strength at the dark core of him.

He let her feast, her eyes devouring him. He had done this for her, to put her at ease. He would not undress her as if she were his to command, to do with as he pleased. He would meet her naked as an equal.

She rose. It was up to her now and she was eager for it. She wanted to be naked with him, wanted him to see her as he had not seen her in their earlier encounters. He too had only seen parts of her, but not the whole, not all at once. She would give it to him, her gift. 'Sit for me, Archer. It's your turn now to look at me.'

She managed the fastenings of her gown with hasty fingers, letting it slide from her body like a curtain falling away to reveal a piece of art. She let the candlelight play across her body, the light casting provocative shadows and highlights over her breasts, over the triangle between her thighs. Archer's eyes went dark and she revelled in his overt response.

She lifted a leg, balancing her foot on his knee and slowly rolled down a stocking, offering him a tantalising view of long, slim limb and feminine juncture. She shifted legs and watched his throat work.

Elisabeta stepped back and lifted the chemise of thin summer cotton over her head, knowing that when she did, she'd be fully exposed to him, every private inch open to his perusal. She wanted to tell him, wanted him to know. 'You're my first...' she began, the words coming awkwardly.

Archer rose from the chair and came to her, drawing her close, taking her mouth in a slow kiss before he spoke, his body bare and hot against her. 'Your first what?' His words feathered against her lips.

'I've never been naked with a man before.'

He smiled, his forehead pressed against hers, his words a sibilant seduction. 'There's nothing better than naked sex. Let me show you what I mean.'

Yes, show me, love me. This was what a wedding night was supposed to be, this reverent consummation of passion. She craved him body and mind. She went easily when he urged her backwards to the bed, his body following her down, covering her with his strength, with his length. This was straightforward lovemaking at its finest if not its most sophisticated. Archer's body was above her, his arms bracketing her head, muscles tensed to take his weight, her legs open to him, his phallus brushing against her curls as he levered himself into position.

He thrust, and she closed her eyes, letting go of everything, letting her senses wrap around the totality of this pleasure, the feel of him moving in her, of her own response to him. He was driving them towards union, towards climax. His command came hoarse and guttural. 'Look at me, Elisabeta, I want to be in your eyes when we shatter. I want you to see what you do to me.'

Her eyes flew open and the intimacy of their act ratcheted to another level. To see him, to see the intensity of his desire in those beautiful eyes, was like seeing to the depths of him. He was exposed intimately to her in those final thrusts, locked to her in gaze and in body in a connection that transcended pleasure. In these moments she was worshipped entirely by his body, by his mind, by his soul. She'd never known anything finer. This was perfection personified.

But perfection could not be sustained. It existed in moments only and it did not solve any of her problems. When she spiralled back to earth, drowsy in Archer's arms, she was still Elisabeta di Nofri, desired by one man who promised her personal protection, but betrothed to another who had no intention of loving her, only possessing her by whatever means possible. She was still a woman who had to make a dreadful choice: to trade her family's pride for her happiness or enter into an unholy alliance in order to preserve it. But she was different. No one could make love the way they had and not be changed by it. But for what purpose? And how?

She didn't need to know, not yet. The night had hours to go, and Archer had stamina to match. But all the slow, lingering lovemaking in the world could not hold back the night and eventually the dark realm of their passion slipped its leash, letting sunrise and reality intrude.

* * *

'I have to go,' she murmured as the sun filtered through the high window. She slid out of bed before Archer could protest, before she lost her resolve. Workers would be arriving. Horses would need to be fed. Her own villa would be expecting her to come and claim her trunks. She was supposed to set out for home today. She reached for her clothes, gathering them up from the floor. The sheets rustled as Archer shifted. She could feel his eyes on her as she pulled on her chemise.

'Go where? To him?' There was heat in his words as he levered up on an arm.

She gave an exasperated sigh as much for herself as for him. 'Archer, what choice do I have?' Why did he insist on this discussion? It always ended in an impasse. She turned to look at him, but that was a mistake. Archer by morning presented a different kind of sensuality, one that was no less potent or persuasive than his brand of midnight seduction. A sheet lay draped across his hips, his torso exposed, muscled and smooth and tanned from days in the sun—days he'd worked shirtless alongside the grooms. The image sent a bolt of uncontrolled lust through her. She was giving up all of this for a marriage with a man who saw her as nothing more than a slave to his pleasure? But she knew why.

'You have every choice,' Archer fired back. 'You want your freedom, well, take it. I am giving it to you.' He waved a hand in the air. 'How can you walk away from this, from me, from what we shared last night?'

That made her angry. Didn't he understand how

brave she had to be to do just that? He'd all but called her a coward. She jerked on her gown and shoved her feet into her slippers. 'My family's honour demands it. Honour is no small thing in this part of the world, in case you haven't noticed.'

Now it was his turn to hurt. Her sharp words had found their target as she'd known they would. He prided himself on being a man of honour. But Archer was not so easily felled.

'Nor is it in mine,' he replied. 'What of your personal honour? Is that a smaller consideration?'

'It is my personal honour to be of use to my family.' She came to sit at the edge of the bed. She didn't want to fight with him, she just wanted him to understand. This decision was not easy. 'When my parents were killed, my uncle took me in without hesitation or reluctance—another mouth to feed, another girl to bring up, another marriage to arrange. He spared no expense. I was older than Contessina and he begrudged me nothing, even knowing his own daughter would need all the same expensive trappings to make her bow to society a few years later.

'Now, he has found me another wealthy marriage to replace the one I lost. If I bow out, I will shame him. Worse than that, I could cause actual physical hurt. I do not want Giuliano or my uncle involved in any duel of honour over me. How would I ever face my aunt again, knowing I had killed her son or her husband? What I do reflects directly on them. Whether I agree with the system or not, my family is responsible for me. I will not have them dragged down because of my selfishness.'

Archer's eyes were hard. 'I understand your argument and in theory I respect your commitment to your family, but I cannot agree to it in practice.'

Elisabeta rose from the bed. She'd failed to persuade him. '*You* don't have to.' She headed towards the door—better to leave on this note than a more dangerous one, a more tempting one.

His voice halted her. 'You're not thinking clearly right now. Will you promise me one thing before you go?' Archer stayed in bed. Smart man. He knew better than to try to force her acquiescence. 'Do nothing hasty. I will be in town soon. I have to bring the horses for the *tratta*. Wait for me. I will think of something. Trust me.'

'And will you promise me something? Stop making it harder than it is,' she shot back. He had to let her go for his own sake. *Stop showing me what is possible between a man and woman. You can stop tempting me with a future that doesn't exist. You can stop making me love you.* But it was too late for that.

She already did and that damning thought followed her home. She had fallen for Archer Crawford. It wasn't supposed to happen like that. He was supposed to have been her tool only, a stranger passing through who could appease her desire, her curiosity, a safe harbour in which to satisfy both. She had not expected any of this to happen when she'd tempted him into the alley. He'd been part experimentation, part discreet rebellion. He was never supposed to part of her future.

Chapter Fourteen

The future was an uncertain thing indeed. If anyone had told him four months ago his uncle would hand him his dream on a platter, he would have been thrilled beyond words. Yet now, the dream seemed tarnished, not exactly the shining opportunity he'd once thought it was.

It was one of the many thoughts that occupied Archer's mind as he sat at the long table inside the villa with his uncle who had come out to see the horses one last time before the *tratta*. Needless to say, it was not one of the thoughts he should have had his mind on. None of the thoughts were. He should not be thinking of the forbidden Elisabeta or what he could do to dissuade her from her stubborn refusal.

'Life at the villa suits you.' His uncle poured them a glass of wine, cheerfully oblivious to his distraction.

'It does,' Archer answered truthfully. His time here had been all he'd hoped, further proof that he'd chosen well in coming to Siena. He was his own man here, as he hoped he would be, and he was connecting for the first time with a family he'd always known existed, but had never known in person.

'The two chestnuts are coming along.' His uncle picked up a cluster of grapes from the platter between them, settling in for a discussion of the horses and which ones Archer would bring back with him for the *tratta*.

Archer nodded in agreement. 'Their legs are strong. They are cornering well.' Archer had studied the maps of the Palio course, the circular track of the race. 'Either of them will be able to navigate San Martino's curve.' It was the most dangerous turn of the Palio course and the bane of many horses. Of course, the horse's skill wasn't the only factor, just the only factor that could be trained for. Successful cornering also depended on whether or not another rider was out to cause a wreck and that depended on what *partiti* had been struck between you and other *contradas*.

'Which other horses do you think we should bring to the *tratta*?' The *tratta* was the official selection of the horses, held three days before the Palio itself. The question was asked casually, but Archer did not miss the honour the question did him. Once more, his uncle had asked for his opinion, a sign that he was willing to be guided by Archer's choice.

'I think there will be two more plus the chestnuts ready to go.' Archer named them, watching his uncle nod.

'What about the grey?' his uncle asked when he finished.

Archer shook his head without hesitation. 'He's too green. The horse is fast, but he is skittish. I don't think he will respond well to the noise and activity on the day of the Palio. I've run some simulations out here with gunfire and they haven't gone well. But he is young. Next year, perhaps.'

His uncle's face broke into a grin, and he slapped his knee with a hearty chuckle. 'Spoken like a true Ricci! One would never guess this is your first Palio, *mio nipote*. There wasn't an ounce of prevarication to your answer either. You've got spine.' His eyes twinkled proudly. 'But we knew that the moment you got up to trouble in Pantera.'

Archer grinned but he was instantly on alert. The conversation was moving on from horses and he wasn't sure he wanted it to. He'd hoped 'out of sight, out of mind' had been good not only for the *contrada* tensions. 'I trust the situation in town has cooled in my absence,' he said neutrally.

His uncle shrugged and waved a hand in dismissal. 'It has. The lady's uncle did his part as well. He announced the engagement, and the wedding will take place the end of August. Oca is satisfied now that it is official. I heard Ranieri gave her a tour of his home and then the bride-to-be took herself off to the country to "reflect". A nice house and full coffers can do much to change a woman's head. Women are eminently practical creatures when it comes down to it.'

So that was how her uncle was playing it. His own uncle was watching him carefully for a reaction. Archer was equally careful not to give one. He knew a different interpretation of the reason for her visit to the country and had a far different understanding of the visit to Ridolfo Ranieri's home. He could not tolerate the thought of all her beauty and passion sacrificed to a man she didn't love, a man who didn't respect her. But she would do it for the sake of her family. Only he stood between her and that decision.

'It is for the best, don't you agree?' His uncle's probe was not so subtle. 'A beautiful, fiery woman left unwed can be dangerous for a family, especially if she's widowed and thinks she might act on her own.'

'In England a widow has certain social privileges,' Archer offered a veiled defence.

'A discreet widow here might manage the same,' his uncle acquiesced but the implication was obvious. Elisabeta di Norfi hadn't been discreet and in her indiscretion had sacrificed that privilege. 'In any case, such a woman isn't for you. You've mentioned you are not intending to marry in the near future. Is that still true?' More not-so-subtle probing on his uncle's part.

'How do you like it out here at the villa with the horses? I'm told constantly about what a fine job you're doing here. The men say they've never seen someone who knows so much about horses and that you're a bruising rider.'

It was the praise, the recognition Archer had once hoped to acquire. Now that it had come, Archer was wary of it, linked as it was to his marital prospects and the direction in which those prospects should be aimed.

'I like it out here very much. It has proven to me that I made the right choice in coming.' Archer could see his uncle's approval in the nod of his head. He ventured the next part. 'I would like to purchase a property of my own. I want to make my home here.

I am done with England.' The words should have excited him. It had been a plan of his for many months as this tour had come together. Today, those words left him empty. Staying meant he couldn't run off with Elisabeta, couldn't take her away from Ridolfo, although it was unclear that was something she'd even allow.

'And done with your father, no doubt?' Uncle Giacomo said shrewdly. 'But I would warn you, distance alone won't solve your problems.' He pointed to his chest. 'Your father is your father, your flesh and blood, your family. He will always be with you.'

His uncle leaned forward. 'You need to work out for yourself if you're running *from* your father or *to* your mother's family.' Hadn't he said something similar to Elisabeta? There wasn't time to think about it. His uncle continued, 'Rest assured, we're glad to have you and to that end, I have a proposition I want to discuss with you. I want you to take over the villa and the horses.' He could live here year-round. It was a generous offer, one that spoke to his uncle's wealth that he could simply give over a villa without a moment's hesitation and one that spoke to the family's generous acceptance of him.

In the Italian view, Archer didn't have a choice. Family was family. Still, not everyone had uncles giving them villas. The offer touched him. The offer changed everything. He had something now beyond himself to offer Elisabeta, a respectable life. What would she make of this offer and what it might afford her? 'You are too good, Uncle...' Archer began delicately, wondering what his uncle wanted in exchange for this generosity. He felt guilty too. Perhaps this was a reward for having given up Elisabeta?

His uncle shrugged and made a small gesture. 'I would be honoured to have your family in this house in the future.'

In those moments, Uncle Giacomo seemed to live his years. Usually energetic, shrewd and sharp, Uncle Giacomo appeared ageless, certainly younger than his fifty-two years. In the letters written to his mother, Uncle Giacomo had taken on an immortal image to a young, impressionable Archer; the older brother who never made mistakes, who was the mainstay of the family through the decades, a fortress of stability, an enduring rock.

Not so now. It struck Archer how much loss his uncle had endured over the years: his younger brother, Pietro, dead on a dare at thirty in an accident that occurred when racing a horse through the cobblestone streets; his sought-after sister married to an Englishman and carried away, never to be seen again except in letters; his own wife childless. For a man who valued family, Uncle Giacomo's had dwindled.

His uncle leaned across the table and gripped Archer's wrist. 'It means everything to your aunt and me to have you here. You must never think of yourself as a burden. Family is never a burden. You're very like her, you know.' His uncle's eyes were sad. 'I wish I could have seen her again. Was she happy?'

'For the most part.' Archer would not lie to this man. 'My father is sometimes a difficult man to live with. He wants his way in all things.'

'Vittoria knew that before she married him. But he was a handsome man and wealthy. He rode like a master and cut a romantic figure. All the ladies in the *contrada* were taken with him.' Giacomo sighed. 'They all found his occasional aloofness romantic. Women, who understands them? All that brooding was attractive to them. I found it tiresome. I always thought the match an odd one. The Riccis are not poor people, but we have no title, we are not a noble family, just a rich one with horses and property. I would have thought your father would prefer a wife with a different sort of background. But in the end, love overrode all those considerations.' He held up a hand when Archer would have protested. 'He did love her, Archer, no matter what you think. Some people just have difficulty expressing it.'

His uncle rose from the table, his composure restored. Archer rose with him. His uncle placed a kiss on each cheek. 'Bring the horses up to town in a couple of days. The Palio track is being laid and there will be unofficial night trials before the *tratta*. Bring a few riders with you—you can't ride possibly ride all four horses at once.'

'Ride?' Archer queried, unable to believe the good luck that had just landed in his lap, and then he questioned it. Perhaps this too was a reward for good behaviour—good behaviour that hadn't happened.

His uncle laughed. 'Just for the night trials. Don't go getting any ideas.' His uncle waggled a finger at him playfully. 'You've done well, Archer. I am proud and your mother would be proud too.' He lowered his voice. 'Did she ever tell you that she rode in the night trials once? No? She did. The riders are all amateurs, the real jockeys don't usually risk it. She was in disguise, of course. No one recognised her except

Pietro and me. We were furious with her for taking such a chance, but who could deny her when she rode so well? Eh?' He clapped Archer on the shoulder.

His uncle felt in his pocket. 'I nearly forgot this. A letter came for you yesterday.'

Archer studied the outside, recognising the firm hand immediately. It was from Haviland, and Archer scanned the contents with a smile. It would be good to see him. 'My friends will be in town for the race.'

'They will stay with us,' his uncle volunteered. 'It will be good to have a house full of young men. We'll see you in town soon.'

Town. A chance to prove himself once more, a chance to move one step closer to his dream if he still wanted it, a chance to make good on his promise to Elisabeta. But it came at a price. He would have to act soon. It looked like Haviland and company was just in time. He could use a friend or two or three.

Archer stayed at the table long after his uncle left. He fingered the letter, his thoughts coming fast. He was excited to see his friends. He'd missed them and he needed them. But when he and Haviland had decided to rejoin forces in Siena plans had been different. He'd thought he'd be riding in the race. He'd also not thought he might be potentially fleeing the city with a woman in tow.

Admittedly, the last was putting the cart before the horse. Elisabeta had not agreed to anything. But the bottom line was still the same: he'd thought things would be different, more settled, when he'd made the suggestion to Haviland.

He wasn't sure how his friends would feel to arrive and then potentially be separated again, especially Haviland, who was arriving with a wife in tow. He wasn't sure at all how Haviland would feel about dragging her into this mess. In fact, he wasn't sure how forgiving Brennan and Nolan would feel. He'd left without telling them, leaving Haviland to explain. And now, he might potentially be doing the same thing all over again when they arrived. He'd invited them to travel across Europe at the expense of cutting down their time in the Alps only to run out on them again.

Archer played with a corner of the letter. These were answers he didn't have—yet. But he would, soon. The Palio had become a dream and a deadline.

Chapter Fifteen

The night trials; a chance to be free, a chance to be wild, a chance to prove to herself, if no one else, that her life wasn't over, a chance to escape reality for just a few giddy moments. Elisabeta twisted her long hair up under a cap and checked her reflection in the mirror, making sure her disguise was intact. Women didn't ride in the unofficial night trials. She laughed a little at the syllogism the idea created: women didn't ride in the night trials; Elisabeta di Nofri was riding in the trials, therefore, Elisabeta di Nofri couldn't be a woman.

Sometimes she wished she wasn't. If she were a man, she wouldn't be facing an unwanted marriage, or a lifetime of men making life-changing decisions for her. She would be free to live in the country, surrounded by her horses, to marry where she would and when she wanted. Her life would be her own. She gave a wry smile. But then there were other things she would have missed, like Archer.

She couldn't change the past or what she was. All she could do was take refuge in the idea that the syllogism would protect her tonight as much as the disguise. People didn't expect to see a woman ride so they simply wouldn't scrutinise her too much. It would be dark as well and that would be additional camouflage.

Who else would be there? Would Archer come to watch the trials? Maybe he would be there to ride. The riders tonight would all be amateurs. The night trials were for the horses, a chance to practise on the Palio track. A thrill of excitement went through her at the prospect of seeing him. She had been patient as he'd asked. Would he bring answers that she could live with? It had taken all her fortitude to leave him in the country. She didn't relish the idea of having to walk away from him again. If she did, this time would be the last time.

There was a low whistle outside her window, Giuliano's signal that all was clear. It was time to go. Tonight, she would ride and ride, and for a little while, no man would stand in her way.

La terra in piazza were the first words to run through Elisabeta's mind when she saw the track. It was well after midnight but even in the dark, she could sense the transformation of the town's central piazza into a race track. The excitement she'd grown up with as a child swept through her anew. The expression *there was dirt in the piazza* also translated into an expression of hope. *La terra in piazza*—there is dirt in the piazza—was one of the first expressions any Sienese learned. It meant not only that the Palio was coming, but that good times were coming again. Everything would be better soon. This year, more than ever, she wanted that to be true. But what good times awaited her?

Giuliano led out one of her uncle's three hopeful contenders, and she grinned when she saw the bay—the gelding was one of her favourites. Giuliano tossed her up with a wink. 'Have fun.'

'Thank you for this.' She squeezed his hand as she gathered the reins and settled on the horse's bare back. All the horses were ridden without saddles or stirrups for the race. She and Giuliano had negotiated something more than a truce for the debacle at the party, each them understanding they bore part of the blame. She was cognizant of his attempts to make up to her for his part in the trouble. She'd done her part too. She'd been the model dutiful niece since her return from the country, going everywhere with an appropriate cortège of women from the household, or with her uncle and Giuliano as escorts. No one could say she'd been indiscreet, giving credence to Giuliano's report that she'd had nothing to do with the Englishman at the party. No one would suspect she was anything but the dutiful bride-to-be.

She wondered if she'd managed to fool Ridolfo, or if he saw through her charade of compliance. The cruel visit to his home still haunted her. He had not said anything to her uncle about the outcome of the visit. He knew very well he couldn't without exposing his part in provoking her. He knew too that her uncle would not tolerate such threats aimed at his niece.

Secrecy worked in his favour. By not telling, Ridolfo had taken away a piece of her leverage. She could not use his threats to break the betrothal. He was a shrewd opponent who understood human nature far too well. He knew how to use her very nature against her.

She would not think about him tonight, not when there were horses to think about. Elisabeta turned her horse towards the track, joining the other riders. That was when she saw *him*, tall and proud on the back of a strong chestnut horse. Archer was here.

Her pulse leapt in recognition, but she could do nothing more to acknowledge his presence at the moment without giving herself away. That would have to wait until later. Until then, she would have a little fun of her own.

Elisabeta lined up in a group that contained Archer and his horse. For these amateur trials, horses usually raced in smaller groups of five or six so the track wasn't as crowded. Someone acted as the starter and there was a rope stretched across the starting line to simulate the race conditions. Around the track, spectators had gathered to take notes on the contenders, most of them were *capitani* who would vote on the ten horses in a few days at the *tratta*.

The signal came to start, the rope dropped and they were off, flying through the straight away and then into the San Martino curve. It was sharp, a few degrees over a right angle, but her horse managed beautifully, not losing pace as he exited the turn and headed into another straight-away zone. Archer was in front of her, riding well, but she knew this track better. She would make her move after the Casato turn.

She did, urging her bay to slowly eliminate the gap between them. Predictably, Archer slowed for the curve, wanting to learn its nuances and degrees. It was a sound strategy. While the San Martino curve posed a continual danger throughout the race, most accidents that happened on the Casato, happened during the first lap. But she had the edge of experience here and she used it to push her mount through the backside of the turn and surge to full speed in the last straight away of the first lap. She knew her own surge of satisfaction as she passed Archer, her horse stretching its legs into the second lap of the race.

The second lap was more difficult. She'd not been in the lead for the first and that made her job more defined. She knew she had to move the horse through the group, had to make up ground. But now, she was in the lead and the ride was different. She had to defend that lead. That meant racing the track with all its inclines, declines and curves, but also racing to prevent others from passing her. She was particularly conscious of Archer behind her, his chestnut yearning to pass.

She took the second lap and moved into the third and final, paying attention to her horse's physical response to the exercise. How was his breathing? How was his pacing? These were the items a rider paid attention to in the trials. They were far more important than winning an unofficial trial. Giuliano would want a full report from her and from the other two riders of the condition of the track, their horses and the horses they had ridden against. He would use her report for planning the *partiti*.

Elisabeta cursed as Archer sped past her in the straight away after the San Martino turn. She'd been overly cautious in the turn, not wanting to tax a tiring mount further and he'd taken advantage of it. Tonight, she wouldn't stand for it. Elisabeta pulled even with him at the Casato turn and surged, forcing him to let her cut ahead unless he wanted to risk being pushed into the wall.

Merda! For the second time the same horse and rider had passed him. That alone was enough to make them interesting to Archer. The derrière on the rider made them even more so. Even in the dark, even with his body and mind filled with the adrenaline of the race, he wasn't so far gone he couldn't tell a woman's backside from a man's. Archer made a final push to catch the pair before the finish line, but there simply wasn't enough ground to make up the distance.

Giacomo and some other men from the *contrada* came out to congratulate him, exclaiming over the horse. Giacomo was already asking questions about the ride: what was the corner like? How did the horse handle at the Casato curve? Archer answered, but his eyes were drawn to the horse and rider to his left. 'Who brought that horse? The one that beat me?'

'Rafaele di Bruno's, I think,' Giacomo replied, eager to get back to the subject of their horses. That information confirmed his growing suspicion. Rafaele di Bruno was Elisabeta's uncle. Since these trials weren't about the *contrada*, but about the horses, it wasn't inconceivable that she had managed to wrangle a chance to ride disguised. After all, he had been given the same opportunity sans disguise. Suddenly, he wanted nothing more than to be done with his uncle's questions. He wanted to be free to go after her.

'I'll write up a report if you like,' he offered to

Giacomo. 'We can go over it in the morning.' He clapped his uncle on the shoulder and disappeared into the crowd of horses and men before Giacomo could protest.

It was no easy feat to find Elisabeta. The area was full of horses moving on and off the track with their riders as the second group came on. There were spectators too, even though it was well after midnight. The *capitani* had brought their *mangini*, which made for at least three people from each of the seventeen *contrada* present, plus grooms and riders. Unofficial these races might be, but they were full-fledged events none the less.

Luck was with him. He caught sight of her finally on the edge of the busyness and alone. He approached, not daring to use her name. He hailed her with a compliment instead, letting his smile and his eyes say the rest of it. 'That was an excellent piece of riding out there.'

She looked at him, letting her face do the same, and he felt his body stir to life as if it had been dead since she'd left.

'How are you?' Archer pitched his voice low, watching her face.

'I am well. How are you?' But it was a lie. Up close, he could make out the tightness of her jaw, the faint show of shadows beneath her eyes.

'It's no good, Elisabeta. I can see that you are not entirely all right. We must talk, we must plan in earnest now if you are to escape this marriage. I have ideas.' He did, just not ideas that she would approve of. She wanted it all. To lose the family was to lose everything. In light of that, no price was too great to pay. It was what he admired about her. But he would have to persuade her otherwise.

She stiffened suddenly, her eyes going to a spot over his shoulder. 'I have to go. Giuliano is looking for me.' She hesitated, her voice so low he nearly missed it. Her body brushed against his ever so slightly, the feel of it erotic for its brevity. 'Archer, light a candle.'

'Yes,' came his hoarse agreement. What would it have been like to have known her earlier? Would he have had a chance to win her? Perhaps being from Torre would not have mattered if his timing had been better.

Archer lit the candle, knowing full well she meant to come to him. He would have liked to have argued with her. He'd gladly have risked going to her, would have gladly risked the consequence of him being caught, but there'd been no time to plead his case. So here he was, at nearly three o'clock in the morning, lying abed alert, and hard, waiting. Hoping. Admittedly a position he was not used to. He was a man of action and this delicate dance of subterfuge was testing him sorely.

Had this been how Haviland had felt in Paris with Alyssandra: this desperation in wanting to seize every moment because it was going to end? Haviland had known the date of that end too, it had loomed on their travel calendar as a day in early June, just as the end for him and Elisabeta loomed as the day of her wedding approached in late August. Haviland had dealt with his desperation by changing the date to for ever and then by changing his circumstances. He'd decided to no longer be a traveller, to no longer be a man seeking a temporary escape from his burdens. He simply gave the burdens up and by doing so those burdens lost the ability to define his life.

Archer couldn't do that. For one, he wasn't temporarily escaping. He'd decided from the outset that this was permanent for him. He wasn't going back. His burdens had been given up. His situation, unfortunately, didn't mirror Haviland's. The fact that he was staying permanently in Siena meant he had to think about the consequences his choices had on others. He wished Haviland were here. Perhaps between the two of them, they would know what he could do in regards to Elisabeta.

A rattle sounded at the doors of his balcony and the doors swung in before Archer could rise and open them. Elisabeta stepped through the gauzy curtains and shut the doors behind her. She looked utterly enticing in her breeches and boots. How anyone could remotely think her a man with all those curves on display beneath those riding breeches was beyond him. He might have been immediately aroused, but he'd certainly not been immediately fooled.

She took off her cap in a flourish that brought her hair down in a cascade of dark waves. 'Your balcony is a little higher up than it looks.' She was flushed and still catching her breath. 'I haven't climbed like that in ages.'

'You took an enormous risk coming here.' Physically, socially, the risks had come in more than one form. The risks had been enormous. Archer launched the pro forma protest as he crossed the room to her. He was far more interested in doing other things besides scolding her. He drew her close for a kiss, forcing himself to linger over it, to savour it, when what he really wanted to do was devour her. He could smell the sweat of her, the scent of horse, and beneath that the remnants of her rosemary-lavender soap. The scent of her spoke her story: animal lover, enticing woman, risk taker, passionate lover of life's adventure. All of it was there and he hungered for it, for her.

Her arms were about his neck, her body pressing against his. She kissed with her entire being, not just her mouth. 'I didn't want to let those breeches go to waste,' she murmured beneath his lips. 'All the same, I think I've had enough of playing the boy tonight.' She stepped back, disengaging their bodies. 'Watch me, Archer. Watch me become a woman before your very eyes.'

She gave him a gentle push, and he sat back on the bed, watching, waiting, the room around him a reminder of the intimacy they were about to share. So many of his encounters took place outside of a bedroom, and certainly all of them took place outside his bedroom. *This*, what was happening here in front of him right now, existed on an entirely different plane.

Elisabeta pulled off her boots and went to work. She drew the shirt over her head and undid the binding around her breasts, unwinding the length of cloth with a slowness that tantalised. But nothing compared to the pleasurable torture of only being able to look at the body revealed to him in pieces and not touch.

His hands ached to take those breasts in his hands, to run his thumbs over the dusky nipples, to trace the rosy-brown aureoles surrounding them, to take his mouth and blow gentle breaths into that navel while his hands traced the sleek lines of her torso.

But his eyes, oh, how they feasted. She drew her breeches down over slim hips, entirely naked beneath as she kicked out of them, and he was breathless—he had seen her like this before, seen plenty of women naked and yet for all of his experience, for all of the women he'd pleasured, he was breathless.

She gave a satisfied smile, luring him with the dancing light in her eyes. 'You've seen me nude, Archer.'

His voice was a desire-laden growl of want. 'But not as often I'd like.' Every last word was true. He wanted to taste, touch, lick and lave, explore and worship each inch of her. His body was tight with the wanting of it, the needing of it as she stood there, brazenly naked for *him*.

'I could say the same of you. So…' her eyes ran over him in a show of anticipated appreciation '…if you wouldn't mind obliging? It's your turn.'

Chapter Sixteen

He was more than happy to oblige. He'd heard the boldness in her voice, but he'd seen the flicker of sad regret in her eyes as she'd made her demand. Not regret over anything they had done, but regret for what was to come—marriage to a man for whom she felt not the slightest bit of physical interest. He understood now why she'd risked coming. This might be the last time. He would make this good for her, for them.

Archer rose from the bed with deliberate slowness, letting the profundity of that thought strike him in full. *Would* this be the last time? Surely with the upcoming Palio festivities, there would be a chance, but a chance only, and certainly nothing that would guarantee a bed being present. He let his hands linger at the waist of his trousers, let her anticipate what lay beneath the fabric.

It was a rather erotic sensation to undress in front of a naked woman, the two of them an antithesis of the other, he in his clothes and she without them. If he were an artist, he would paint her as she was in this moment; sitting nude in a chair, legs crossed, hair falling over her shoulders, looking entirely composed, as if she sat this way every day. That was, until one looked in her eyes and saw the wildness, the want, the hunger that lurked brazenly.

Archer crossed his arms and lifted his shirt up and over his head in a fluid motion that left his chest bare and exposed. He felt her eyes run over him, saw the appreciation grow in them as she took in the tanned, defined musculature of his torso. 'I've always thought Adam would look this way.' Her words came with a breathless hitch to them and he knew a moment's pride in her appreciation. When had a woman ever taken time to savour him thusly? To enjoy simply looking upon him? Yet she did, each time as if it were the first.

He gave her a slow, sensual smile and watched her come alive with it. He opened the fall of his trousers and pushed them from his hips. She came to him, running her hands down his chest, skimming the surface of his skin with her fingertips, nails brushing nipples. He could feel them harden as she passed over, could feel the temperature of his body rise with each touch until her hand dropped low and closed over the core of him.

She held his gaze as she held him, let him see that her quicksilver eyes had become nearly black with desire. 'I've decided it is so much better to see you,' she whispered, running her hand the length of him. Already hard, he felt himself jump in her grasp, his cock taking on a life of its own, twitching its pleasure.

She gave a husky laugh. 'It's like a frisky stallion.'

She gave him a gentle push backwards, urging him to sit on the edge of the bed, a seductive smile on her lips. 'Let's see if we can't tame him a bit.' She knelt before him with a wicked look. 'Open your legs for me, Archer.'

She spread his thighs apart, hands firm on either side of his groin, perhaps to steady herself, he thought. Then, she took him in her mouth, and he knew it wasn't to steady herself, but to steady him. He could scarcely breathe from the exquisite contact of her mouth with his tender head. When he did breathe, all he could manage was a series of trembling pants, his hands gripping the edge of the bed. There wasn't enough stability in the world to anchor him against this.

Elisabeta licked his tip, giving a small moan of delight as she moved on to tongue the rest of him, to nip at his length with gentle teeth. She returned once more to his tip, upping the intensity of their play, sucking hard, turning the tantalising tease of her mouth to an insistent pressure of pleasure. Archer felt his body gathering for its climax, his balls tightening in anticipation of release. He arched back and let it come, let it fill her hand, pleased that the act held her in thrall. She did not shy away from his completion, but instead seemed to share in the awe of it with him. They had done this *together*. It added credence to his wildest of options—marry Elisabeta—and his hope that she might agree. What woman would walk away from this?

Amazing. Positively amazing. But how to tell him? How to convey the emotion rocketing through her at what had transpired? Her eyes held his, unable to look away. All she wanted to do was look at him, to memorise every line and plane of him, the feel of him, the taste of him. Her hand was still warm about him where he pulsed with half life, the tension starting to leave his body.

'I've not...' she began, faltering for words.

I've never done that to another man with my mouth before, never thought I would want to, never thought a man would compel me to madness, but you do. You have me climbing into bedrooms in the dead of night, risking everything for one more moment of pleasure, one more night of impossible hope.

Archer put a gentle finger over her lips, his voice quiet. 'No words, Elisabeta. They would be inadequate anyway.' He drew her up then to his lap and she straddled him so that they were bare skin to bare skin. It was simple, beautiful contact. He kissed her long and slow, letting their mouths play. 'I can taste myself on your lips, Elisabeta,' he whispered. 'That is a heady reminder of the pleasure you've brought me and the pleasure I owe you in return.'

'Owe?' she murmured, biting at his lower lip. 'Lovers give, Archer, they don't owe,' she reprimanded gently.

He grinned, and she could feel his mouth widen in a smile beneath her own. 'Give, then. It is a prelude to the pleasure I will *give* you.'

'When?' Elisabeta teased, moving her hips against him and feeling the first flares of new life in his groin.

'Soon, very soon.' Archer gave a low rumble of laughter. He leaned back, taking her with him so that they lay against the pillows, side by side, able to look each other in the eye. This was comfortable intimacy, with him propped up on an arm, looking down at her as if they had all the time in the world, as if the night weren't fleeing.

'Tell me about your uncle's villa and the horses,' she prompted. She wanted to use every minute of their short night to her benefit. She wanted to touch him, to make love to him, and when that wasn't possible, she wanted to know him as she'd come to know him in the country. She wanted the closeness that came with knowledge, even if it made it harder to let him go.

'He has offered the villa and the farm to me. My uncle has been all that is generous and gracious. He has welcomed me as a son. I have only to breathe a wish and he sees it granted. Do you want a horse farm? Here, have the villa. Do you want to ride in the Palio? Here, take my horses and ride them in the unofficial trials. Do you want a bride? We will find one for you.' Archer shook his head with a chuckle. 'I think all I would have to say is "I want to marry on September fifteenth" and I would only need to show up. It would all be there for me.' He grinned.

Elisabeta's hand stalled on the muscled ridge of his biceps. What did she say to that? Everything changed. Taking on the villa implied a permanence she hadn't anticipated. Always she'd thought there'd come a day when Archer would leave, later if not sooner. It was what made him safe. He would leave and take this secret affair with him along with her heart. But now? Now there would be no more talk of running away, no more sense in even contemplating that fantasy. He meant to stay. He'd been given a farm. He'd been given his dream. She was all that stood in his way.

Stay. The word had riveted all of her attention. She'd barely heard the rest. He was staying. She'd not bargained on that.

How perfect.

How awful.

How perfectly awful.

'What?' Archer studied her in the silence. 'Have I rendered you speechless with my insensitivity for the Italian way?'

'No, not at all.' She gathered enough control over her voice to turn the conversation coy. 'I was just wondering, *do* you want to marry on September fifteenth?' Perhaps he did. It had struck her anew that if he stayed, he would eventually marry here. It would be quite the torture for them both: he watching her marry Ridolfo and she having to tolerate whomever he chose. Of course, all that assumed current feelings remained constant and perhaps that was a large assumption to make indeed.

Archer came up over her, his mouth teasing hers, his renewed erection flirting with her core as his hips pressed. 'I could go sooner or later on the date, depending on the girl. Do you know anyone who's available?'

'Archer, don't,' she warned. These were things they could not say to one another even in jest. 'This changes nothing.'

'It changes everything,' Archer was quick to respond. 'I have something to offer you, here. You needn't marry him. You can marry *me*, we can have our life in the country. Choosing me no longer means choosing to flee in shame.'

Marry Archer? It was a stunning idea, one that went far beyond his original offer of protection. But it wasn't enough. 'Marriage won't be rid of the scandal. The scandal will still be there. His offer is on the table before yours. The engagement is official.'

'I will find a way around it if you would have me. It is merely the last obstacle. Will you? Have me?' Archer queried. He wound a curl around one long finger.

If he stayed, he would be here, but out of reach. She didn't dare seek him after her marriage, not after the horrors Ridolfo had promised to inflict. He would not tolerate it. No one respected a man whose wife was unfaithful. An affair would disgrace her family, her *contrada* and herself. Yet to encounter him, to know Archer was nearby, would be torture to consider. To know that pleasure was at hand and she could not take it. It would be a Sisyphean task. He was offering her everything and yet it was nothing without the one thing she wanted as much as her own freedom to choose. 'I won't be a pity project, Archer. I don't want you to marry me just to save me. You would come to resent me.' And yet, she wanted to say yes. He'd very nearly found a way for them to have it all—her freedom, his dream of a horse farm in Italy near his mother's family. But it was a plan born of desperation, born of spontaneity. He'd never once spoken of love and she would not trap him. He would come to hate her for it. She'd never meant to embroil him.

Archer gave a rueful smile, his eyes amber coals

come to life, his dark hair falling forward over his face, skimming his shoulders. 'I would not have offered if I didn't mean it, if I didn't want it. Let me show you how much.' Then he silenced her with a kiss that was long and slow and obliterating.

'You're playing with fire now, Archer,' she warned between hot kisses.

He turned serious, There was no joking now. 'Then come for me, Elisabeta, and let us burn together.'

He was ready for her again, evidence of his arousal pressing against her stomach, and she was ready for him, ready for the pleasure, a different sort of pleasure than what they had shared earlier. His hand cupped her breast, running the flat of his palm over her nipple until she felt it peak for him, and he took the straining peak in his mouth, laving it with his tongue as she'd done for him. She arched for him, pressing her body against his, wanting this foreplay and yet wanting more than this. She wanted it all. 'Take me, Archer,' she urged, her legs widening for him so that he was cradled between her thighs and there was no question of his welcome.

He did not deny her. He slid home in one powerful thrust, a guttural cry escaping him at his reception. She could feel her own slickness as he entered, could smell the scent of her arousal mingling with his, could feel her body live the words of her mind, *Yes, this is and more...* And there *was* more.

His body set the rhythm and hers followed, hips rising to join his, legs wrapping about his waist, holding him tight as they sought release together. She revelled in the feel of his body pumping into hers, primal and alive in these exquisite moments. She revelled, too, in her own body's response; the rising of the pleasurable ache she now knew signalled the approach of climax, the racing of her pulse. They were near, so very near, she felt the signals in her body and in his. Archer gave a final thrust and they reached out to grab it together, soaring, falling into pleasure, into the impossibility of perfection,

She must have slept. When she awoke, it was with a languorous sense of satisfaction permeating her bones; her body was exquisitely sore with loving, her lover's body lay against her, his arm draped across her in wondrous possession. The sun fell warm across the sheets. *The sun was up!* Panic set in. She had not meant to stay so long. She'd meant to leave before sunrise.

'Archer!' she gave a frantic whisper. 'I've got to go!' In the distance she heard the church bells sound the hour and her panic eased slightly. It was only six, but it was still far later than she'd meant it to be.

Archer stirred and opened sleepy eyes that made her heart flip. What she wouldn't give to lie abed in the mornings with this man and rekindle the passions of the night. 'There is still time. It will be all right. People will be sleeping late because of the trials. I'll walk you back.' He rolled out of bed and reached for his discarded breeches.

'No, that's far too incriminating.' Elisabeta shook her head, hurrying into her clothes. She twisted her hair up in a hasty bun—it would fool no one on closer inspection and there was no time to bind her breasts. 'If anyone questions me, I'll tell them I was out on business with the horses. But if I'm seen with you, there will be no good explanation.' She could see Archer didn't like the plan. It was not in his nature to let another take risks on his behalf. *He* was the rescuer.

'Are you sure? Perhaps I could go part of the way with you?' Archer insisted. He was all protective warrior, ready to leap to her defence as he had been at the ball, her safety his first concern and the primal woman in her thrilled to the knowledge that this bare-chested warrior had been hers.

She went to him and put a hand on his chest. 'I'm sure, Archer. It is better this way.' Better in case she was seen, better because a swift goodbye was better than a prolonged one that left time for regrets. Now, it was all a rush, all of their efforts focused on the getaway and not the import of what her leaving meant. But their eyes caught at the last moment. She wasn't going to get away that easily. His unresolved proposal passed between them. His hand covered hers where it rested against his chest.

'I will come to you, tonight. You are to take no more risks. Let the risks be mine from here on out.' He kissed her hand and then her lips. He tugged at that hand and led her towards the bedroom door with a wink. 'I know a better way out. It's called the stairs.'

He would come for her. A thrill of excitement surged through her at the idea of an illicit assignation in her room. But he was coming for more than her, he was coming for an answer.

* * *

The *troia*! She had dared to go to him, that English *figlio di puttana*. Ridolfo Ranieri spat into the gutter and pressed himself against the brick of the building. It would not do to be seen now. His man had woken him with the news and he hurried out to watch and wait so he could see it with his own eyes. Elisabeta di Nofri had climbed into the Englishman's bed the moment he returned to town and now she swaggered down the empty street as if she hadn't a care in the world.

Ridolfo passed a hand over his eyes, his anger growing. He'd not accepted his cousin's explanations, or Rafaele di Bruno's or that son of his Giuliano's the night of the party. He'd suspected something more was up. A woman that beautiful couldn't be entirely innocent of attracting the wrong sort of attention. Those sort of women encouraged it. He'd set his own spies on the di Bruno household to watch her every move. He'd just about been willing to give up. The past weeks had passed without incident; she had seemed reformed enough from her reflective retreat in the country, but then the report had come that his man suspected she'd gone to the trials in disguise and it had all unfolded from there.

Rafaele di Bruno and Pantera would have to pay for this treachery against Oca and his cousin. He was a wealthy man, respected for his business acumen in the community, but she was making him look like a fool. Only a weak man tolerated such behaviour. But most of all, Elisabeta would have to pay and so would the Englishman for their treachery against him. Anyone who crossed Ridolfo Ranieri would live to regret it. Timing was everything and the time was not yet, but soon. Very soon, the Englishman would receive a most unpleasant surprise.

Chapter Seventeen

'This is a grand surprise indeed!' Archer thumped Haviland and the others on the back in genuine delight as he stepped into the *loggia* to find Uncle Giacomo holding court with his friends. 'You've arrived early. I wasn't expecting you until tomorrow,' Archer exclaimed. 'This is even better, you are here in time for the *tratta*. Today, the horses are selected for the Palio.' He stepped back to survey the group with a smile. 'I am glad you are here. Please, eat. There's prosciutto and melon, bread and coffee, always coffee in the morning.' By Jove, it felt good to see them! Nolan and Brennan were obscenely tan from days spent outdoors on the mountains and Haviland looked…happy. His earlier worries seemed foolish.

Haviland laughed as everyone took their seats. 'You sound like your uncle. He's been feeding us since we walked in.'

Giacomo grinned and shrugged. 'It's what we do.' He rose from his chair. 'I will leave you gentlemen to catch up. I have errands to run before the *tratta*.' He wagged a finger in Archer's direction. 'Don't forget to come to the *tratta*, though.'

'He is fond of you,' Nolan commented as the older man left the room.

Archer smiled. 'I am fond of him too. It has been good beyond words to meet him and my mother's family at last.' He looked around the table. 'Where's Alyssandra, Haviland?'

'Still in bed,' Haviland replied slyly. 'Perhaps where you'd like to be? Tell us, who is she?'

Archer feigned ignorance. How did Haviland know? His friends had only been here for a few minutes. 'What makes you think there's a she at all?'

Nolan tutted and shook his head. 'It's no good pretending, old man, all the signs are there: sleeping late, the dark circles. You've been up all night, several nights in a row. I've been around Brennan enough to know what that looks like.'

Archer pushed a hand through his hair, prevaricating. Did he tell them? He tried to sidestep it once more. 'It's a busy time with the race. I just got back from the countryside.'

Brennan gave a hoot of laughter. 'This is *not* about a horse, Archer. How stupid do we look?'

Nolan shot Brennan a glance. 'Perhaps he thought we were so stupid we wouldn't notice he was gone.' Nolan's quicksilver eyes turned on Archer. 'Why didn't you tell us you meant to leave us in Paris?'

There it was. The reckoning he'd feared. They would be angry they hadn't been told, as if not being told reflected in some way on the quality of their friendship being less than the quality of friendship he held with Haviland. That wasn't the case at all.

The decision wasn't about them. It was about him. 'I apologise…' Archer began. 'The decision wasn't meant to offend anyone.'

'We would have come with you,' Nolan insisted. 'Old Haviland could have got married by himself or we could have caught up.'

Archer shook his head. Nolan wasn't going to be put off. It was time for the truth, the real reason he hadn't told them. 'No, you had plans for the Alps. I didn't want to get in the way of that when I wasn't sure how things would turn out here.' The words seemed inadequate to convey all he felt, but that was it in a nutshell. He hadn't wanted to fail in front of his friends. What if his uncle hadn't been welcoming? What if he hadn't liked Siena? He would have brought them along for nothing. This was simply something he had to do on his own.

Silence descended on the table. They understood. Each of them had their own demons, their own dreams, their own risks that had to be faced alone. Brennan smiled, breaking the solemnity. 'Well, that answers part one of the stupid question. Let's get back to the other part. Who is she?'

Now it would be Archer's turn to be the idiot. What would they think once he told them about Elisabeta and his mad scheme? Archer stalled for time and helped himself to more melon. 'It's complicated.'

Nolan leaned forward. 'It always is with a woman. Do tell.'

Archer looked at them. They were his best friends, no matter how wild they were. He could trust them with this as perhaps he should have trusted them with his decision to leave Paris early. He lowered his voice.

'It's private. My uncle feels that I shouldn't see her. She's from another *contrada* and she's betrothed to a loathsome man.'

Nolan grinned. 'She's forbidden, the daughter of a rival and pledged to another? Lucifer's balls, Archer, Shakespeare would be drooling on himself, "two households both alike in dignity" and all that. The only thing missing is a hero's proposal of marriage to whisk her away to a happy ever after.' Nolan paused, Archer feeling the weight of his gaze. Nolan always saw too much in others.

'Oh, hell, Archer, you didn't?' Nolan gaped at him.

The others were looking at him too in stunned surprise.

Haviland was the first to recover. 'When?'

'Just this morning.'

'At a most opportune time, no doubt, when she was thoroughly ploughed—' Brennan winked '—and refusing you was the furthest thing from her mind.'

'I didn't "plough" her,' Archer corrected.

'Of course not, you *made love* to her.' Nolan chuckled. 'Good Lord, you're besotted with her.'

'He's not besotted, he wants to rescue her,' Haviland said shrewdly, sounding far too like Elisabeta. Haviland, always the voice of reason, steepled his hands. 'Marriage is a big step. Are you sure it's for the right reasons? If you want to rescue her, perhaps we can find another way.'

Archer blew out a breath. 'This is why I didn't want to tell you. I knew you'd try to talk me out of it.' Marrying Elisabeta was admittedly a mad idea, but one that had slowly taken hold since the countryside. Still, Haviland's comment had hit its mark.

Was that what he wanted? Or had his subconscious prompted it because he knew their *affaire* couldn't go on this way without resolution? 'If you knew her like I do, you'd understand.' They had not watched her with the horses in the country, hadn't seen her heart etched on her face when she spoke of her family. This was a woman who loved deeply and without reservation even at the expense of great personal sacrifice. To have the love of such a woman turned his way, to share a life with her, would be a treasure beyond imagining, beyond deserving.

'Well,' Archer said, filling in the silence, 'it hardly matters yet. She hasn't accepted.'

'Why ever not? You really should have asked her after you ploughed her,' Brennan put in. 'Women will say yes to anything after great sex.'

'Even you, apparently,' Nolan ribbed him.

'For the second time, I didn't plough her. That's so crass, Brennan,' Archer protested.

'Will we get to meet this paragon?' Haviland asked before Nolan and Brennan could degenerate the discussion further.

'You will likely see her at the *tratta*.' Archer stood up. It was as good of an opening as any to change the subject. 'In fact, we should get going if we want a good spot.' He smiled at his friends. 'I *am* glad you're here.' And he was even if they were shocked by his news. They would stand beside him come what may.

The *campo* in front of the Palazzo Pubblico was full, everyone gathering for the *tratta* late that morning. The excitement of anticipation filled the air as Archer and his friends joined the Torre *contrada*.

The unofficial late-night trials were over and now the horses for the race would be chosen. Then, that afternoon, the chosen horses would be assigned to the neighbourhoods. They would waste no time after that. The first official trial would be held that night. There would only be three days remaining before the great race. He would have responsibilities for his uncle as one of his *mangini*. It would be harder to slip away, nigh on impossible if Giacomo was to be believed. The nights before the race were manic, with *capitani* and *mangini* arranging secret *partiti*.

A certain anxiety underlay Archer's excitement. With all the activity of the next three days, what would become of him and Elisabeta? Had last night literally been that, their *last* night? Would the affair merely fade into the background as the Palio took centre stage? It would be a convenient out for her if she meant to reject his offer. With her wedding to Ridolfo lurking on the calendar in two weeks, they would simply run out of time.

She had not rejected the idea of marrying him, but she had not affirmed it either. Had it crossed her mind too that he might be her salvation, her way out? Or was she too noble to impose on him? Perhaps she feared his affections only stemmed from the desire to rescue her. How did he convince her otherwise? How did he convince anyone otherwise? Those who knew him knew he'd not come here to marry. He'd said it out loud often enough. His plan to wait had made sense in the beginning. He was starting a new phase of his life away from England, away from the grief of his mother's passing. It was hardly a 'good time' to start a new intimate relationship, but Elisabeta offered him a relationship of mind and body and soul, something he'd never had before. He was too smart to throw it away.

If his parents' marriage had shown him the risks of love, Siena was showing him the beauties of it. If he could have that, what wouldn't he risk for it? Was it possible? Elisabeta thought it was. It was why she resisted being bartered away in marriage to Ridolfo. If it was possible for her, was it possible for him? For them together? He'd based his proposal on the hopes that it was. These were the thoughts that kept him well occupied through the early stages of the *tratta*.

'Seriously, Archer…' Nolan leaned close amid the crowd, sensing his distraction '… I ache for you. You have fixed your attentions on a woman you cannot have. But have you thought it through? What can come of this infatuation but trouble? If your rivals, or her rivals, learn this affair has continued…' He let his words trail off, his eyes sad as they communicated his meaning.

Archer winced. He hated how astute Nolan could be. Even after only one day, Nolan seemed to grasp the intricacies of Sienese life. If Oca learned of this, it would mean they had grounds for revenge. They would believe that not just Archer, but Torre had violated the truce after the Pantera party. Archer's proposal would bring a feud to Torre.

'The Palio is dangerous enough,' Nolan said lightly. 'We don't need to invite more trouble.'

'Her fiancé's *contrada* isn't even racing in this one,' Archer said defensively. The remaining three slots for the Palio had been drawn while he was in the countryside. Oca would not be among the ten *contradas* in the contest. But that wouldn't stop Oca from trying to negotiate contracts that would prevent their rivals from winning. It was horrible for a non-racing *contrada* to have its enemy *contrada* win. It was almost as bad as losing it yourself.

Brennan nudged him. 'Look, here they come!' A cry went up from the crowd as the first horses were sighted, being led through the crowd to the courtyard of the Palazzo Pubblico where their health would be determined. Conversations began immediately as the horses passed by. All about him, Archer could hear snatches of conversation: would Jacopi's Morello be selected again after winning in July? Would this horse? Would that horse? See how this one holds his foot, perhaps it is a strained ligament? Didn't that one suffer a fall in one of the night trials? The energy in the piazza swelled, contagious and rambunctious. It was hard not to get caught up in the excitement.

'There's my uncle's horses!' Archer pointed a little farther down the line of animals being brought in. Not only would they know today which horse Torre would get to race, but they'd know if any of his uncle's horses, *his* horses, would be racing too. He'd worked hard with them for this moment.

If an owner's horse was chosen for the Palio, the owner was paid a handsome stipend for the honour although there was no guarantee that horse would race for the owner's *contrada*. One of Uncle Giacomo's horses might race for one of the other neighbourhoods. There was another bonus as well for the owner if his horse went on to win. As Giacomo had been fond of telling him, there were a lot of ways to win or lose on the Palio—it was more than simply crossing the finish first.

The crowd quieted a bit as the last of the horses, twenty in all, disappeared into the palazzo's courtyard. Now they would wait for the doctors to ascertain the health of the horses. This was paramount. A sick horse would not be replaced. If a *contrada*'s assigned horse became ill or injured, they would not be given a replacement, which was why Archer's job of guarding the stable was so critical. *Contradas* were not above trying to render another's horse unable to race.

The crowd grew restless waiting for news. Archer searched the gathering for signs of Elisabeta. There were plenty of women here—perhaps she'd come. But if she was here, he couldn't find her. At last the announcement was made. All the horses had been declared sound. Archer let out a breath he hadn't realised he'd been holding. His uncle's horses had passed. Archer knew a moment's relief. They'd been horses he'd personally recommended. He would have had some answering to do if those horses had not been found sound.

The energy of the crowd started escalating again. People got out little scorecards to take notes as the *capitani* separated the horses into groups of four or five to run mock races, but the races held little appeal for Archer. He knew these horses. He'd raced alongside them for three breathless nights and he'd already passed on his recommendations to his uncle. The crowd held all of his attention now. Was Elisabeta here? Archer's gaze scanned up to the balconies lining the perimeter of the square, a smile spreading in slow satisfaction across his face. There!

He spied her sitting at one of the balconies, and his breath hitched for a moment as he let the beauty of her wash over him. 'She's there, on the balcony.' He pointed her out to Nolan and the others. She was stunning, dressed in white, holding a parasol to match. The white was an ideal foil for her dark hair. Even at this distance with a crowd and half a piazza between them, one could sense the vibrancy of her, the life that radiated from her. She leaned forward to hear one of her companions and then she laughed. He knew the sound of that laugh. He could hear that laugh in his mind despite the noise of the crowd. He knew how her eyes would be dancing at this moment as she made her response—something witty and funny.

Nolan let out a low whistle. 'She's gorgeous. No wonder you've proposed.' Archer barely heard him. He was too busy letting his imagination conjure up another fantasy, one from the near future; one of Elisabeta sitting at a balcony with a small dark-haired child on her lap, his child, *their* child, anxiously awaiting the outcome of the *tratta* to see whether the horses from their stables in the country would be selected to run. Aunt Bettina and Uncle Giacomo would be with them, the women laughing together. Then, Elisabeta would spy him in the crowd and give him a wave and the world would vanish as it did now. Maybe later that night they would lie in bed celebrating their success and he would tell her the story of his first *tratta*, of how he'd looked up to see her all in white and perhaps that was the first time he knew, really knew, that she was meant to be his.

A heavyset man lumbered out on to the balcony and exchanged words with Elisabeta as he took up a seat behind her. Immediate, primal dislike surged through Archer. Beside him, Nolan murmured, 'Is that the bastard she's to marry?'

Ridolfo was turned out in splendour today. He wore his wealth in his clothes and his paunch. His money had no doubt secured the luxury of a balcony as well. Only a rich man could afford such indulgences. Ridolfo leaned close and the life seemed to go out of Elisabeta. Her gaze no longer looked out over the piazza, but down at her hands, her mouth no longer moving in sparkling conversation.

The mayor had begun drawing the horses and the crowd boisterously awaited the announcement of each result. After the first five drawings, both of his uncle's chestnuts had been assigned to other *contradas*, which was both good and bad news. Archer wouldn't have minded Torre drawing one of its own mounts. One of them had gone to Pantera. He did not remember who had drawn the other. Aside from Jacopi's Morello, the Torre horses were very promising competitors. Jacopi's Morello, the bay that won the last Palio, was still available, though.

Perhaps later, he'd reflect on the irony of it all: here he was, in the piazza on the most important day before the race he'd waited his whole life to be part of. He should be drinking in each moment, seeing each moment as part of the fulfilment of a dream, and yet all he wanted was for it to be over. He wanted to escape, to go to Elisabeta.

Around him, the Torre men were getting nervous about him. Seven *contrada* had already been drawn. The mayor drew again. 'The next horse is Jacopi's Morello!' Torre held its collective breath. There were only three *contrada* left in the other urn. The slip of paper came out, the name was read. 'Torre! Jacopi's Morello goes to Torre!'

'We got the bay, we got the bay!' Someone next to him grabbed Archer and kissed both his cheeks. Men went crazy with excitement, pumping fists and hitting each other rather heartily on the back in congratulations as if they had anything to do with the luck of the draw.

His uncle came out of the building and spied him, throwing an arm around him as they were pushed along in the wave of Torre men going to claim their horse. 'You know what this means, right?' Giacomo yelled over the cheers as Archer's hand closed in possession over Morello's bridle. 'It means we're going to have to work our butts off! I'll be out negotiating *partiti* all night, and you, *mio nipote*, for the next three nights, will be guarding this horse with your life!'

The prospect, the acceptance, should have thrilled him. The day had been a success beyond words. His uncle had two favoured horses in the Palio, horses that had been brought to town on his recommendation. He'd proven his worth to his uncle on those grounds, and his uncle's *contrada* had won the prime horse for the race. It would be his honour to watch over that horse and he was cognizant of what that opportunity meant. He'd be able to prove his worth to the *contrada* now that he'd proven it to his uncle.

But all he could think of as someone started a loud rendition of the Torre neighbourhood song was that it left damn little time for Elisabeta.

Chapter Eighteen

Damn her! She had been watching *him*, that blasted Englishman. How she could find him in that sea of people down there was beyond Ridolfo, but somehow she had and her face had lit with a soft smile, her eyes had danced. He'd watched her come alive and he hated it. She never looked at him that way. She should. He was Ridolfo Ranieri, the richest man in Siena. Any woman in town would understand the honour it was to be his wife.

But not Elisabeta di Nofri. No, she had not only flirted openly with the Englishman, she'd gone to him, sneaking out in the middle of the night dressed as a boy. How dare she sit there, pretending she was innocent? 'Your gaze is too bold,' he snapped. 'A modest woman would keep her eyes downcast.' The wedding was only two weeks off. He would teach her manners by then. No woman would make a fool of him by openly hungering after a foreigner. He watched the life seep out of her, her eyes going to her lap, and felt a sense of satisfaction. A man who couldn't master a wife was no man at all in his opinion.

His satisfaction was short-lived. Torre had drawn Jacopi's Morello. Did he imagine it or did his bride's shoulders straighten infinitesimally in defiance at the announcement as if to say 'hah, it serves you right for making me look away'?

Down in the piazza, he could see the Englishman and his *contrada* celebrating. Fate had shown undue favour to the Englishman since his arrival. Ridolfo stood to go back inside, an idea forming that would separate his bride from the Englishman for good. There were plans to be laid. He would have vindication and she would unwittingly be part of it.

When he was done, the Englishman would be sorry he had ever met Elisabeta di Nofri, and Elisabeta would be grateful for the protection of her fiancé. He was already imagining the ways in which she might show that gratitude. He would speak to her uncle tonight. The time had come to set his plan in motion. There would be partying and celebrating in the *contradas* like Pantera and Torre who had drawn good horses. But tomorrow, Elisabeta would be the agent of her own downfall.

Elisabeta tried not to stare. She tried to be involved in the conversations going on around her as the *contrada* dined at long tables set up in the street. But her gaze kept going back to the table where Ridolfo sat with her uncle. They were deep in animated conversation. Giuliano was already out performing his duties as a *mangini*. With her cousin gone, she had no way of knowing what Ridolfo discussed with her uncle.

A nervous ball formed in her stomach, and she pushed away her plate. Ridolfo had been positively possessive at the *tratta* today, his words and his touch all designed to remind her of her submissive place beside him as his wife. They also reminded her of another proposal she had yet to answer.

Archer had been serious. He would brave the consequences of his proposal for her. Could she be brave too? If she loved him, was it fair to reach for the happiness he offered or was it perhaps more fair that she cut him loose from this entanglement? If she loved him, should she set him free? Or should she embrace that love with all its risks? But love for Archer wasn't the only consideration. There was her family too. Loving Archer would hurt them. Perhaps it was better that she couldn't see him tonight after all. He'd be busy with the horse and she was no closer to an answer to their dilemma.

From the table, her uncle motioned for her to approach, and she rose with dread. What would Ridolfo want with her now? Would he seek further atonement for having caught her watching Archer this afternoon? Had he told her uncle?

'Niece,' her uncle began in casual tones, 'I want to know more about this chestnut we've been assigned. I think Torre will talk to you. Tomorrow, I need you to go to Torre's stables and ask the Englishman about the horses.'

'Of course, *Zio*, I would be glad to go.' She *was* glad to go too—it would give her an excuse to see Archer.

* * *

Elisabeta had been so glad, in fact, that it didn't occur to her until the next day when she set out for Torre that she should be suspicious. Why her? Why not Giuliano? Why ask at all when her uncle was an excellent judge of horseflesh himself? Surely there was nothing about the chestnut that her uncle couldn't divine already. Something was afoot. It was a good thing she was going to see Archer; she could at least warn him so he could take measures to protect himself from whatever came next.

Protecting Morello was no small matter. Archer yawned. He'd been awake the previous night and nearly all day. The only break he'd had was when the grooms had come to get Morello ready for the first official evening trial and then again in the morning for the next trial. There would be six official trials in all. He'd gone with the grooms to watch Morello run this morning at the second trial. Now, Morello was being brushed and settled for the afternoon before going out for the evening trial.

Archer wished he could do the same. He was bone tired in part from having been up for days and in part because there wasn't much to do in the *contrada* stable except play cards and keep Nolan's card-playing tendencies on a leash. He didn't need Nolan fleecing his relatives.

It might be a prestigious job to guard the horse, especially when the horse was a favourite to win, but it was an unexciting one. So far, there'd been no trouble at the stable, at the track or on the streets. He'd been warned that often unhappy *contradas* didn't hesitate to start a scrap in the streets if they thought their horse or rider had been treated unfairly during a trial.

The most he'd had to guard against were too many neighbours stopping by to pet the horse, or too many of the *contrada*'s marriageable girls stopping by to smile at him—probably encouraged to do so by his uncle. While it had taken no small amount of diplomatic skill to keep the neighbours and girls away without hurting feelings, it was hardly the stuff of which excitement was made. And still, the issue of Elisabeta plagued him. Being unable to see her meant being unable to have his answer. He was restless, eager to do something about it and frustrated because he could do nothing while the Palio loomed.

Archer pushed a hand through his hair and squinted at the far end of the stable. Someone was there, leaning against the wall. He blinked. Not someone, but a woman.

Surely it wasn't her? That would be almost too good to be true. But it was. His blood began to thrum, his pulse began to race. Elisabeta was here, as if his very thoughts had called her to him.

He strode forward, his weariness falling away with each step. 'Signora di Nofri, what a pleasant surprise!' He took her hands, letting his smile say for him what he could not say out loud in front of the others milling about the stables.

'Signor Crawford, it is good to see you.' Her greeting was formal, polite, but her eyes danced. She was not indifferent to him. Her thumbs moved over his, secretly, hidden within his grasp. 'I came to congratulate you on your good luck in drawing Morello. My uncle says that horse will not disappoint you.'

'And Pantera's horse will not disappoint either.' Archer smiled to confirm they weren't entirely talking about horses.

She blushed and looked away demurely at the veiled compliment. 'Thank you.' Something was on her mind. Now that the pleasantries were disposed of, she was distracted. Archer waited for her to decide her approach.

'I have a question to ask about the chestnut. My uncle thought you might have some knowledge.' The question was odd. The *contradas* didn't seek out one another's advice on horses. Instantly suspicious, Archer took her arm.

'Come walk with me. There is a more private place where we can speak.' Perhaps it was the crowd she wanted to avoid, although in truth there were only two grooms remaining. It might be that there was no question at all, but an excuse to speak with him. Perhaps she'd not come with a question, but an answer. His pulse sped up in anticipation.

He led her to a quiet place in the stables, an empty stall where they wouldn't be disturbed. 'Now, tell me what's on your mind. Have you come with an answer to my proposal?' It didn't matter to him what it was. It was enough right now to hold her, to run his hands down her arms, to simply see her.

She held his gaze. She was trying to tell him something beyond words, but he could not puzzle it out. 'Ridolfo and my uncle wanted your opinion on his weight. They were worried about him being too thin.'

He was disappointed. She'd not come of her own accord, but that was telling too. She was the messenger. Ridolfo had sent her. Her uncle had sent her. That they had let her come or perhaps *insisted* she come had made her nervous. She too suspected something.

Archer bent his lips to hers in a soft kiss meant to reassure. 'Did they send you to spy on Torre?' he asked between kisses.

'I don't know.' Her arms slipped about his neck, and he drew her close, his body hungry for the feel of hers.

'I saw you at the *tratta*.' His mouth pressed a kiss over the pulse beating at the base of her neck, his hands moving in slow motions up and down her back. 'You were beautiful dressed all in white.'

She gave a little gasp as his teeth nipped at her throat. 'I saw you too.'

'Is that why you looked away? Ridolfo caught you?' Their private glances had been marked even in a crowd. Had she been sent as a warning? Was she being forced to act as a pawn in some act of *contrada* revenge? Primal protectiveness surged in Archer. She was his no matter what arrangements had been made by other men, and he would not have her subjugated thus.

'I came so I could warn you, but I don't know about what, only that I think they're plotting something.'

She was beautiful in her concern. All the feeling she didn't dare admit to him with words shone in her eyes. His body pulsed with life, with arousal. He had her backed against the stall wall with no one around and her own body was willing. He could have her and in moments it would be over. This would not take long, so great was his need, and hers too. He just needed a sign from her.

'Archer.' His name came from her lips, a gasping moan of a word as her hand sought him through his trousers. 'Archer, I want you, here.' She drew the length of him against her hips and pressed herself to it. 'Please, Archer.'

They had done this before—they were good at walls. He lifted her and her legs wrapped about him, their bodies coming together effortlessly, his phallus thrusting deep and hard, hitting the core of her the first time. He delighted in her moan of satisfaction, recklessly not caring how loud it was or who might hear. Maybe some small selfish part of him wanted her to be heard, wanted them to be discovered, wanted to spill deep inside her and find purchase. If so, the betrothal to Ridolfo could be broken. She would have no choice then. She would have to choose him. But his conscience was greater. He could not trap her by taking from her the one thing she'd come to him to save.

Her head went back against the wall, her body arched as he thrust again. He felt her hands brace against his shoulders. Oh, this was heaven what they could do together, knowing he could render her senseless, push her to a point where all things seemed possible, a point where she could walk away from her obligations and walk to him. She moaned. He felt her body clench around him, feeling his own body approach its point of no return, its final hill. Ecstasy awaited at the top of this thrusting climb. He wished they were naked, wished he could feel his bare skin against her. But it was enough to move against her, his mouth at her shoulder muffling his cries, enough to climax with her into satisfied bliss, each of them heaving hard against the other.

'I wish it would get old.' She sighed, her neck arched against the wall, her breaths coming in pants.

Archer laughed softly. 'Why would you ever wish that for something so wonderful?'

She opened her eyes and held his amber gaze. 'Because then it would be easier to let you go.'

'Don't.' After all that, she was still insistent on avoiding his solution out of some misguided idea that she could save him from a mistake. His hands were still wrapped about the round globes of her bottom, his phallus still lingered in her, her legs still wrapped about him. 'Don't let go, Elisabeta.' He gave her a sensual, confident smile that betrayed none of his frustration.

'Why let it end, Elisabeta, when it doesn't have to?' He kissed her when she would have protested the obvious: she was pledged to another. 'The solution is simple. Marry me instead.' He spoke the words so softly, she thought she might have imagined them, heard them because she wanted to hear them, her desperate dreams come to life. But the offer didn't make accepting it right.

'Do not sacrifice your hopes for me. You can have it all. I can bring you only scandal if you stay and only heartache if you go,' she whispered back, taking his mouth in a kiss of her own, feeling him stir inside her again. 'You didn't come to Siena for me.' He would come to resent her eventually if she let him give up his hopes. Had he realised yet that there would be a price for marrying her? 'I am not your dream, Archer.'

'True enough, Elisabeta,' he argued. 'You were not my dream, marriage was not my dream then, but it is now where you are concerned.'

'No, you want to rescue me, Archer,' she murmured at his ear, her fingers playing through the ends of his hair. 'It's what you do.'

'I would want *this*, I would want *you* even if you were not in this predicament.' Archer was determined and her arguments were tired ones. They had lost their power. She had nothing new to throw at him. He sensed that he had her close to breaking. It meant she was open to his proposal, wanted it in fact.

'Archer, it isn't only about us.'

'Maybe it should be,' he said fiercely. 'Maybe that's what has been complicating this from the start. Let this be about us and only us.' He heard the possession in his words, felt her body rouse to it, the way a woman's body has always roused to a warrior's desire knowing that he would fight for her.

There was the pounding of boots in the aisle outside the stall, a shout. 'Signor Crawford! Morello needs you!'

Archer dropped her with haste, moving his body in front of hers. 'What is it, boy?' he barked, striding out of the stall and taking command while she used the time to assemble herself.

'It's Morello, he won't eat his hay.'

Archer flashed her a brief look: *Is this what you feared? Did you know?* He questioned the boy. 'Was anyone near the horse or his feed?' He could only be in so many places at once. He was supposed to watch the horse, there were horse boys to watch over the feed.

The boy was pale when he answered. 'No, *signor*, not around the horse.' Archer started down the aisle to Morello's stall, the boy in front of him. Beside him, Elisabeta was trembling, her quick mind assembling pieces and assigning blame.

'This is all my fault, Archer. I should not have come. This is Ridolfo's revenge. He has gone after the horse because of me.' If Ridolfo had done something to the horse, the man would have to answer to him. The horse was innocent in all of this. She was struggling to match her step to his long strides. 'This is my fault for reaching for what wasn't mine, for not playing by the rules and being a dutiful niece.'

Archer shook his head. 'We'll talk about it later.' He would sort motives out once his temper had cooled. Right now, taking care of Morello mattered more.

At Morello's stall, Archer bent down to grab a handful of hay. He smelled it, cracked it open and examined it with a careful eye while the stable hands looked on. He passed some to the others with an explanation. 'Morello won't eat it because it's been tampered with. It's got angelica on it. Horses don't like bitter tastes. It wouldn't have hurt the horse necessarily.' He turned to Elisabeta, hoping to give her relief. 'But it would have starved him if we had let it go on for a day or so.' Just long enough to keep him from running in the Palio.

It wouldn't have hurt the horse *this* time. But this was, Archer feared, the opening salvo designed to act as a calling card and to put Torre on guard. Perhaps even to provoke Torre to violence. Everyone knew Torre and Oca were not above brawling in the streets.

Archer began querying the other boys now—was there any time in which the food was unguarded? He was patient with them, not wanting to pass blame. One of the boys pointed a finger at her. 'The food was unguarded when she came. She needed to know where to find you so we brought her inside. You can't trust anyone, especially not a woman.' The boy flashed accusing eyes at Elisabeta, and Archer felt his world crumble.

What she had done would be all over the *contrada* by evening. His uncle would know she'd been here and that disaster had nearly followed in her wake. Already, the other boys were shooting daggers at her with their dark eyes.

'It's not like that, Archer. I came to warn you.' Elisabeta wasn't afraid to argue but he was afraid to listen, afraid to admit that he had been duped. All of her talk about loyalty to family first, all of her reticence to respond to his proposal made sense. She had made no secret in the beginning that she'd only wanted sex, only wanted pleasure. She might not want to marry Ridolfo, but in the end family and tradition were too difficult to overthrow. And who knew, perhaps she had cut a deal more to her liking if she performed this one service.

And yet, she'd run to him. She'd been afraid in the countryside, afraid of life with Ridolfo. That sort of terror could not be feigned. 'I think you should go.' He would decide later if his words were a dismissal or protection. Whatever safe haven he'd created for them was gone now.

Chapter Nineteen

Her uncle feted her as a hero when she returned. Never mind the tear-splotched face, never mind the anger that roiled inside her. Ridolfo made sure everyone knew what a grand service she'd done for Pantera and for Oca. Her desire to warn Archer, to protect him, had been used against her. She never should have gone, thinking she could warn him. There'd been nothing to warn him about, *she'd* been the threat, the distraction that led to tampering with the hay.

She could not forget the way Archer had looked at her, his sharp mind tallying up the strikes against her. She knew what he'd been thinking in those moments; she'd used him and then betrayed him. Nothing could be further from the truth. Today, she'd been so close to saying yes. Now, he would never ask again. Unless, when he had time to cool his thoughts, he would come to see it differently, come to see her words as truth. She had come to warn him, nothing more. Ridolfo had set her up. He was still setting her up.

The story was told over and over at dinner, embellished until it reached epic proportion; how the Pantera beauty had distracted the Torre stable long enough for the *mangini* of Pantera to leave heavy traces of angelica on the hay and leaves of angelica buried deep inside the haystack.

The only quirk to the story was that the Torre *mangini* had figured out what had happened far more quickly than they would have liked. They would have preferred Morello off his feed for a day, too weak to make a good show at the races, but essentially none the worse for the prank.

She hated the story. Hated that everyone, even those beyond the *contrada*, would hear her part in it and assume she'd done it willingly when in fact she'd done it accidentally. She'd not had any intention of setting up the prank. She thought she'd known the reason Ridolfo had sent her: nothing more than a cruel snub to Archer and perhaps a strong reminder to her of what she couldn't have. Perhaps even as a reminder to her that he was powerful and she was not. But she'd been wrong.

Once this story made the rounds, Archer would want nothing to do with her. It would confirm for him that his *contrada*'s accusations were right. She'd spoken to him so many times of the importance of family loyalty. Archer would think that was where she sided and why she'd resisted his proposal. He would feel used and betrayed. He would think there had only been sex between them, a sex that meant nothing beyond its physical pleasures, that she'd strung him along.

Beside her at dinner, Contessina squeezed her hand, caught up in the excitement of the story and entirely oblivious to her own distress. 'You're so brave, Cousin! I envy you.'

'So brave, that I fear Torre might seek retribution,' Uncle Rafaele called down the table in good humour. 'Contessina, you might do us a service and stay the night in your cousin's room in case they try to steal her away. They've already crashed one party, I wouldn't put it past them.'

Ridolfo nodded his approval, and Elisabeta knew the matter was settled. Ridolfo was fat, not stupid. He suspected she would run, that she would try to reach Archer one last time, all of which assumed Archer would still have her after the debacle of today. Now the chances of running were slim indeed with Contessina in her room. She might as well suggest they put a lock on her door too. Which they probably would now that everyone would view it as protection and not imprisonment. Only she and Ridolfo would know the difference.

He knew, though, there was no question of it. His narrow eyes had studied her throughout the meal in a most uncomfortable manner. He was watching her, assessing her. His gaze was part that of a butcher or horse trader assessing his newly acquired product and part shrewd businessman calculating his next move and hers. He was drinking heavily. She had lost track of how many times his glass had been filled during the long meal.

This would be a night to avoid him, something she'd been successful in doing thus far. Ridolfo seldom came to the house, but the days before the Palio made for new alliances. With Oca not running, Pantera's involvement with the race was critical to him, his one personal connection. Of course, Oca had their other alliances, but they were not Ridolfo's personally. He knew his leverage rested with Pantera and with her.

Elisabeta rose from the table to go with Contessina and her aunt and the other women of the house, but Ridolfo's voice stopped them all. 'Rafaele, I would speak with our lovely heroine for a moment if you will permit it?'

Her uncle could not refuse, nor would he see any reason for it. With the wedding two weeks away, it was a perfectly natural request. 'Please, Ridolfo, use the garden,' her uncle offered. She shot a covert plea for help in Giuliano's direction just in case she still had an ally in the room. She wondered if he knew of Archer's nocturnal visits? If he did, he'd said nothing, his time consumed with the Palio.

At least the garden was somewhat public given that it had no doors or windows and was out in the open. She wouldn't be in a confined space with him and she supposed there was plenty of statuary and dirt to throw at him if it came to that. Surely it wouldn't. If the garden was public for her it was public for him too.

Ridolfo insisted on touching her, taking her arm on the short walk to the garden, his hand dropping to the small of her back as they strolled among the shrubs and artwork. She tried not to flinch. His touch was nothing like Archer's. Where Archer's touch caressed and teased, inspiring visions of glorious pleasure to come, Ridolfo's touch was heavy and possessive. His touch claimed, marked and invited no images of pleasure. Quite the opposite, in fact: images of servitude and punishment for disobedience. He was a man who would have his justice.

'The *contrada* thinks you a heroine…' Ridolfo began, harmlessly enough. He smiled in the lantern-lit light, revealing yellowing teeth behind his lips. It was something one could ignore at a distance, but up close it was impossible to dismiss. Archer's mouth on the other hand was clean, full of straight, white teeth.

She had to stop. She was only making this worse on herself if she let every thought lead back to Archer. Archer had all but repudiated her today. No, that wasn't quite true, he'd also offered for her, offered to declare his intentions publicly. But that was before Oca's treachery was discovered, before she'd been implicated. Did his offer still stand? A small kernel of hope had stubbornly kept flaring throughout the evening that Archer would understand she had been used, that he would come for her. But then she'd remember the flat look in his eyes and the kernel would retreat only to resurface a few hours later.

'I did not ask to be a heroine,' Elisabeta replied modestly. Ridolfo liked humility in women. Perhaps, like a fire that could not burn without oxygen, his wrath could be deprived of fuel as well. If she was humble, there would be nothing for him to take issue with. She had to keep her temper.

'Heroine or whore is the real question.' Ridolfo's tone became harsh. 'Your uncle can spin the tale however he likes. It's good for me if you're painted with a kind brush. But you and I know the difference, don't we?' His hand moved to grip her arm in a tight vice. His beefy sausage fingers were digging in hard. 'You went to his bed at least once. I saw you leave him early in the morning after the first night of the unofficial trials.'

'You saw me? Or your spies saw me?' Elisabeta spat. So much for keeping her temper. At the first provocation her temper soared, but anger was better than fear. It was fair to say that she was more than a little frightened. Her strength was no match for Ridolfo. Her arm hurt where he gripped it, and she'd been caught. He or his minions had seen her. But she would not give Ridolfo the satisfaction of her fear. She would, however, not hesitate in letting him see her anger. She would give him a fight.

'I was alerted immediately and I came to see it with my own eyes.' He shook her arm. 'How convenient it was for you. Your uncle was out of town that first night and you took every advantage of his absence to blacken his name; riding on the track, dressing as a boy, sneaking off with the Englishman, going to his bed.'

His face was close to hers now, his breath a lingering menu of the evening meal. 'I came down to the street and saw you myself. It is a hard thing to see your fiancée's betrayal with your own eyes, but I would not believe it of you any other way.'

'Of course you believed it of me. You wouldn't have spied on me otherwise,' Elisabeta dared to contradict him.

'Not spies, guards. They were for your protection,' he sneered. 'After the incident at the party, I didn't dare leave you unguarded. Such a jewel like yourself should never be left unprotected. *Never*, Elisabeta.'

His message was clear. This was a mere precursor to what her married life would be like. There would be guards, escorts, everywhere for her. The town would look at such gestures with approval. A man should protect what he loves, what he treasures. No one would see anything wrong with the wealthy Ridolfo employing men to watch his beloved. But she would know otherwise. Every day was to be imprisonment with gaolers everywhere. She yanked at her arm, struggling to free it, but Ridolfo was too strong.

'We are not done yet. There is the issue of consequences for your infidelity.' They'd reached the edge of the garden where a wall separated the private home of Rafaele di Bruno from the city streets. Elisabeta would have preferred to be closer to the interior of the house, closer to the chance of family or servants walking by. Being out here beyond the lanterns, beyond family, was unnerving, especially when she sensed Ridolfo had orchestrated it this way on purpose. This was not an accidental destination.

'I am not your wife yet,' Elisabeta reminded him. 'Until then, your official jurisdiction over me is in question. My uncle is my guardian at present and even that is somewhat nebulous given that I'm a widow and of age.' Her case sounded stronger when she voiced it out loud. Her confidence urged her on. 'You have control over your consent to the betrothal and that is all. You may end this arrangement at any point.'

She had pushed him too far. She saw it in the narrow beads of his eyes a fraction of a second before she felt it in his grip, in the pressure of his body pushing her back to the wall until she was pinned between the rough brick and the fat of his stomach. 'You would like that. Perhaps that's what you've been after all along. Did you want me to catch you with the Englishman? Did you think that would be enough?' He was breathing hard now, angry and excited all at once. His cock stirred against her leg in frightening arousal.

'I have wanted you in my bed for quite some time and I will have you. I have built a trade empire by negotiating for anything I ever wanted and I've got it. You are no different, Elisabeta. I wanted you and I shall have you. Used goods or not.' He was rough with her now, his hands tearing at the laces of her bodice, her attempts to push them away only encouraging him to press her harder into the wall where breathing became difficult.

'I had no illusions about being your first, although I doubt that boy husband of yours made much use of you. But I will be your last and I will be your only from here on out. You will not put another man before me, ever again.'

'Ridolfo, please.' Elisabeta pushed at him with both hands, starting to fight him in earnest as his weight crushed her and his intentions became brutally obvious. She forced her gaze to stay on him, like a wolf in the wild faced with a foe. To look away would be to admit defeat and that would be a grievous mistake at this critical moment. 'You are not thinking straight. You will regret this in the morning. You don't want us to come together like this.' She tried not to cringe as she said the words, tried not to imagine other times, other walls, with far more pleasant outcomes.

'What I don't want,' he snarled, his free hand working open his trousers, 'is to go to the altar with you with no assurance there isn't an English bastard already in your belly. At least I can muddy those waters and why shouldn't I? You've already played the *troia* so you shouldn't mind doing it one more time. You might even like what I have to offer you if you give it a chance.'

Elisabeta kicked at him, but the close proximity of their bodies rendered the kicks impotent. If only she could render the same for him. She struggled, but that seemed to incite him further. She bit at him and earned the back of his hand and a string of cursing. That was when she screamed, not caring who it brought as long as it brought someone. He had brought her out here solely for this purpose.

Noise was not what Ridolfo wanted. He wanted absolute privacy for this reckoning. She'd taken that from him and she was going to pay. She was falling before it registered that he'd thrown her. She was on the ground, on all fours, scrambling for distance and freedom, her knees struggling in the folds of her skirts, when the kick came, his foot finding her midsection between belly and ribs. It took all the wind from her. She had nothing left to struggle with, she could barely breathe. That was struggle enough. Panic welled. She had to fight that at least. Panic would only make it worse. The one thought passing through her mind was that she was going to suffocate right here at Ridolfo's feet. Although she should have been more concerned about Ridolfo would do next.

Ridolfo was cursing, his rage out of control. If he kicked her again, she would be finished. He might have done it if there hadn't been the rush of running feet on the gravel. The footsteps sounded overloud to her. Perhaps they were meant to be. The sooner Ridolfo heard them, the better.

'What has happened?' It was Giuliano and he was on his knees beside her instantly, his arm about her as he helped her to stand.

'It is none of your concern what happens between a man and his intended,' Ridolfo reprimanded.

She could feel tension rippling through Giuliano's body. He would not accept that explanation. 'She is my cousin before she is your wife and she's not even that yet,' Giuliano replied, his body ready for a fight. That was not what she wanted. She wanted no more men fighting over her or because of her. A horse had been risked today on her behalf. Archer was targeted for violence because of her. She would not have Giuliano suffer too.

'Please, Giuliano, let it be.' Elisabeta spoke each word haltingly, her breath still in the process of returning. She put a hand on Giuliano's arm and turned him towards the house. 'Just take me inside. I am sure Contessina is waiting for me.' She hated speaking the words, hated giving any sign of outward complicity with Ridolfo, but she hated more the idea of Giuliano hurt because of her. She could sacrifice a little pride for his safety.

'You're protecting him,' Giuliano growled ungraciously as he helped her back to the house. 'Did he hurt you? What a stupid question, of course he did. You were on the ground and in pain. What did he do? Did he hit you? Kick you?' Her face was too transparent.

'He kicked you, didn't he?' Giuliano pushed a hand through his hair. 'I should challenge him, that *porca miseria.* I should call him out. The fat bastard probably can't fire a pistol or wield a sword with any dexterity. I will skewer him like the pig is he.'

She felt some her temper returning. 'Do you think that's what I want?' She tugged at Giuliano's arm. 'Why do you suppose I covered for him? Not to protect him, but to protect you.'

'I could beat him,' Giuliano protested indignantly.

'That's not the point. I would not have you do murder for me. You would live with that the rest of your life.'

'So, better you live with him the rest of yours?' The colour had risen in Giuliano's face. 'He will hit you again. You are too stubborn,' Giuliano said quietly, helping her up the stairs.

They paused at the landing for her to gather her breath. She gathered her thoughts and her courage too. If she meant to do it, she needed to do it now or it would be too late. 'I need you to do something for me, Giuliano.'

'Anything, Cousin.'

'Go to Torre and see if you can learn what Archer thinks of me. If there's a chance...'

She didn't finish the sentence, her words choked off with emotion, but Giuliano knew. He squeezed her hand. 'I will find Archer and he will come for you.'

Elisabeta cut in swiftly, alarmed by the potential behind those words. 'Not by force, Giuliano. Promise me. Archer has to come of his own free will. I won't have him any other way.' It was quite a gamble to take. Who knew what Archer thought of her now?

Chapter Twenty

'What do you think of your lovely widow now? Maybe it's a good thing she delayed on answering your proposal,' Nolan asked as they sat around the long table in the *loggia*, drinking wine and talking late into the night, or maybe it just seemed that way to Archer. He'd been up for days, literally.

By rights, this should have been a joyous occasion, the kind of evening young, single men lived for. There was good food, good wine and excellent company. They sat around the table catching each other up on their adventures since Archer had left Paris. Alyssandra, Haviland's new bride, had discreetly excused herself an hour ago, sensing the need, no doubt, for male bonding. Archer wished he could go too. Sleep sounded good. Forgetting sounded even better. For obvious reasons, it was hard to fully celebrate when the issue of Elisabeta weighed on his mind and now Nolan had brought it to the fore with his question.

'They are calling her the Hero of Pantera,' Nolan

went on. 'I heard it in the streets on my way home. Pantera is saying she ruined Torre's hay.'

Whether *she* did was debatable, but the hay *was* ruined. They'd had to put in a special order.

'I envy everyone's quick pigeonholing of Signora di Nofri, when I am still sifting through the afternoon's events and trying to figure out what they mean,' Archer replied drily. *She's mine after all, why shouldn't I be the one who decides her story?* But was she really his?

'It is because you love her.' Nolan leaned forward across the table. 'There's nothing to sort through. It's very simple. They used her to gain access to our stables in order to conduct sabotage. Fortunately, you were too smart for them and it backfired. Our stable boys understood right away the part she'd played and were more than happy to expose her. Pantera and Oca won't be able to play the di Nofri card again.'

'Our stables?' Archer raised an eyebrow at Nolan. 'How quickly you've become Italian.'

'You're just prickly,' Nolan replied, pouring some more wine.

Archer smiled neutrally at his friend, unwilling to argue the facts. He was prickly on Elisabeta's behalf. He knew what no one else did. He'd seen what no one else had; the wariness in her eyes. He'd heard the carefully worded sentences and he believed he'd accurately translated their code. She'd known she was being sent as part of some nefarious purpose, but she hadn't known what that purpose was. Neither had she been in a position to refuse to come. If he was right, walking into the stables must have been akin to digging one's own grave. She knew eventually she would be exposed and she could do nothing to save herself. But she could save him, so she'd come to put him on guard, to see him one more time.

That was the theory he liked, at least. And if he was wrong? If she had used him, he was a fool who put the *contrada* at risk. So he sat and endured his friends' well-intended ribs. Elisabeta was right. There was something to be said for keeping one's business one's own. He'd never had his life as exposed as it was now.

'It's quite the Romeo-and-Juliet story, sans poison though,' Nolan said rather cheerily. 'A story of two people torn apart by forbidden love.' He gave an exaggeratedly dramatic sigh. Archer caught a sly look from Haviland that said they'd talk about this later.

A footman interrupted the party. 'Signor Crawford, there's a man outside. He wants to speak with you.'

Archer didn't show the slightest hesitation. He was out of his chair, almost in enough time to avoid Haviland's warning hand on his arm. 'Perhaps I should come with you? It might be a trap. The messenger may not bring a verbal message, but a more physical one,' Haviland warned.

Down the table, Nolan reached for the wine bottle. 'Oh, I *do* love Italy. There's adventure around every corner, even at the dinner table.'

Archer shot him a censorious look. Haviland had a point. 'All right, I appreciate it.'

'We'll come too.' Nolan and Brennan set aside their napkins and stood, not waiting for any argument. Archer smiled. He'd missed them, all of them, sorely since Paris. It felt good to know they had his back once more.

Haviland clapped a hand on Archer's shoulder as they made their way to the street. 'My goodness, I leave you alone for six weeks and look at the trouble you've got into.' He winked. 'Perhaps I should have left you alone a lot sooner.'

'I know, just look what happened to you,' Archer jested. 'You break free of the old home front and the first thing you do is run off and get married.'

'Isn't rebellion fabulous?' Haviland laughed.

'I hate to break up the bonhomie,' Nolan put in impatiently, 'but do either of you have a blade? A knife?'

'I do, in my boot,' Archer replied, earning a classic raised eyebrow of enquiry from Haviland. Archer shrugged. 'It's Palio season, you always go armed if you're *mangini*.'

'I've a knife too in my boot, but that's because I was travelling, *not* because I was wandering around your quaint little town here,' Haviland said with dry humour, shooting another look at Archer.

'Draw them, I see the man over there.' Nolan nodded towards a quiet, dark part of the street, perfect for an ambush or for staying discreetly hidden if one didn't want other late-night strollers to notice.

But Archer noticed who it was immediately. It was Giuliano, and Archer thought Haviland's recommendation to come with friends might not be amiss. Giuliano wasn't simply a messenger. He was one of Rafaele di Bruno's *mangini*, his son and Elisabeta's cousin. Just his being here suggested something was afoot.

Giuliano shook his head and held up his hands at

the sight of the blades. He let them approach before he quietly stated his purpose. '*Signori*, I come peaceably and secretly on an errand from Elisabeta. May we speak somewhere less public?'

'Come inside and take some wine with us,' Archer offered before Nolan could suggest the *loggia*. The *loggia* was open to the street and Giuliano would not want to be seen lounging with them after the events of today.

Wine was brought to a small room that opened on to the fountain and the internal courtyard. Giuliano made the requisite small talk as wine was poured; complimenting the vintage and asking about Morello.

Archer shifted in his seat, anxiously wanting to get on to the real business. He decided to help that business along with a direct question, his tone terse. 'Morello is fine. How is Elisabeta?'

Giuliano's dark eyes settled on him. 'I think that will depend on you, Signor Crawford. She risked much to come to you today and she was sorely used by Ridolfo. In turn, she was accused of treachery by your *contrada*.'

Archer turned the glass in his hand, wanting to appear unaffected. This was not new. He had suspected as much, but did that make it true? 'She has come through it well. I hear tell they are calling her the Hero of Pantera even though the mission was unsuccessful in achieving its ends.'

Giuliano gave a dismissive shrug. 'All is not always what it appears, *signor*. She has been crafted a hero and pitting the two of you against one another has made for a delicious Palio tale, sure to become legend: the beautiful Pantera woman attempting to lure the skilled Torre horseman; the Torre horseman outwitting the lady at each turn. It is the stuff of romances.'

Giuliano paused and said grimly, 'If all of this is done in the name of the Palio and the *contrada* we can preserve her reputation. Otherwise, she is nothing more than a common *troia*, a traitor to her *contrada* and a cuckolder of her fiancé.' There was no small amount of concern behind Giuliano's words.

'You said you came with a message and yet you sit here and slander my friend!' Nolan would have leapt for Giuliano if Archer had not stayed him with an out-thrust hand. His own temper was rising, but not for the same reason.

'Sit, Nolan. We will not draw blood in my uncle's house.' Archer thought he caught Haviland mutter under his breath something to the extent of 'I never thought to hear those words spoken together in a sentence'.

'You said her well-being depended on me. What would you have me do?' Archer asked calmly.

'You are the only one who can decide how the grand epic will end,' Giuliano replied. He'd given up any pretence of nonchalance. He leaned forward in earnest, hands braced on his thighs. 'Will you allow this story to have a happy ending?'

Archer studied him. Giuliano was tense, his jaw tight. There was something more at work here. He had not come as an ambassador of Pantera, which suggested the 'happy ending' he sought was not one where she married the wealthy merchant and lived for ever as the Hero of Pantera. Hope stirred. 'I think it depends on which happy ending you have in mind, Signor di Bruno,' Archer replied.

Giuliano's shoulders relaxed fractionally and he smiled. 'You understand my predicament, *signor*. I am grateful. Will you walk with me? I would speak with you alone.'

'I prefer you speak in front of my friends. Their advice maybe useful and we have no secrets among us.'

'All right,' Giuliano agreed. 'But what I am telling you must be kept in strictest confidence. I would not have anyone know what has happened. Elisabeta has asked me to come and ascertain her standing with you. You repudiated her this afternoon, most convincingly.'

'I had no choice,' Archer replied. 'I am not afraid to fight, but the fight must be prudent. At that moment, it was not. There was always the chance that my *contrada* was right and that she had used me. I would not be the first man to be blinded by love. I needed time to sort through it all and to think what would be best for us. To contradict my *contrada* too soon would not have served her well.' Archer slid a glance at Giuliano. 'You are right when you say she is either the hero or the whore. To have fought for her today would have branded her the whore you and I are so intent on avoiding.'

'You say you will fight for her? That you love her?' Giuliano pressed.

Why was it so hard to say the simple word? Was it that he didn't trust Giuliano not to make a fool of him, not to turn this into a deadly game? Or was it because there would be no turning back? Italian or English, a man's word was his bond. He gave Giuliano a hard look. 'I cannot play games over this. If I tell you the truth, may I have your word you will not use it against me?'

It was Giuliano's turn to waver. He drew a breath. 'Yes, let us have plain speech between us.'

Archer gathered his courage, thinking it was far easier to ride an unbroken horse than to confess his feelings. 'I love her. I would marry her and make a life with her either here or in England. My father is an earl. I am a second son, I will not inherit, but I have my own resources. I have the family string and my uncle has offered me his villa—'

Giuliano cut him off. 'I don't need any other qualifications.' But Archer could see that the brief recitation had pleased him. 'She cannot marry Ridolfo.' There was urgency in his tone overlaid with worry and genuine concern. 'I know she resists your offer because she is concerned about the family and the scandal, but I cannot allow those things to stand in her way any longer. Something happened tonight that has changed all that.'

Archer listened in appalled silence as Giuliano recounted the scene from the di Bruno garden. His fists clenched at his sides. 'Ridolfo knows, then,' he said grimly when Giuliano concluded. What else could have provoked such an act of violence? This was his fault. He'd left her open to harm. He should have fought for her today in the stable. He should have defended her with words at least. But that would not have stopped Ridolfo from knowing.

His blood was humming with the need for revenge, the need to see her and know for himself Elisabeta was all right. Dear God, Ridolfo had kicked her, had thrown her to the ground. What sort of man treated a woman that way? But he knew. One who threatened to tie her up, to compel her into sexual congress against her will, with drugs if needed.

'What do I do next? I have offered,' Archer repeated. He had done all he could do up to a point. She had to make the choice. 'I will not force her to exchange one unwanted wedding for another.'

'Your offers have been private ones,' Nolan put in, twirling his knife absently. He grabbed the knife hilt and leaned forward in earnest. 'What makes Ridolfo's offer so damning is that it's public. That's where the scandal lies. Face is at stake. Your offers, my friend, are private ones likely made at the most private of times. No one knows of them but the two of you.'

'Go on.' Archer's interest was piqued. Nolan was onto something. He needed to make an ally of her uncle, of her family.

'You need to declare your intentions. You need to go to her uncle and show yourself,' Nolan explained.

'I will go tonight.' Archer was halfway out of his seat.

Giuliano shook his head. 'You will get only one chance. This is a more delicate negotiation than you realise. Listen carefully, you are to come to my father's house tomorrow in the morning after the fourth trial and then you will make your best offer,' Giuliano said solemnly. 'Your uncle will know what you need. I will tell Elisabeta.'

His uncle Giacomo would be disappointed. He might lose the villa, might lose the dream, might even lose the family he'd just discovered. 'If my uncle does not approve, we will have no choice but to leave,' Archer said slowly.

'Can you live with that?' Haviland interjected. 'Think about yourself. Your dreams are here. Once sacrificed, they won't be regained.'

Then came Nolan's persistent question, quietly voiced and in all seriousness. 'Archer, is she worth it?'

'Yes,' Archer said solemnly, holding Giuliano's gaze. A horse farm could be made anywhere. He could go back to England and mend fences with his father. Perhaps this trip had been about coming to grips with that—his father had loved his mother and been unable to cope with her illness and her loss. His inability to do so had driven him to make poor decisions. Perhaps it was time to forgive him for that and get on with life.

Archer rose. He offered his hand to Giuliano. 'Tell her I will come to her tomorrow. I will not fail her. I must speak to my uncle.'

'About what?' Giacomo strode into the room. 'I heard we had a visitor.' He eyed Giuliano.

Archer drew a deep breath. The words were hard to find. He did not want to hurt this man, this brother of his mother. 'About Elisabeta di Nofri, *Zio*. I wish to offer for her.'

His uncle's eyes were shrewd. 'She is pledged to another.'

'A man who is unworthy of her,' Archer replied evenly.

'I know. I heard.' His uncle nodded to the corner by the door—he'd been eavesdropping. 'Still, there will be vengeance over this,' his uncle warned. 'Torre will be embroiled. It is not enough to merely offer for her.'

'He's right.' Nolan stepped forward, and Archer glared at him. Whose side was his friend on anyway? 'We have to disgrace Ridolfo, cause him to lose face so that Pantera can walk away from the match, so that the other *contradas* will be sympathetic to Pantera's choice.' Then Nolan added cunningly, 'And so you can stay. If Ridolfo loses face, you won't have to leave.'

Archer's eyes flitted between his uncle and Nolan. 'If that is acceptable to my uncle?'

His uncle did not hesitate. 'Of course it is. Did you think I would withdraw my offer of the villa and the horses over this? You are family. What did I tell you? Family is never a burden.'

Archer felt an enormous weight lift. One hurdle down. 'I will go tomorrow.' He smiled for the first time since that afternoon. Either way, the end would be the same. Elisabeta would be his. It was amazing what making a decision could do for a man. He felt good, he felt awake when he should have been dead on his feet.

Giacomo gave him a sly look. 'No, you don't. There is no "I" in Siena, just "we". *We* will go to di Bruno's.'

Archer nodded his assent. 'Of course I meant "we".'

'I hope that "we" includes us this time?' Nolan interjected, gesturing to the group.

'You needn't be involved—' Archer began, his guilt rising over having them here with so much unsettled. Guilt too over wanting them here in spite of it.

'Needn't be involved?' Nolan protested. 'We didn't come all this way to miss out on the fun. Of course we're in.'

There would be no gainsaying Nolan once he'd made up his mind, especially when that mind was apparently backed by the others. Archer raised his glass, more than happy to acquiesce. 'Well, then, I guess that's decided. *A domani*—here's to tomorrow!'

Chapter Twenty-One

'*A domani*? There will be no blood spilt in the house? Are you sure this is what you want? This place is just this side of crazy, Archer, and now you're attempting to marry a woman you've known for only a month. A woman who, I might add, is promised to another.' Haviland paced the bedroom while Archer finished dressing. The morning trials were over and they were free to make their way to di Bruno's.

'Not attempting. I *will* succeed. Attempt implies there is a margin for failure.' Archer inserted cufflinks into their holes at his wrists. 'Are you trying to talk me out of this?' He fixed Haviland with a stare that was part-scolding and part-stubbornness. Haviland's efforts would be futile. His mind was made up.

'It's just happening so fast,' Haviland protested.

Archer grinned. 'Says the man who married a woman he'd known for barely six weeks.' He was too happy this morning to take Haviland's concerns seriously. Haviland was merely trying to be a good friend, much as he had done for Haviland when their positions had been reversed in Paris.

'You're completely transformed,' Haviland ventured. 'You speak Italian flawlessly, you carry a knife in your boot all of the time, you've been climbing balconies.'

Archer laughed. 'First, I've always spoken Italian. You know that. I was raised on it. I just didn't have a chance to use it in England. Second, Siena is no different than London where you and I carry swordsticks and I've never been a monk.'

'We carry swordsticks to fight off the occasional ruffian, not to cross the street and talk to our neighbours.' Haviland warmed to the debate.

'It's Palio season,' Archer said, as if the Palio explained everything. To most Sienese, it did. Perhaps he really was starting to fit in. Archer wondered if this was how his father had felt when he'd first come to Siena? Had he too felt transformed by the energy and pace of Siena, the different customs and lifestyles? Archer tried not to think about his father too much, tried not to think about history repeating itself. His father had come to Siena not seeking a bride and had found one, just like him. His father had fallen head over heels in love, just like him. Like father, like son, seemed aptly applied for the occasion. But he hoped that was where the similarity ended. Were the Crawford men destined to love intensely but tragically? He was his father's son, but he hoped he was his mother's too. There was a knock on the door and Archer grabbed up his coat. It was time to go.

Downstairs was organised chaos. His uncle had indeed taken care of all the details. His uncle and his friends were turned out in their best. The *contrada* page was there dressed in full costume and out in the street along with a whole *comparsa*, or delegation, complete with flag throwers and a drummer waiting to accompany him. 'The only thing missing is the *duce*,' Archer joked with his uncle.

Giacomo slapped him on the back. 'You are the *duce*, Archer. It's the perfect role for you to play today.'

'The *duce*?' Nolan queried with a laugh. 'That's sounds rather dubious in English or French.'

'Get your mind out of the gutter,' Archer scolded good-naturedly. 'In the Palio parades, every *contrada* has a *duce*. He's to be the most handsome young man in the neighbourhood.' He fixed Nolan with a serious stare. 'You have to behave today. This is important, everything hinges on this embassy.'

Giacomo squeezed his shoulder reassuringly. 'Don't worry, we will do our best.'

They were coming! Elisabeta could hear the drums and the singing before she could see the *comparsa*. She flung open the doors to her little balcony and stared down the streets, her fingers gripping the railing. Archer was coming! Giuliano had told her as much last night. But to see it and to know it would not be a covert effort, but a public one with all of Torre behind him, was more than she hoped for.

The burgundy flag with Torre's pale blue-and-white decorations, bearing the Torre symbol of a crowned elephant and a tower, came into view. 'Contessina! Come help me dress,' she called to her cousin. She wasn't going to miss a minute of this. Elisabeta flung open her wardrobe and riffled through her gowns. Normally, she wore the standard fare of the white underdress with a dirndl-style overdress, but today she wanted something more sophisticated. 'There! This one, I think.' She pulled out a seldom-worn gown of pale sage and held it against her as she danced across the floor.

What a difference a day made, she thought as Contessina helped her into the gown. Everything had been so very bleak yesterday and last evening had been positively dire. But this morning, Archer was coming for her. She fastened a strand of demure pearls about her neck while Contessina worked on her hair. 'Nothing too fancy,' she suggested. 'It is just eleven o'clock in the morning.'

'A neat chignon, then.' Contessina smiled at her in the mirror. 'Isn't this exciting! Two suitors vying for your hand.'

Exciting didn't begin to describe it. Exciting, because Archer was coming, but also nerve-racking because Archer *was* coming and there was no guarantee his suit would be accepted. Her uncle had much to weigh in the balance when considering this about-face. That was precisely what it would be too—she was publicly promised to Ridolfo and now Archer would make his suit public as well. To change direction now would cause someone a loss of face, either her uncle or Ridolfo, not to mention Pantera and Oca as a whole.

Elisabeta slid her feet into matching slippers and made her way downstairs, her stomach full of butterflies. The impact of this on the *contradas* was no small matter. Her uncle was the *capitano*, no one but the *priore* had as much prestige in Pantera. Would he risk that status by neglecting his commitment to

Oca? Would he risk the face of Pantera? Oca would hate them and a *contrada* grudge was no small thing. People still talked about Pantera's interference with the Aquila rider in the 1752 Palio which led to Torre's victory. She had no doubt someone would bring that up again today.

Her uncle and his men were already assembled, her aunt and Giuliano were there and, to her dismay, Ridolfo was there too looking thunderous with his Oca contingent. Elisabeta took the seat between her uncle and aunt. 'What is he doing here?' she whispered to her uncle.

'You are publicly committed to marry him. He has every right to be here and defend his claim should he want to,' her uncle answered sternly, reminding her of the gravity of the situation. Then the doors opened and Archer stood framed in the doorway, surrounded by the splendour of Torre and all worry fled for the moment. Archer had outdone himself. She'd seen him in the clothes of a working horseman and in the guise of a weary, dusty traveller. Today, he came as a nobleman's son.

He wore polished black boots into which went fawn-coloured breeches tailored to perfection. Everything about him bore that same stamp of perfection from the tamed sheen of his hair to the impeccable knot of his cravat. He sported pristine white linen beneath a pale blue silk waistcoat and a coat of burgundy with a generous shawl collar that fell to his knees in neat, full folds. The colours, she was sure, were calculated to pay tribute to Torre and serve as a reminder that, for Pantera, an alliance with Torre would have benefits. Torre was one of the more powerful and prestigious neighbourhoods even if it was the most contentious. Torre was the only *contrada* with two enemies.

Archer bowed to her uncle, and she noticed for the first time the rapier that hung from his belt. For decorative reasons, she hoped. The other men in his cortège were similarly attired. They must be his English friends. His greeting might have been in the English style, but he spoke to her uncle in his flawless Italian, hardly even sparing her a glance, but that was by design. This was to be approached with the formality of a business transaction. Still, she hung on every word.

His case was well presented. He laid out his credentials: the son of an earl and a son of Torre. He was Sienese through his mother's family, proving he was more than an upstart Englishman. He was half-Italian too. He laid out his wealth: the horse farm, the string of racing thoroughbreds, the sport of kings, in Newmarket, his annual income, which sounded staggering to her. He outlined his position with his uncle at the villa, which he'd be given upon his marriage, and his obligations with his uncle's horses. He had no intentions of merely absconding with her to England. He meant to stay and become part of Sienese life. He was welcome in his *contrada* and had some standing in it already through his uncle, who had shown him great personal favour.

With each argument, Elisabeta's hopes rose. He was an eminently suitable gentleman. More than that, her hope rose that he wouldn't have to choose between his dreams and her. There was hope for her too; that she could have the life she'd always wanted;

a horse farm in the countryside, a loving husband by her side, eventually children, a *private* family. It was all so close, she could almost reach out and touch it. Her joy was nearly overwhelming. She wanted to run to Archer and throw her arms about him for making it possible.

Archer finished speaking. He took a respectful step backwards and gave her uncle a small bow to indicate he'd concluded. Those present in the receiving room were nodding their heads in approval. All her uncle had to do was say yes. Elisabeta very carefully kept her eyes downcast, not wanting to give away her excitement.

'These are indeed practical considerations when taking a wife...' her uncle began. 'Signor Crawford, you have comported yourself well today. You have much that recommends you and for that you are to be applauded. Your responsibility speaks well of you. However, there is still the issue of my niece's previous betrothal. You are aware, I believe, that she is currently promised to another?'

Beneath her lashes, Elisabeta watched Archer calmly accept the pronouncement. Her uncle would not make this easy for Archer no matter how impeccable his credentials. Her uncle simply couldn't. If he was going to concede his arrangement with Oca, he would have to make it look difficult. Perhaps Archer had anticipated as much as well.

Archer let his voice fill the receiving room for all to hear. 'I am aware of that, Signor di Bruno. I would not dare to intrude on another man's arrangement except for the fact that I am compelled by love. My feelings for Signora di Nofri are such that I cannot, in good conscience, ignore them and know that I had been true to myself or to her.'

'What of Signor Ranieri?' her uncle enquired patiently. 'Are his feelings of no consequence?'

'I cannot speak for his feelings, only my own. But I was led to believe this match was made for purely political reasons and that love had very little to do with it. If you are looking for political gain, I assure you Torre will prove most valuable in that regard. There is nothing Oca can offer that Torre cannot match or exceed.'

Bravo! Elisabeta thought. Her Englishman had learned to think like a true Sienese. This was the stuff of the classic Oca-Torre rivalry. Ridolfo was halfway out of his seat, huffing with the exertion of sudden movement and making his way towards her uncle before Archer had drawn a breath.

'This is an outrage!' he cried. 'We had an agreement and you've let this Torre swine come to argue it. He has no grounds. This agreement is not contestable.'

Elisabeta thought Ridolfo had made a rather poor choice in vacating his seat and coming to stand side by side with Archer. Ridolfo did not fare well in the visual comparison. Where Archer was immaculate in his attire and temper, Ridolfo's clothes fit poorly, his trousers baggy to accommodate his paunch, his linen wrinkled, his cravat drooping after a morning in the sun at the trials. Never mind that most men in the room looked the same. He looked unkempt next to Archer and that was all that mattered.

Where Archer's delivery had been polite and well paced, Ridolfo's angry outburst had been emotional and not businesslike in the least. He looked like a petulant child denied a treat. How could her uncle possibly prefer Ridolfo to Archer? How could anyone in the room blame him for entertaining Archer's offer? Yet, her uncle hesitated.

'She is to be my wife and everyone knows it,' Ridolfo protested. 'There is no reason to break the agreement.'

Elisabeta gripped the arms of her chair until her nails bit into the centuries-old wood. This was the sticking point. There was no reason. On her uncle's other side, Giuliano leaned over to speak into her uncle's ear. She thought she noticed her uncle's hand clench the arm of his chair, his face settling into stern features.

His eyes had narrowed to shrewd slits when he spoke again to Ridolfo. 'It seems there is reason after all. My son informs me you exhibited untoward behaviour involving violence towards my niece last night in my own home.'

Elisabeta sucked in her breath, daring a look at last directly at Archer. Giuliano had taken a huge risk, but it was masterfully done. The news had come from a credible source, not Archer himself, who would have appeared to have been biased. Ridolfo was not the only one who'd engaged in untoward behaviour in her uncle's home. If Ridolfo wanted to press the issue, she and Archer could be exposed. But that, too, would be risky on Ridolfo's part. If Ridolfo made it public knowledge she'd been sexually engaged with Archer, her uncle would feel compelled to allow Archer's suit and at the same time it would put Ridolfo in the role of the cuckold. No, she didn't think Ridolfo would take the chance.

Ridolfo made a short incline of his head. 'I am most regretful of my actions last night.'

'As well you should be,' her uncle continued. 'My niece is dear to me and I will not give her in marriage to a man who would mistreat her. You have nullified my need to honour the contract. Even if there was no counter-suit in the offing, I would still nullify it.' Elisabeta fought the urge to smile triumphantly as her uncle's words settled on the assembly.

'No!' Ridolfo fairly exploded. 'I was well within my rights, she…' He jabbed a finger her direction and Elisabeta froze. It was her worst fear. In his anger, he would risk exposing her. But his words never materialised. Archer's rapier was out in a flash and pressed to the soft skin of Ridolfo's throat.

'You will not slander her name within my hearing without paying the consequence.' Archer's voice was deadly cold, his hand steady.

Ridolfo's eyes bulged. He sent a silent plea towards her uncle. Her uncle nodded his head and Archer lowered his rapier. 'I demand recompense for this assault,' Ridolfo growled, one hand at his neck massaging the spot where Archer's blade had been.

'What would you have me do? Signor Crawford was only acting the gentleman,' her uncle cajoled, reminding Ridolfo that while Archer had played the gentleman, Ridolfo had not.

'I demand a chance to win her back.'

'What do you propose?'

'The Palio. Torre wins the Palio, Signor Crawford wins his bride.' Ridolfo spread his hands. 'Oca does not have a horse in the Palio so I can't simply wager my *contrada*'s horse against his. Besides…'

Ridolfo gave an innocent shrug '…Torre has the favoured horse. Chances seem fair to me. After all, I saw her first.'

Elisabeta held her breath. How could her uncle refuse without appearing to be the boor? But this was the last thing she wanted. It had almost been settled. She had the sensation again of having been so close. Only now instead of being within her reach, it was slipping away. To win, Torre would have to beat Pantera, who had already won the first Palio and who had a favoured horse as well, one of Archer's uncle's own excellent chestnuts. Would her uncle give up a Palio victory in order to secure her marriage to Archer? He could arrange to lose if it came down to it, but if anyone suspected such a thing, there would be hell to pay. No one with any honor willingly lost a Palio.

But it wasn't her uncle who answered the challenge. It was Archer's voice who filled the room. It was Archer's eyes that were on her, full of open affection as he spoke the two words that would feed the *contradas'* gossip for days: 'I accept.' A general upsurge of excitement spread through the room, everyone exclaiming at once. Elisabeta felt her uncle's hand cover hers where it lay on the arm of her chair, urging her towards restraint. She was not to undo Archer's efforts with any rash protests. But by the saints, had he any idea what he'd done? Oca might abide by the decision out of a sense of sportsmanship, but Ridolfo would not. She had to see Archer. She had to tell him. Archer had all but signed his death warrant.

Chapter Twenty-Two

'People have been killed in feuds for less!' Elisabeta blurted out the moment Archer strode into the dim interior of the parish church. The only light came from the candles on the votive rack. Her voice echoed off the stone walls. It sounded desperate and angry. She didn't care. Let him hear her concern. The church was empty and here he'd have sanctuary should Oca attempt anything. 'Do you have any idea what you've done?' He looked so alive, it was impossible to imagine anything could harm him. But she knew better. Vitality was an illusion. Lorenzo had died young. Youth did not protect one from mortality.

Archer's hands closed over hers, warm and pulsing with life. 'I know exactly what I have done. I have made it possible for you and me to be together.'

How could his voice be so steady, his hands so firm when he'd wagered so much on a single race? 'Our lives are staked on that race, Archer.'

He shook his head. 'With your permission, I have no intentions of abiding by any outcome of that race. If Torre should lose, will you come away with me?'

The pressure on her hands tightened infinitesimally, the only sign that perhaps he too shared some of her anxiety. 'It won't be a tidy getaway, but I'll have Amicus saddled and waiting. We can slip away during the celebrations right after the race.' He paused. 'It will mean, of course, that we won't be able to return. I don't think we'll exactly be welcome if I disregard the agreement.'

Elisabeta smiled. She understood the source of his anxiety now. It wasn't over the race. He'd already decided the race ultimately didn't matter. His anxiety stemmed from whether or not she would assent to living away from Siena now that the decision mattered. They'd spoken of it once before, but not with any definitive conclusion.

Her answer was more important than he realised. There was something he'd overlooked. 'Archer, whether Torre wins or loses, we can't stay here. If you are willing to forgo the agreement, you can assume Ridolfo Ranieri is too. If we stay, Ridolfo won't stop until you're dead. You have done more than offend him and he'll have the long-standing enmity between Oca and Torre to cover his motives.'

'I disagree. Torre will win and you will leave Ridolfo to me. But if it comes to leaving, will you?' Archer asked again, his eyes on her, solemn. She felt every ounce of the weight of that gaze. Elisabeta pulled her hands free and turned away from him, overwhelmed with guilt. Her foolishness had brought them to this.

'I've destroyed your dream.' She bowed her head and shut her eyes, trying to squeeze out the reality of what she'd done. His dream of becoming part of his Italian family had been shattered because of her. He couldn't stay no matter what happened on the race track. Even if she refused him right now and swore an oath to marry Ridolfo, Archer could not stay. He'd publicly declared himself. It was a touching but futile gesture.

She could feel him come up behind her before his hands even rested on her arms, warm and reassuring. His voice was private and intimate at her ear. 'You are my dream now. I think you have been since the moment I saw you in the piazza, from the moment I danced with you, from the moment you popped a forkful of *risotto alle fragole* in my mouth, I have loved you. You are like no other woman I've ever met. I mean to keep you, Elisabeta. I mean to love you for ever, whether you come with me or not. England, Austria, Siena, it doesn't matter where I am if you're with me.' He kissed her then, a sweet, lingering kiss just behind and below her ear and she was lost, but Archer wasn't done. 'If there's anything you're guilty of, it is having ruined me for other women. I'm not in the habit of begging, but I will beg for you. Please, Elisabeta, don't let me live my life without you.'

The words were quietly spoken and they meant all the more because of that. These were private words spoken from the very heart of a man. There would not be a prettier proposal ever and it was all hers just as this man was all hers. She turned towards him, her arms going about his neck. She pressed a kiss to his mouth, her voice a whisper against his lips. 'This means yes.'

Archer broke their kiss and stepped back, going

down on one knee. Her hand still clasped in his. 'Then let me make it official. Will you marry me? Right now? I do not want to wait until after the Palio.'

Tears threatened, and Archer rose to his feet, misunderstanding the reason for them. He'd pushed for too much. 'I'm sorry it is not a glamorous wedding. We'll wait if you want.'

She shook her head and swiped at the unwelcome tears. 'No, it's not that. It's just that I've never made such a monumental decision on my own before. This is all up to me.' She bit her lip, studying his face. 'I was never asked when I married Lorenzo. It was all arranged. Even the betrothal was done with a proxy. I never met Lorenzo until the wedding. No one has ever asked *me* before.'

'Then I am doubly glad I did.' Archer's thumb ran over her knuckles in a soothing caress. 'And you're wrong, you know. You have already made a monumental decision on your own, the night you crossed the piazza. *You* chose me first and today I choose you. Shall we? I have a priest and witnesses. It will be legal and it will stand up to scrutiny should it need to.'

Archer had thought of everything. On her periphery, a dark-robed figure entered the church from an interior side door followed by two distinct male figures: Giuliano and the man she recognised as Archer's friend Haviland. Her pulse quickened. This was going to happen! Archer had planned this for them, but also for her.

Archer smiled at her and the tears threatened again, but she managed. 'I will marry you, right here, Archer.' It was with foreboding that she said the words. She saw the practical wisdom of it, the victory of it and the sadness of it as well. A legally binding marriage would make her safe from Ridolfo regardless of what transpired. But she saw the romance of it too, and chose to embrace that instead of the grim reality: the next two days could see her a widow for the second time. She forcefully shoved the morbid thought away. She would not think of this good, handsome man lying dead.

Archer gripped her hand, reading her thoughts. 'I don't think Ridolfo will find me easy to kill. And there is still a chance Torre could always win.' She thought of the lightning speed with which Archer had drawn his rapier this morning and hoped he was right.

'Are we ready?' the priest enquired in gentle tones, asking them to stand before the altar, with Haviland and Giuliano on each side. Elisabeta nodded. She was ready. With Archer beside her she could face anything, a new life in a new place, a life away from all she knew if it came to that, and it most assuredly would.

The ceremony might have been impromptu, bereft of any of the traditional trimmings. There was no veil for the bride, no flowers, no music, no audience to fill the pews to brimming capacity, but Elisabeta had had all that before and it had not made that wedding any more special. Yet, this wedding was indeed the stuff of her dreams. She would remember every moment of it, every detail of it; the dress she wore, how the candlelight from the votives had flickered across the planes of Archer's face, how he had looked every inch the proud bridegroom as he repeated his vows to her, meaning each word.

It occurred to her vaguely that she was hearing his full name for the first time as he spoke it, 'I, Archer Michael Wolfe Crawford…' It was a beautiful name, a strong name. By the time it was her turn to say the vows, tears were streaming freely down her face. No wedding could be finer. He slid a simple gold ring on her finger, kissed her tenderly, sincerely, and it was done. She was his. More importantly, he was hers. If he thought the vows to love and protect were his alone to keep, he needed to think again.

Giuliano kissed her on the cheek and hugged her close. 'Be happy, Elisabeta. I'll wait until after the Palio to tell Father.' He winked. 'Maybe I won't have to.'

Haviland kissed her other cheek and offered felicitations. 'Make him happy.' She had no doubt she'd have Haviland to deal with if she didn't. But it was an irrelevant worry. She meant to make Archer happy, so very happy, and apparently she could start right away. There would be no wedding breakfast and she'd assumed the honeymoon would have to wait as well, but she was wrong. A small room in a quiet street away from the excitement of the Palio and the upcoming *prova generale* had been arranged for them.

'We've got to make it legal in all ways, of course.' Archer had winked at her as Giuliano and Haviland left them at the door.

It was the small room they'd met in once before, a lifetime ago when they'd merely been two people in a furious *affaire*. So much had changed. The room was furnished only with a bed, a bureau and a small table. But the room was well provisioned for them with a basket of food and water for washing in an ewer atop the bureau. If the ewer was chipped or the quilt on the bed plain, it seemed unimportant. 'I get the sense you had an idea of what you were doing when you got up this morning,' Elisabeta said slyly, sliding her hands up his shirtfront and working his studs free. Had it only been two days since they'd been together? It seemed much longer, an eternity.

His hands rested at her waist, letting her undress him, his mouth slanting to steal playful, errant kisses. 'How does it feel to be the Honourable Mrs Archer Crawford?'

Elisabeta wrinkled her nose. 'That sounds awful. No one will actually call me that, will they?'

Archer laughed. 'Only on invitations and only in England.' He paused. 'I mean to see Torre win that race, Elisabeta. Leaving isn't a foregone conclusion. I will fight for you and our life here.'

She didn't want to argue or point out that perhaps Ridolfo meant that as well and with the same intensity if only for different reasons. She gave him a coy glance, her hands finished with his shirt. They dropped lower, cupping him appreciatively. She loved the feel of him coming to life in her hand. 'I think the better question is how does it feel to be the *husband* of the Honourable Mrs Archer Crawford?'

He nipped at her ear. 'It feels quite good.' He worked the laces of her gown and slid it down her shoulders, while she worked his trousers and then his boots. It wasn't the most graceful of undressings, but it was fun. In the midst of the laughing and oc-

casional collision of hands, they could forget the potential danger that waited outside in the streets. They
could forget that Oca might be lurking to wreak their
revenge, or that many obstacles lay in front of them
before they could truly claim their lives together. In
this tiny room, in this afternoon, being together was
simply enough.

Clothes discarded, Archer scooped her up in his
arms and carried her to the bed. He towered over her
for a long moment, looking down at her with warm
eyes, his arousal full and straining. His nakedness
was glorious, but hers made her suddenly shy. She
reached for a sheet, but Archer was faster.

'Don't. You're beautiful.'

'It's broad daylight,' Elisabeta stammered.

'All the better to see you, my dear.' Archer grinned.
'There's a reason my middle name is Wolfe.'

'*One* of your middle names,' she scolded as his
weight came down on the mattress and he took up
his place beside her, his head propped on one hand.
'That's a lot for a girl to remember.'

'Will you let me devour you?' His amber eyes
glinted mischievously. 'There's something I've
wanted to do, but I've been waiting for the right time.
I think today is it.'

They'd already done so much, much more than
she had ever experienced before: walls and hand-
driven consummations, seductive undressings and
multiple climaxes. Him on top, her on top. The va-
riety had seemed endless to her. Only the wall had
been repeated but that hardly counted, since it hadn't
been the *same* wall. 'I can't imagine what else there

would be.' But she gave him a challenging smile as she said it, daring him to prove her wrong.

'Oh, there's more, I promise.' He gave her one last infectious smile and went to work, or was it that he went to 'pleasure' instead? It started out relaxing at first, the soft caress of his mouth trailing kisses over her throat, down her neck to her breasts, where he stroked each of them in turn with his tongue, the relaxation starting to ebb as her body began to fire.

She gave a long shudder of delight, and he moved on, blowing a gentle breath into her navel, his hands lightly bracketing her hips with their grip. She ruffled his hair with her hands, liking the weight of his head against her stomach, but Archer wasn't done. He started to move down her again and this time there was nothing relaxing about it. Each touch of his mouth to her skin aroused. He kissed her hips, kissed the inner sides of her thighs, and her body tensed with anticipation, guessing his final destination. He meant to kiss her there, at the private juncture of those thighs! She was too aroused by the prospect to be embarrassed, to be anything but eager for his mouth on her.

Even so, this was more than a kiss. His breath feathered her curls, and she could feel her own dampness. The kiss didn't stop there. His tongue went to work on her furrow, his hands bracing her thighs while they parted her private folds so his tongue could lick the intimate length of her. 'Archer!' The sound of his name was nothing more than a mewl as he took her in a long, slow stroke.

He was enjoying this too, she could feel it in the pressure of his hands at her thighs as his desire rose, spurred on by hers. Then his tongue found the little pearl at the top of her cleft and she thought she'd go mad. His hand had done an admirable job there once before, but it was nothing compared to the exquisite pass of his tongue over its tiny, slick surface. Her mewls became full-bodied moans as she lost control.

He licked once, twice more, she gave a wanton scream and then he was mounting her, his own desire driving him to join her in the madness. She drew him to her with her arms, with her legs about him, and she met him with her hips, her mouth, tasting her own arousal on his lips. This was a frenzy of sensory pleasure. They crested quickly, their moans intermixed with incoherent love words, the sheets tangling about their legs as they seized their passion, plummeting into it head first. Most importantly, when they fell, they fell together.

Archer lay beside her, catching his breath, his head thrown back on his pillow, his hair a tousled mess, the faint sheen of sweat on his brow. Dear heavens, she'd married a sexual madman. A wicked smile played across her lips at the thought. Their lives would be full of adventure, in bed and out, at this rate. He rolled his head to the side and caught her gaze with a smile. 'What is going through that head of yours?'

'I was thinking you looked well used, not unlike a stallion put to stud.'

'Mmm.' He sighed, turning on his side to face her. 'I like that image. Perhaps it's an image we might improve on as the afternoon proceeds.' He gave a sensual laugh, drawing a finger down her breastbone in a gesture that raised delightful goose pimples on her arms, his voice low, his eyes wickedly mischievous. 'Every stallion needs a mare to cover. Roll over, my dear.'

They did improve on the image, in her estimation, that long afternoon. She found that she rather liked playing the mare to Archer's stallion. She revelled in the power of her lover-cum-husband, the strength of him as he held her by the hips and thrust confidently into her from behind, her body opening to take the entire length of him. Best of all, she loved the feel of his hot seed filling her deep in her womb. There was no longer any need for hasty withdrawals. Today was about beginnings of all types.

She was pleasantly exhausted as the heat of the afternoon gave way to evening's shadows. Even in their quiet street, the sounds of people preparing for the fifth trial, the *prova generale*, and arguably the most important trial of the six, drifted up to their little room. The hours of their honeymoon were fast coming to a close.

'We have some time yet,' Archer murmured, pulling her back down to him when she would have risen. 'We have until after the trial. No one will expect us until the *cena* tonight. Come, sleep with me and we'll see if I can't find the strength to pleasure you once more before we part.'

Elisabeta snuggled down next to him, a hand on the flat of his stomach. There would be parties tonight. Each *contrada* would host a large dinner in celebration of their Palio entry on the morrow. There would be food and brave speeches about their chances for winning the race. It was a grand night, but the thought of the evening's festivities dulled when she thought of spending them without Archer. She would have to pack tonight too. There would be much to do in case they had to flee. There were farewells to see to as well, notes perhaps to leave behind. Tonight would be a night of celebration, but also of sadness.

She must have dozed. When she woke, it was with a jolt of awareness that something was wrong. She sat up quickly, gathering her wits. Archer was already up, partially dressed and at the little balcony overlooking the street. There were people in the street and it was noisy. 'What has happened?' Archer called down to the crowd.

A voice filtered up from the throng, clearly not recognising him. 'The fighting has started between Oca and Torre. The Torre *fantino* is hurt. The rider from Onda drove the Torre horse into the wall at the San Martino turn! The jockey fell, crushed between the wall and the horse. Torre got even, though. In return, Torre took Oca at the Bocca del Casato afterwards. Torre got the better of it there, but it won't bring the *fantino* back.'

'And the horse?' Archer called back, but the man had moved on and no one else hollered back.

He was stricken when he turned from the window. 'We have no rider. Torre has no rider. Oca put Onda up to it.'

'Of course they did. Onda is your enemy and the only one of your two enemies to be riding in the race. Now that Oca can't trust Pantera, they have to use their other alliances.' Elisabeta reached for her clothes, dressing as Archer put on his boots.

'I have to go.' Archer raked a hand through his hair, worry plainly etched on his face. She could read his thoughts. It would certainly put a quirk in their plans if Torre couldn't race. How would they get away then? What if Ridolfo tried to come for her? She put her right hand over her left where her gold ring rested on her finger. He couldn't. He couldn't take her, she reminded herself. She was married to Archer now, quite irrevocably so. The church would have to support Archer's claim.

'What do you mean to do?' But she knew before she asked.

'Torre needs a rider. I mean for that rider to be me.'

'Archer, no! It's too dangerous. It would be the perfect opportunity to do you harm. You don't know how that race is, what people will do.' She couldn't lose him, not now.

'I do know the race, Elisabeta. I've been on the track.' Archer came to the bed and took her hands. 'Who better than me to race? My stakes are higher than anyone's. Tomorrow, I will race for us.'

'Your uncle may not approve…' Elisabeta began.

'He will. I can be quite persuasive.' Archer was all confidence. She wished she had half of his optimism. Archer was always so sure of himself, so sure he could make things happen. She loved that about him, it was more than part of his charm.

'I'll walk you back,' Archer offered, but she could see the need for haste on his face. He could hardly wait to get to his uncle's. She would not stop him.

Time was of the essence. His uncle would want to make a decision about a rider as soon as possible.

'I'll be fine. I know the back streets and I'll wait for the crowds to thin out,' she assured him. She knew how volatile the post-*prova* crowds could be. It was not uncommon for *contradas* to brawl as Torre and Onda had this afternoon because of a real or imagined slight to a horse or rider during the trials.

He kissed her once more and was gone, his footsteps fast on the stairs. Elisabeta pulled the sheet up to her chin. The honeymoon was over. What had she done? Her fear had driven her to this, her recklessness, her selfishness had all led to this. What had she been thinking to go through with the secret wedding? It had been entirely selfish.

The wedding gave her protection, but it did not give her or Archer a solution. A little sob welled up in her throat. She couldn't cry now. If she started, she might not stop. She'd married an innocent man, dragged him into the mire of her life, because she needed protection. But not just for that. Perhaps protection could be justified. She'd simply wanted him. Now he would pay for her actions.

Elisabeta rocked on the bed, keeping the tears at bay. This was what happened when one acted impulsively. She should never have crossed the piazza, should never have gone into the alley with him, should never have invited him to the masquerade and put him in Ridolfo's way. She should never have encouraged Archer by going to the country. Yet she had done all those things and they had led here; to a secret wedding, to a clandestine wedding 'night' in a rented room, to a man she loved, a man she had chosen.

The last thought gave her pause. It changed everything. A man she loved. She did not regret that. This worry, this pain, this was the price for love. Archer was no fool. He knew what it would cost him, what it would cost them. They would have to fight for this marriage and he had been willing to do that. She should be willing to do no less.

Torre might win tomorrow, a hopeful little voice whispered in her mind. She might be worried for nothing. Elisabeta smiled in the gathering dusk, the long shadows creeping across the floor of the room. The Palio was impossible to predict. There were so many variables one couldn't control even if one had a good horse and a good rider.

Did it really matter if Torre won? On the surface winning certainly solved several of their problems. But that no longer seemed to be the paramount issue. Their marriage was not about the race. It was about something more—about love, about freedom of choice, about two people who had found each other in this wide world. Archer had chosen her not just because he could protect her, but because he wanted her, just her.

Elisabeta rose from the bed and gathered up her clothes, a sense of calm settling over her. Wedding days were not for tears and doubts. They were for celebrations and hope. She had Archer now and nothing could change that. Just the thought of Archer was enough to make her smile. The race tomorrow might decide where they lived out their future, but it didn't decide their future. For weeks the Palio had been a deadline she was dreading, now she could hardly wait. The Palio signified her hope. The future was coming and Archer was in it. *La terra in piazza* indeed.

Chapter Twenty-Three

The *contrada* was in high spirits when Archer returned. Having comported themselves well in the brawl against Oca and Onda, the men of Torre were still celebrating. Drink flowed and there was much cheering and singing of the Torre song through the streets. The crowd was particularly thick as he neared his uncle's house. People had begun to gather for dinner. Archer wished he could share in their merriment. Perhaps they had not yet realised that while they'd won the street brawl they were without a rider.

Archer felt his throat tighten as he made his way towards his uncle's table, the words *be careful what you wish for* suddenly pounding in his head. He'd come to Siena for the chance to ride only to be disappointed early in that particular quest. Now the thing he had wanted so badly was available once more, but at a time when there was something greater at stake. How would he make a quick getaway, how would he disappear with Elisabeta if he was in the race? It was a trade-off he'd considered on the way over. They had planned to slip out of town unnoticed in the victory celebrations, if Torre didn't win. If he was on the track, it would be much harder to do and he would be so much more conspicuous. But that was what the marriage was for, he reminded himself. If they had to be conspicuous, so be it. The church stood behind him as of today.

Archer wound his way through the tables that had been set out in the streets for the *prova generale cena*, the supper that traditionally followed the fifth trial. At one table set up on a dais, his uncle was already seated with the Priore of Torre and other *contrada* officials. His uncle waved him over to take the remaining seat. Archer noticed that his friends were seated close by, and from the look of things they were in the thick of the impromptu celebrations. Nolan was sporting a bruise on his jaw and was busy apparently re-enacting a particular episode from the brawl with many gestures, having no Italian to speak of. His storytelling efforts were met with laughter from those around him, and Archer smiled to himself. Nolan had the ability to make himself at home wherever he went.

Up on the dais, Archer greeted the *priore* and the other officials with the traditional kisses before taking his seat. 'How is Morello? I heard there was difficulty at the trial,' he asked as soon as small talk had been dispensed. The sooner he got to the point the better. He wanted the issue of a rider settled immediately and he was prepared to fight for it.

His uncle shrugged, apparently not sharing his same sense of urgency. 'Morello is fine, thank the saints, because you only get one horse. The rules are clear. If your horse can't run, you can't race. There are no substitutes for an ill horse. Maybe after dinner you will take a look at his leg and wrap it for the night as a precaution.' But there was a twinkle in his uncle's eye and a secret message of congratulations passed between them. His uncle had helped him plan every aspect of his day. His uncle knew very well where he'd been.

Archer splayed his hands on the tablecloth and looked from him to the *priore* with grave seriousness. 'However, we cannot say the same for our *fantino*, our jockey. He is not able to ride. We need a rider, a good rider. We have the best horse according to the odds makers. It would be a shame to waste the horse on a rider who doesn't know his business.' He paused and looked meaningfully at his uncle. 'I think the rider should be me.'

His uncle sat still, his face inscrutable. Archer expected no less. His uncle could not risk being accused of undue favouritism, not yet. This had to be his fight alone. The *priore* shook his head. 'The offer is much appreciated, but it's not how things are done.' He smiled to soften the refusal, but Archer would have none of it. Archer leaned forward, his words rapid and earnest.

'Injuring a *fantino* the day before the race is also not how things are done. I would suggest that tradition has been exceeded. We no longer need to be bound by past practice. In fact, we do not ever need to be officially bound by the rules regarding the *fantini*. The idea that a *fantino* does not come from a *contrada* is a normative practice only. There is nothing in the rules that bans a rider from a *contrada*.'

The *priore* gave an exasperated sigh. 'It is not the preference.'

'Preference be damned,' Archer interjected swiftly. 'I am not going to see this *contrada* lose the Palio because you want to stand on preferences.' Nor was he going to lose Elisabeta because an incompetent *fantino* was aboard Morello. He wanted control of his destiny.

The *priore*'s eyes narrowed. '*Signor*, be careful you do not ask this solely for yourself. We all know of your wager with Pantera and with Ridolfo Ranieri.'

Archer would not be cowed by the implication of selfishness. 'Of course I ask it for myself. Who else has as much staked on the race as me? My bride of choice, my future happiness, my ability to stay in Siena with a clean reputation, all lie on the line tomorrow. Ridolfo is scared. We all know who precipitated the attack on our *fantino* today and why. Only a fool would ignore that reality. But it doesn't matter. Even without Elisabeta on the line, I would still be here asking for the honour to ride for this *contrada*, for my uncle who has worked so hard to ensure we have a victory.'

'And I would still be saying no,' the *priore* said firmly.

'I am the best rider. I've ridden in the night trials. I know the course, Morello knows me. Best of all, I am one of you, but still a newcomer,' Archer replied evenly. 'I will personally race anyone who says otherwise on my horse, Amicus, tonight to prove it.'

The *priore* shot a nervous glance at his uncle. Archer's gaze did not waver. He was getting to the *priore*. The man had nothing to stand on but tradition and while that was no small thing, Archer knew he had made compelling arguments.

His uncle leaned forward, joining the debate for the first time. He spoke directly to the *priore*. 'The way I see it, Archer is the best choice. I cannot negotiate a *partiti* for another *fantino* of any merit tonight. Ranieri has deep pockets and he's not left anyone open to a trade. Anyone I could find tonight who is not already riding tomorrow is not a rider who is prepared for the race. It would put us at a severe disadvantage. My nephew has put himself forward on his own. Remember, this recommendation did not come from me. But it is a good recommendation. He would not have offered if he could not do the job. I think he rides. I think he is our best hope.'

The *priore* sat back, hands clasped across his stomach, his jaw tight. He nodded his head. 'You are the *capitano*, Signor Ricci. If you say it is the best decision, then it is. Signor Crawford will ride.'

The sun had fallen, and the streets were lit with lanterns as the food was brought out, heaping plates of risotto and pasta, loaves of freshly baked bread, and bottle after bottle of wine. The atmosphere was merry. Toasts were drunk, songs were sung. The *priore* gave a speech, and his uncle gave a speech about the greatness of Torre, recounting their past victories and reminding everyone of the superiority of their horse and of their rider. Gobbo Saragialo might be injured, but Torre would rise on his nephew's shoulders.

This party would go on all night, but those at Archer's table had work to do. His uncle excused himself shortly after the speeches ended to take care of last-minute negotiations, sensing a need after today's altercation to take precautions against Onda who was riding tomorrow. Archer excused himself as well to take a look at Morello.

Morello was no worse for the trouble. Archer ran a hand down each of the gelding's legs to be sure, but he could find no telltale heat. He could have gone back to the party then. Since he was now the *fantino*, someone else had been given the duty to watch over the horse for the night. But Archer let the groom go get a plate of food. The truth was, Archer welcomed the quiet of the stable over the riotous atmosphere of the dinner. He had no desire to return to the party. If he couldn't be with Elisabeta, the stable was a good second choice. He leaned his head against Morello's and rubbed the horse's shoulder affectionately, muttering soothing words.

'Can you just imagine how crazy it will be when you win tomorrow?' a friendly voice drawled behind him. 'This place is insane! I mean that in the best of ways.'

'Hello, Nolan. How much have you had to drink?' Archer chuckled. He didn't need to turn around to know who it was. He could picture Nolan with a bottle in each hand.

'Not nearly enough, but plenty more than you, my friend. You of all people should be celebrating.' Nolan leaned beside him on the stall door. 'You're talking to horses again.'

'Always. They're good listeners.' Archer laughed and rubbed Morello's nose.

'Amicus looks good. I saw him today. He's filled

out. Everyone says he's a prime goer,' Nolan said casually.

'How would you know? You don't speak Italian.'

Nolan shrugged. 'It's not hard to guess what people are saying.' Nolan could read people better than a fortune teller. It was an enviable skill. 'Do you know what else I heard today? I heard you married Elisabeta di Nofri in secret.'

Archer tried not to look disturbed. 'If you heard it, it's not a secret, so I think there's a flaw to your logic.' If Nolan knew, who else knew? Was the entire *contrada* in on it? Would Torre keep his secret at least for a day? It was impossible to imagine an entire neighbourhood being very successful at it.

Nolan took a swig of rich Chianti straight from the bottle. 'That is fine, fine wine.' He passed the back of his hand over his mouth and winked at Archer. 'You'd never guess my father's a viscount.'

'No, one certainly wouldn't,' Archer replied drily.

'So, you are now a happily married man. Or perhaps unhappily married since you're here and she's not. Not much of a wedding night, I suppose. Still, a pretty ingenious plan, Arch. Win or lose tomorrow, the girl is yours.' Then Nolan sobered. He wasn't nearly as drunk as he pretended. 'I can't imagine Oca or Ridolfo will be appreciative of your efforts. Once they find out, it will make today's brawl look like a stroll in Hyde Park. Have you thought of that? There will be blood, primarily yours.'

'If I win, it won't matter. No one needs to know I stole a march on Ridolfo,' Archer answered quietly. 'If I win, he'll have to accept the terms of our arrangement.' He'd thought of little else since learning the news he was going to ride. There would be no discreet escape now. He would be the focus of public attention. The only way to contain Ridolfo and to avoid bloodshed was to win. Winning would protect his family and Elisabeta.

Nolan nodded in agreement with the wisdom of it. 'One victory solves much, but you're going to need a helluva a ride, Arch. This isn't like races in Newmarket. You've got Onda to worry about because they're Torre's sworn enemy. You've got Pantera to worry about because they've won once already and they've got a good enough horse to do it again. Who knows what Oca is up to? No doubt their allies have been paid well to make life miserable for Torre tomorrow. Besides that, you don't really know if you can trust any of the *contradas.*'

Archer gave Nolan a half grin. 'You've grasped the intricacies of the Palio quite nicely for a newcomer.'

'It's all about networks and who you know. That's what I do best.' Nolan shrugged, trying not to make too much of it. 'I like it here. This is my kind of place, I understand it.'

'Looks like you were pretty handy in that fight today.' Archer elbowed him in the ribs.

He nudged Archer in return. 'I am to be handier still. We all thought it was best if you didn't sleep alone tonight in case Oca tried anything or in case someone told them you were going to ride for Torre. So guess what?' His face split into a wide mischievous grin. 'You're spending your wedding night with me. I drew the lucky straw.'

* * *

Archer was still the recipient of drawing lucky straws or the unlucky ones depending on how you looked at it the next evening as the horses lined up for the Palio. He had indeed spent his wedding night in bed with Nolan who had promptly passed out and would have been absolutely no use if Oca had tried to break in. Now, with the hours-long Palio parade and the ride-the-horse-inside-the-church blessing behind him, his pants wetted down along the inside of his legs to allow for better traction against the horse's bare sides, the traditional *nerbo* for a whip in one hand, Archer had drawn the *rincorsa* position at the start.

It was not a position he would have chosen for himself. While nine of the ten racing horses lined up at the rope in an assigned order, the *rincorsa* horse, the tenth horse, stayed behind, waiting to be summoned onto the track when the official starter, the *mossiere*, had everyone situated to satisfaction. Then, and only then, would the tenth horse be allowed to enter the track. He would enter at a gallop behind the other horses when the starting rope dropped. While other horses would need a few strides to get up to speed, he would already be at speed. But there were disadvantages too.

Morello pranced beneath him, and Archer turned him in a circle, stroking the horse's shoulder with his free hand and keeping up a running patter of words to keep the big animal calm. Perhaps to keep himself calm too. He'd looked around the *campo* for Elisabeta. He thought he'd caught sight of her on the balcony she'd used for the *tratta*, but the light had been too dim for him to be sure. He hoped she was safe. He wasn't sure what would happen after the race.

There was no time to think about those things now. He could not afford to think about the future even if it was just a few minutes away nor could he afford to think about Elisabeta. All of his thoughts had to stay centred on Morello, the track, and everything he knew about the dangerous turns at the San Martino and Casato corners. The horses were nearly lined up now to the *mossiere's* satisfaction. It was nearly surreal to think that in a few minutes it would all be over.

Archer received the signal from the *mossiere*, getting permission to enter the track. He drew a breath and didn't rush his entrance. Archer had a little power of his own to control the race. The *mossiere* could not start the race until some part of his horse set foot on the track. A fair start usually assumed the *mossiere* dropped the rope once the *rincorsa* horse had started galloping, but not all of them followed that rule. His uncle had gone that morning to bargain a last-minute *partiti* with the *mossiere* just in case Torre drew the tenth spot.

Archer gathered his reins, looked once at the sky and thought of his mother. This would have been a proud moment for her. 'Are you ready, boy?' he asked Morello, edging him forward. Morello's ears flicked back. He was listening, he was ready. 'All right, let's go win this.' Archer circled Morello once more, signalling for a gallop, and the big horse leapt onto the track nearly at full speed. The rope dropped and the race was on.

Morello surged ahead of the pack still trying to

gather its speed. Archer took advantage and pushed Morello forward into the straight away. Even a slight lead would allow him the luxury of slowing to a safe pace through the San Martino curve. His uncle's statistics flashed through his head. This was the corner that posed the most likely risk of a fall on first and second laps. Safely through, he gave Morello his head. The bay wanted to run and Archer let him. A good rider knew when to respect his horse's wishes and Archer did all the way through the Casato curve when he reined Morello in.

The first lap was complete. The other horses had their rhythms now. A few moved to press him for the lead in the straight away as the second lap began. One of the riders leaned over to smack Morello with his *nerbo* as they went into the San Martino corner, causing the bay to take the corner faster than Archer would have liked. Archer could feel the horse's hooves slip coming out of the turn, could feel Morello lose his balance. Archer shifted his weight, helping Morello keep his feet. He would not go down! A horse screamed behind him, and Archer resisted the urge to look. Someone had crashed, a horse had gone down in the dangerously angled curve, but not him, not Morello.

The noise of the crowd was starting to rise to a fever pitch as Morello and two others raced neck and neck in the backside straight away. A challenger was on each side of Morello, and Archer saw the peril immediately. Between them, they could crush Morello. But it was either that or take his chances between them and the wall. Neither choice was an acceptable risk. Archer swatted Morello with his own *nerbo*, asking for more speed, the only option was to break free of these two and extend his lead.

Morello answered, the horse, too, wary of the challengers. Archer navigated the Casato curve at full speed. For whatever reason, most crashes at Casato occurred in the first lap only. Archer played the odds and took the chance. The crowd yelled its approval as Morello raced through without mishap. 'One more lap,' Archer yelled to the horse. He could feel the bay tiring. The horse had taken the race at full speed from the start. But other horses, other riders, were tiring too. Archer's own legs felt the effort of riding without a saddle.

The two challengers had fallen back. But a new one had risen. The bay representing the Giraffa Contrada gave chase after the San Martino turn and Archer urged Morello to run. Even exhausted, the horse was all heart. Morello ran. Giraffa's bay didn't give up. Through the second straight away they went, into the last turn and then a sprint for the finish, Archer laying on his *nerbo* in encouragement, his voice yelling hoarsely to Morello over the roar of the crowd. 'Go, go, go!' He could not lose—everything hinged on Morello crossing the finish line first.

Morello seemed to sense the urgency and found a last burst of speed, crossing the finish line half a length ahead of Giraffa's bay. The crowd noise was deafening. He saw his uncle surge down from the special stands constructed for the *capitani* and other elite guests, Ridolfo among them. Onda and Oca were on the move.

His uncle grabbed Morello's bridle, leading them quickly towards the exit from the track where they

could be swallowed up by cheering Torre. Giacomo
pumped his fist into air. 'We did it, *mio nipote*! We
did it!' Archer let himself savour the victory, let himself savour the elation of having been part of it. This
was a dream too. But the best dream was coming towards him. Elisabeta, dressed in a soft blue summer
gown, pushed through the crowd with her uncle and
Giuliano beside her.

Archer slid from Morello's back and made his
way to her, his strong strides parting the crowd. Her
uncle was beaming, and Archer's last reservations
about Pantera not honouring the agreement slipped
away. He had won her fairly. He would not need his
secret marriage as leverage. He had eyes only for her,
her eyes shining, her hair falling down, her mouth
wide with a sensual smile. Perhaps if he'd had eyes
for the crowd he would have seen the trouble before
it was too late.

As it was, he only 'saw' it through Elisabeta, her
shining eyes going wide, her mouth forming a warning scream. Behind him, Morello was skittish. There
was motion behind him making the horse nervous.
Someone was on the move and coming up fast. With
no more than Elisabeta's silent scream to warn Archer of disaster, Ridolfo lunged from the crowd, knife
in hand, sending Morello's hooves into the air.

Archer turned, not waiting for Elisabeta's scream
to confirm the danger. The choice saved his life, but it
was not enough to avoid the blade entirely. The blade
took him along his arm instead of in the back, and
Archer went to the ground. The older man had the advantage of surprise and it was working for him, that
and his weight. The heavy bulk of him pinned Ar-

cher, but Archer was strong. He got his hands around the man's neck, his leg around Ridolfo's, seeking leverage to try to throw the man over. He squeezed with all his might, ignoring the fire in his arm. There would be time for pain later. He would not lose this fight...not with happiness so close.

Suddenly, arms grabbed Ridolfo, a knife flashing at Ridolfo's throat as he was hauled off Archer. Haviland was there, helping him scramble to his feet. Archer's first glance was for Elisabeta, to assure himself she was unharmed, his second was for the man with the blade.

Nolan held a knife to Ridolfo's throat, his eyes lit with unholy fire. 'Say the word, Archer, and I'll do him right here. There's no shame in it, he's turned backstabber.' Nolan would do it too, Archer realised, urged on by the crowd's adrenaline and his own brand of craziness.

The crowd had pressed about them, drawn by the spectacle. Now, they shouted their approval at Nolan's bloodthirsty suggestion. Archer reached out his good arm to Elisabeta and wrapped her in his embrace. He cast a glance at his uncle, who stood in a phalanx of the *capitani* from the *contradas*, all of them arrayed against Ridolfo. His uncle spoke. 'Ridolfo Ranieri broke his promise to abide by the agreement he struck with Pantera. He attempted to kill a man who did nothing more than fairly win a wager and claim his prize. His fate should be decided at the hands of the man he attempted to wrong.'

Archer took a deep breath. Ridolfo was sweating now, realising how close to death he was, how foolish his attempt had been. Archer wanted it ended quickly. He wanted nothing more than to be alone with Elisabeta, away from the crowd. He was starting to feel light-headed from the fight, the race, the lack of sleep. He had to keep his feet. There remained only this last thing to do, this last thing to settle before he could claim happiness. He felt Elisabeta's arm steady him about the waist and he found the strength for this final task.

'Nolan, drop your knife. I will not mark this celebration of Torre's victory with blood. Ridolfo Ranieri will live with his shame. However, he will do it elsewhere so that all of us may have a fresh start. He will leave Siena, never to return. He has until midnight tonight to make arrangements and take whatever he would like.'

The crowd roared its approval and he was hoisted onto Morello's back, Haviland's hand there to steady him. There was still the victory parade to manage, but sitting on Morello helped. 'I want Elisabeta,' he managed to tell Haviland, and she was there, swinging up behind him and wrapping her arms about him as much for herself as for him. He was glad for her presence.

'You've been strong for me for so long,' she whispered, her body pressed against his, warm and alive. Her hands slid over his where they rested on the reins. 'Let me be strong for you now. Better than that, let us be strong together.'

Archer grinned and waved to the crowd with his good arm. 'I like the sound of that.' He'd not come to Siena looking for trouble any more than he'd been looking for it when he'd stepped outside the Antwerp Hotel so many months ago, but he'd found it all the same, and more—he'd found a family, he'd found love. These two things were the true home-lands of the heart wherever they might exist on the maps of men.

Epilogue

The Ricci Villa in the Tuscan countryside

In Archer's opinion it was the best wedding breakfast ever, even if it did take place five days after the wedding and was 'lightly attended' by Italian standards. There was just the bride's family and the groom's family along with four of the groom's friends.

Archer looked about the long table set beneath the olive grove at his friends assembled and his new bride, his heart full of happiness, fuller than it had been for a long time. The grief he'd carried from England was put aside, no longer able to dominate his life. Grief might have driven him to Tuscany, but happiness would make him stay. The others would move on, but this was his home now and he had no regrets that his tour ended here. He'd hoped from the beginning that it would. He just hadn't counted on such a glorious ending.

They didn't have much longer. He could hear the commotion of horses and carriages in the courtyard.

Haviland and Alyssandra would continue their own honeymoon in Florence, studying at the Italian fencing schools for a few months before returning to Paris for Christmas with her brother. Nolan and Brennan had talked of slowly making their way to Venice for the winter revels of Carnevale. Archer chuckled at the thought of those two unleashed on Venice without him or Haviland to chaperon.

Archer raised his glass. He wanted to make these last moments count. For the occasion, they'd opened some of the champagne Haviland had brought from Paris and now it sparkled in long flutes. 'A toast, first of all to my lovely wife who is brave enough to embark with me on this journey called life wherever it may lead us. Second, to my friends, who stood beside me during great uncertainty. I could not ask for better companions. To Brennan, safe travels wherever the road takes you. I hope the women of Europe can survive you on the loose. To Nolan, whenever you find that special someone, I wish you a better wedding night than mine.'

'Hear, hear!' Haviland called out as they all clinked glasses and drank amid the laughter that followed.

When they had swallowed, Archer raised his glass once more, solemn this time, his injured arm wrapped carefully around Elisabeta's shoulder. 'One last drink, everyone, to the future, when we meet again.'

* * * * *

COMING NEXT MONTH FROM

HARLEQUIN®

:H:ISTORICAL

Available August 18, 2015

THE COUNTESS AND THE COWBOY (Western)
by Elizabeth Lane
Widowed Eve Townsend heads to the Wild West with a grand title and not
a penny to her name. Could cowboy Clint Lonigan be the breath of fresh air
this countess needs?

MARRIAGE MADE IN SHAME (Regency)
The Penniless Lords • by Sophia James
Despite his reputation, Gabriel Hughes, Earl of Wesley, shies away from
intimacy. Until his convenient marriage to Adelaide Ashfield awakens a
desire he never thought he'd feel again!

TARNISHED, TEMPTED AND TAMED (Regency)
by Mary Brendan
Fiona Chapman is a tarnished woman, or so the gossips have it! But she
won't succumb to Major Luke Wolfson's charms, not unless he makes her
an honorable proposal...

THE REBEL DAUGHTER (1920s)
Daughters of the Roaring Twenties • by Lauri Robinson
Wild child Twyla Nightingale will stand on the sidelines no longer: her feet
are firmly on the dance floor! Forrest Reynolds sees the challenge in her
eyes and takes Twyla for a dance she'll never forget!

Available via Reader Service and online:

FORBIDDEN TO THE DUKE (Regency)
by Liz Tyner
When the Duke of Harling catches Bellona Cherroll trespassing on his land,
he knows he *should* avoid her. What *does* he do? Invite her to live under
his roof!

HER ENEMY HIGHLANDER (Medieval)
Lovers and Legends • by Nicole Locke
Impulsive Mairead Buchanan's only goal is to track down her brother's
murderer. Until an encounter with Caird Colquhoun proves to be a distraction
she can't ignore...

**YOU CAN FIND MORE INFORMATION ON UPCOMING HARLEQUIN® TITLES,
FREE EXCERPTS AND MORE AT WWW.HARLEQUIN.COM.**

HHCNM0815

REQUEST YOUR FREE BOOKS!

◊ HARLEQUIN®

⚜ISTORICAL

Where love is timeless

2 FREE NOVELS PLUS 2 **FREE GIFTS!**

YES! Please send me 2 FREE Harlequin® Historical novels and my 2 FREE gifts (gifts are worth about $10). After receiving them, if I don't wish to receive any more books, I can return the shipping statement marked "cancel." If I don't cancel, I will receive 6 brand-new novels every month and be billed just $5.69 per book in the U.S. or $5.99 per book in Canada. That's a savings of at least 12% off the cover price! It's quite a bargain! Shipping and handling is just 50¢ per book in the U.S. and 75¢ per book in Canada.* I understand that accepting the 2 free books and gifts places me under no obligation to buy anything. I can always return a shipment and cancel at any time. Even if I never buy another book, the two free books and gifts are mine to keep forever.

246/349 HDN GH2Z

Name	(PLEASE PRINT)

Address		Apt. #

City	State/Prov.	Zip/Postal Code

Signature (if under 18, a parent or guardian must sign)

Mail to the **Reader Service**:
IN U.S.A.: P.O. Box 1867, Buffalo, NY 14240-1867
IN CANADA: P.O. Box 609, Fort Erie, Ontario L2A 5X3

Want to try two free books from another line?
Call 1-800-873-8635 or visit www.ReaderService.com.

* Terms and prices subject to change without notice. Prices do not include applicable taxes. Sales tax applicable in N.Y. Canadian residents will be charged applicable taxes. Offer not valid in Quebec. This offer is limited to one order per household. Not valid for current subscribers to Harlequin Historical books. All orders subject to credit approval. Credit or debit balances in a customer's account(s) may be offset by any other outstanding balance owed by or to the customer. Please allow 4 to 6 weeks for delivery. Offer available while quantities last.

Your Privacy—The Reader Service is committed to protecting your privacy. Our Privacy Policy is available online at www.ReaderService.com or upon request from the Reader Service.

We make a portion of our mailing list available to reputable third parties that offer products we believe may interest you. If you prefer that we not exchange your name with third parties, or if you wish to clarify or modify your communication preferences, please visit us at www.ReaderService.com/consumerchoice or write to us at Reader Service Preference Service, P.O. Box 9062, Buffalo, NY 14240-9062. Include your complete name and address.

"Would you partner me for the next waltz, my lord?"
There it was out, said, blunt and honest.

He was good at hiding things, but still she saw shock
on his face, and questions.

Lost in the consternation of this Adelaide was not
cautious with her next words. "Lord Berrick wants me
to marry him."

It was as if the world around them no longer existed,
the people and the noise relegated to a place far away,
lost in the ether of what each of them was saying, words
under words and the colour of the room stark in only
black and white.

Gabriel Hughes stood very still, a grinding muscle in
his jaw the only movement visible. "And what do you
want?" he asked finally.

"A home, though it is only recently I have come
to realize that a place to be and live is important. My
chaperon has been quick to tell me that when Bertie
brings a bride to Northbridge I shall be...in the way."

He turned towards her, using the pillar as a barrier so that they were cut off from the hearing of those around them, but she knew that it would not be many seconds before the world around them impinged again.

"You would be bored to death with Freddy Lovelace in a week."

"Could we meet privately, then?" She made herself say the words, hating the desperation so obvious within them.

"Pardon?"

"I need to know what it would be like to touch a man who might make my heart beat faster before I settle for one who does not. Your reputation heralds a great proficiency in such matters, and I thought perhaps you might…"

"Hell, Adelaide."

The horror of everything spiraled in her head. She had asked for something so dreadful that even the most dissolute lover in all of London town could not accommodate her.

"I…can't."

His voice was strangled and rough, the words like darts as she turned on her heels, hoping he did not see the tears that were threatening to fall as she walked briskly from his side.

Don't miss
MARRIAGE MADE IN SHAME by Sophia James,
available September 2015 wherever
Harlequin® Historical books and ebooks are sold.

www.Harlequin.com

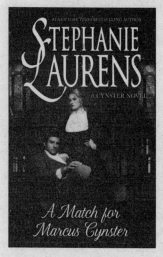